CROOKED PARADISE #3

EVA CHANCE
& HARLOW KING

Ruthless Queen

Book 3 in the Crooked Paradise series

First Digital Edition, 2021

Copyright © 2021 Eva Chance & Harlow King

Cover design: Jodielocks Designs

Ebook ISBN: 978-1-990338-11-3

Paperback ISBN: 978-1-990338-16-8

1

Mercy

IT TURNED OUT HUMAN REMAINS WERE DIFFICULT TO get off of grass, especially remains that had recently exploded.

At least I wasn't right out in the middle of the mess anymore. From the living room window, I could see the Noble lackeys who were hosing down the front lawn. The blood that had painted the grass looked thinner now, but the blades shone faintly red under the morning sun.

When I breathed, a metallic taint remained in the back of my throat. I'd rinsed my mouth out in the shower several times, but I couldn't quite get rid of it.

An hour had passed since the unknown man had burst apart all over the lawn outside the Noble mansion. Even now, the visceral violence of the moment replayed in the back of my mind over and over. That and the moments leading up to it. The

video he'd played for us... That creepy-ass dude
who'd claimed he was going to take over Paradise
Bend now that Colt and the Steel Knights were
destroyed...

It all left me with a clammy sensation wrapped
around my gut.

Wylder and his inner circle were lounging on the
sofa and armchairs around the room, but none of them
looked remotely relaxed.

"Do we have any idea who this Xavier guy is?"
Rowan asked the room at large, as if he knew exactly
what I was thinking. "Did any of you recognize him?"

Wylder shook his head. "No, never seen that fucker.
I think I would have remembered him."

Anybody would. The X shaped scars on his cheeks,
raised and pinkened with age, had shown clearly even
on the small tablet screen. And the way he'd spoken, so
chilling and impassive, was burned into my memory.
The man had to be a psychopath, maybe even a worse
one than Colt.

I tore my gaze away from the window and started
pacing. "I've got no idea either. What the hell does he
want with us?"

With *me*. He'd addressed me directly in the video. A
shudder ran down my spine.

Kaige got up and caught my shoulders in his hands.
"Mercy, come sit down."

I almost argued, but his expression was so
concerned I gave in. I didn't think I could feel any
worse on my ass than on my feet anyway. And Kaige
didn't show emotions other than flirtiness and rage very

often, so when you got something else from him, you knew it was a big deal.

I sank onto the sofa between him and Wylder, and he slung his arm around my back. I let myself lean against the hard planes of his brawny chest. When I looked up at Rowan, I thought I saw a flicker of something in his bright eyes, but he looked away.

Wylder had a nonchalant air, but I knew that was only a front. I wondered if he and Kaige had discussed the threesome we'd had the other night on the terrace. Not that now was a great time to be thinking about that interlude, as spectacular as it'd been.

Gideon seemed oblivious to the rest of us, clicking furiously at his tablet with one hand as he raked the other through his jagged blue hair. Then he let out a short exclamation of victory. "Here it is."

"Here's what?" Wylder asked, leaning forward.

"I was checking the CCTV footage in the area. I figured a guy wouldn't walk up here with a bomb in his stomach unless he had a reason to believe *not* following orders would be worse."

"And?" Rowan asked.

"See for yourself." Gideon held up the tablet to us.

I squinted at the grainy image from a traffic cam. It only took a moment to recognize the row of shops in the background, just a couple of blocks away from the hill in Paradise City where the Noble mansion stood. And then another moment to notice the beefy figure at the corner of the screen, whose frame and salt-and-pepper hair in its short ponytail immediately triggered a sense of recognition.

That was Xavier.

He was standing by a car parked at the curb. With a motion that looked almost careless, he shoved another figure—the young man who'd appeared at the mansion's doorstep—away from him, down the street. The man hesitated for a second and then passed out of view.

Xavier lingered, glancing down at what I assumed was his phone from time to time. Gideon sped up the footage. Finally, Xavier got into the car and drove off.

A chill ran down my spine. "He was so close. He must have been monitoring things to make sure the guy went through with it." And then triggered the explosion when he was done. What had Xavier threatened to do to the guy if he'd chickened out?

"He's been here before, much closer," Wylder said, his voice grim. "He confessed on the video that he was the one leaving those grisly things around the house—first the dead cat and its tail and then the dug-up corpse."

I didn't want to focus on those gruesome memories. I finally had my answers about who'd been leaving me the horrible "gifts," but I couldn't say I was at all comforted. The realization that this psycho had been right outside my bedroom, just inches from the place where I'd been sleeping, made my skin crawl.

"In what part of his fucked-up brain did he think those were gifts?" Kaige growled. His body curled tighter around me as if he could somehow shield me from the rest of the world.

I placed a hand on his thigh. "I don't think he

expects us to see them that way. He wanted to scare me. I just don't know why."

"That is the strangest thing," Gideon agreed, shutting off the video feed.

Wylder scowled. "Why does he want anything from any of us? The video was meant for Dad to see. It was a warning. This Xavier asshole wants to establish something here. He's coming for us, and he wants us to know it."

Wylder was right about that. Xavier had practically called for war on the streets of Paradise Bend.

Not that we hadn't been fighting already, with Colt and all the other gangs he'd brought in...

I paused, a startling thought emerging from the confused haze in my head. "Do you think Xavier is the mastermind behind Colt's takeover of the Bend? I mean, we knew Colt had help from outside in the form of drugs and weapons. There were those strange men who just stood back and watched when he confronted us, and whoever he was taking orders from on the phone. We assumed the people backing him just left, but that never made much sense to me. What if it was Xavier?"

Rowan knit his brow. "That's a good point. We never figured out who his biggest backer was, did we? It'd make more sense than Xavier coming out of nowhere, completely unconnected."

Kaige frowned. "But he seemed happy that Colt's gone."

"Typical kingpin strategy," Wylder said with an edge in his voice. "Use whoever you can to clear the way and then kick them aside when you don't need them anymore. Xavier let the locals go into the line of fire to take down the Claws and whoever else was going to stand up against an invasion, and now he's ready to step up himself. Which'll be easier if Colt isn't there complaining about how *he* was the one who was supposed to take the throne."

Gideon rubbed his mouth, shifting his silver lip ring. "It's odd that Xavier would decide to reveal himself to us, though. What did he gain from that?"

"More fear and intimidation, or at least that's what he's probably hoping for," I said. "The guy's obviously psychotic, and he likes a spectacle. Who else would throw rotting body parts around?"

Rowan nodded. "He wants us to panic and make mistakes that'll play into his hands. But that's the last thing we should do. We don't know how powerful he is or how far his reach extends. Whatever moves we make, we need to be careful."

"And protect Mercy," Kaige spoke up. "Obviously the motherfucker has something against her."

I nudged him gently with my elbow. "I think I've proven enough times that I can take care of myself."

Kaige huffed. "Of course you can. You're the most resilient woman I know, but we're not leaving anything to chance. I think you should stay inside until we catch that piece of shit."

I rolled my eyes. "Are you suggesting that I lock myself in my room?"

"If it comes to that, I'll do it myself." A sly grin

twitched at his lips. "And maybe even give you some company."

Even in the middle of this mess, he just couldn't help himself, could he? I had to laugh, the tension in my chest easing just slightly. The reprieve didn't last long before the uneasy ache returned, though.

I eased out of Kaige's embrace, running my hands back over my hair. "I feel like even with Colt gone, nothing has changed. It's almost as if we're back to square one." And somehow this situation felt far more dangerous than before. There were crazier people than my ex-fiancé out there. People who were willing to go to some very extreme lengths to make a point.

"Don't think like that," Rowan said.

"I can't help it." I smacked my fist against my knee. "I don't care how powerful or insane this guy is; we can't let him win. I don't want an outsider to swoop in and take control of my home."

"That won't happen," Wylder said firmly. "We're going to protect Paradise City *and* the Bend, and send this prick packing. No matter what he throws at us, we're fighting back by whatever means necessary. We'll be smart about it, sure, but this isn't the time to cower in a corner."

Just as I was about to agree, Axel sauntered into the room. The bald, tattooed man didn't look particularly pleased with any of us. "Boss wants to see you," he said curtly, fixing his gaze on me. "Now."

I raised my eyebrows. Why would Ezra Noble want to see *me*? Shouldn't he be strategizing with Wylder and the rest of the top Nobles members?

"What does he want?" I asked, getting up.

Axel shrugged. "Beats me." Something told me he knew the reason but couldn't be bothered to divulge it. He might be one of Ezra's most trusted men, but he always seemed to go out of his way to antagonize his boss's son and anyone associated with Wylder.

Of course, Wylder and his inner circle had plenty of reasons to be wary of any interest Ezra showed toward me regardless. The man had tried to set me up to be murdered not too long ago.

Wylder stood up too. "I'll go with you."

"We'll all go," Rowan said. Gideon turned off his tablet, and Kaige sprang to his feet beside me.

Axel folded his arms over his broad chest. "Boss wants to see *her*. Alone."

"We're going," Kaige insisted.

"Since when are you a package deal?" Axel asked, irritation creeping into his voice.

I looked at the guys. His question set something off in me. Axel might not have meant it that way, but we *were* a package now. We were a team. Our near-death stand-off against the Steel Knights last week had cemented an invisible bond between us. I could feel that in my gut... and possibly a few other places too.

Wylder ignored Axel and ambled out of the room. Axel grumbled under his breath as we all followed.

Since I wasn't a trusted member of the upper echelon, Axel directed us to Ezra's audience room rather than his official office. "It's your funeral," he muttered, pushing open the door, but he hadn't put up that much of a fight against the guys coming along. He probably liked the idea of Ezra getting pissed off at them.

I glanced around and found all four of the guys' faces were set in similarly determined expressions. Kaige squeezed my shoulder.

Whatever Ezra had in store for me, I wasn't going to face it by myself. I'd faced every problem I had alone for most of my life, so I'd have survived on my own—but I couldn't say I wasn't glad that I didn't have to.

When we entered, I was surprised to see Anthea standing beside the sofa. I'd expected Ezra to be alone, but a few men from his own inner circle were also there, flanking him where he sat in the leather armchair that could have passed for a throne.

All eyes focused on me when I walked in.

Ezra cocked his head at Axel. "I only asked for the girl."

"They insisted," Axel said.

Ezra's eyes narrowed as he turned his gaze toward me. Not a good sign. "Very well. They'll need to be informed soon enough anyway. Take a seat, Mercy."

The cheerful daylight streaming through the nearby window did nothing to ease the knot in my stomach. Just like during our previous meetings here, I sat down on the sofa opposite Ezra. His chiseled features were just as difficult to read as usual, but I thought I picked up a hint of strain he wouldn't normally have betrayed.

For everything the head Noble had been through, somehow I suspected this was the first time he'd had a man explode on his front lawn.

I looked from him to Wylder, who moved to join his

aunt near the window. Father and son were strikingly similar in features, and no matter how many times I saw them together, the resemblance was jarring. Not least of all because Ezra's deep green eyes held none of the warmth I'd found in Wylder's.

"So, we finally know who's been targeting you," Ezra said.

I took a deep breath. "It looks that way. I've never seen that guy before, though, and I—"

Ezra held up a hand to stop me. He turned his head to look at Wylder. "Clearly the conflict we're dealing with goes far beyond Colt Bryant and the Steel Knights. You and your men spearheaded that problem. How could you have failed to notice that a larger power was involved?"

Wylder took a few steps forward. "We didn't fail to notice it. We were aware almost from the start that there was some outside presence. But we had no reason until now to believe that they were interested in the Bend—or Paradise City—for themselves rather than acting based on some deal they'd made with Bryant."

"Or you chose to ignore the signs," Ezra said coldly. "And thanks to your recklessness, we have a bigger problem than the Steel Knights. A problem that seems in part to have something to do with our guest." His gaze flicked back to me.

I stiffened in my seat, but Wylder spoke first. "I don't believe we were reckless. If this Xavier was in the picture all along, then we'd have had to deal with him either way. We got rid of Bryant, which means now we can focus all of our attention on this newcomer and whoever he's brought with him. We'll simply track him down and put things in order."

"Will you?" Ezra's eyes swept over to Kaige, Rowan, and Gideon, who'd stopped just inside the door. "I have left things up to you so far, and look where that got us."

Anthea stepped up beside Wylder, her chin raised defiantly. "He did take care of Colt. I'm sure he'll be able to neutralize the new threat too."

Ezra flat out ignored his sister. He liked using Anthea for her skills with poison and other surreptitious killings when it suited him, but from what I'd seen, he didn't have much more respect for women than any other man I'd met in this life.

"Whoever this Xavier is, the most disturbing fact is that he managed to trespass on our property several times and was able to get away with it. That puts my life along with yours and Anthea's and everybody else under my authority in danger."

Wylder's jaw ticked. As if Ezra really cared about anything other than himself and maintaining his image of power.

"The disturbing things he talked about were objects he left behind specifically for you," Ezra said, turning back to me. "And that suggests that he has some kind of personal vendetta against you."

I gritted my teeth. "I have no idea who this guy even is. I've never seen him before today."

"Your assurances, unfortunately, don't do much to ease my mind. The man is obviously deranged. He blew up a human being on our lawn—God knows what he'll do next. As long as you're staying in our home, I can't help but think he'll continue to target you here and therefore us. That makes your presence a liability that eclipses any help you could possibly offer us."

My gut tightened in anticipation of what he would say next.

"Dad," Wylder said, his jaw clenching. "She's the one who took down Colt in the end. She was instrumental in our plans every step of the way."

"Do you think I haven't considered that?" Ezra said sharply. He pointed at me. "I'm not being unreasonable. I won't bargain with a terrorist, so I have no intention of handing you over to him. But you can't expect me to harbor you and offer my protection any longer. Consider all ties between us severed. I want you out of the mansion within the hour."

My heart lurched. Shit. I should have seen this coming.

"It isn't just me he's after," I had to say. "His message was mostly aimed at you. I don't think me leaving will actually solve your problems. And I've been nothing but loyal to the Nobles the entire time I've been here."

"She's right," Kaige jumped in. He pushed forward and might have barged right in front of me if Rowan hadn't grabbed his arm. "You can't just throw Mercy away after everything she's done for us. She could be the key to taking this bastard down."

"When she may be the entire reason he's set his sights on us in the first place, that's hardly reassuring," Ezra said in an acidic tone. "And loyalty means very little when it comes with so much chaos. We hadn't had any problems with Bryant until you turned up here, and now yet another menace has come at his heels. I can't consider that a coincidence."

"Dad," Wylder started, his voice rough. I knew how hard he was trying not to show that I mattered to him for any reason other than business—because the last time he'd cared about a girl for other reasons, his father had murdered her in front of him—but it was obviously taking all of his self-control to hold back.

Ezra didn't even let him get out his protest. "I've made my decision. It's not open for negotiation. Miss Katz, go pack whatever things you have here and be out the front door before noon—that's an order."

"This is ridiculous!" Kaige said. "Mercy's one of us now."

Wylder's hands balled at his side. I could sense the tension in him pulling tight like a bow about to let loose an arrow. How much would he damage his own standing with his father if he spoke up too much for me?

I pushed myself to my feet even though my insides felt like lead. I didn't know where I was going to go or who I'd be able to turn to outside these walls, but I couldn't stand here and watch the Nobles tear into each other when they needed to be focused on the problem that threatened us all.

Ezra wasn't going to change his mind. As touching as it was to hear the guys speaking up for me, I knew that. What happened to me didn't really matter as long as this psycho didn't lay claim to the streets where I'd grown up.

"Fine," I said, the single syllable making my stomach turn. "Fine, I'll leave."

Mercy

ALL FOUR OF THE GUYS GAVE ME MATCHING LOOKS OF muted horror. Their gazes burned into me, but I tuned them out, focusing only on the man who held the power of life and death over everyone in this room.

"Thank you for everything the Nobles have done for me," I said, nodding to Ezra. Not that *he'd* done all that much for me—but he'd like to think I believed he had.

Without another word, I strode out of the room. I only had an hour to figure out where the hell I was going from here, and I suspected the clock was already ticking.

Kaige caught up to me in the hall. He grabbed me by my elbow and whirled me around so I was facing him. "What were you thinking?"

"Ezra was going to kick me out anyway," I said, meeting his furious gaze head on. "Might as well leave with my dignity."

Gideon stalked up behind the bigger guy. "Is that what it was about? We wouldn't have let him run you off."

"Really?" I said, keeping my voice low. "And how would you have stopped the head of all the Nobles?"

Rowan joined us just as I finished speaking. He grimaced. "We could have tried to speak up for you more. There's a psychopath on the loose out there, and he's already made you a target. We don't want you adrift on the streets."

"I know." I didn't want to be out there either. But— "Ezra had made up his mind. I could see it. The only thing arguing about it would have done is cause more tensions between all of you and him when everyone in the Nobles should be tackling the Xavier problem. If you deal with him, then you won't need to worry about me, right?"

Rowan gave me a look that seemed to say he'd worry about me regardless. I didn't know what to make of it. There was so much history between us, good and bad, and even now that I knew and understood why he'd taken off on me years ago, I still couldn't say exactly where we stood.

But it was Kaige who spoke first. "I'll come with you."

I raised my eyebrows at him. "Don't be ridiculous. This is your home. You belong here with these guys and Wylder." Who was conspicuously absent from this conversation. Probably trying to keep the heat off of me by hiding how much he cared, but somehow it stung a little anyway.

"And so do you," Kaige said fiercely.

"Yes, you do," Rowan added. "Even if my behavior at first suggested otherwise."

"We were wrong," Gideon said matter-of-factly. "And after what we went through with Colt, you're undeniably one of us."

Unexpected tears pricked at the back of my eyes. Just weeks ago, I'd lost my entire family. Somehow I'd found another one in the last place I'd ever thought I would.

But to make sure I didn't lose them too... I had to leave them.

"Thank you," I said. "Maybe when Xavier is taken care of, we can convince Ezra of that too. For now, I'd better get packing."

"Wylder will find a way to fix this," Kaige insisted, but I could see from the flicker of doubt in his eyes that he didn't totally believe it either.

———

When I reached my room, I was reminded all over again of how little I had here *other* than the guys. A few changes of clothes, bought used and roughed up over my time here. A handful of origami figures I'd made out of scraps of paper that weren't important enough to bring with me anyway. Some basic toiletries.

I touched my pocket, tracing the outline of the bracelet my mom had given me for my sixth birthday— just a few months before she'd disappeared from my life. I still had that. I was alive; I'd gotten my revenge on the man who'd taken so much else from me. Things could be worse.

I was stuffing my clothes into a backpack when the door swung open. Wylder strode inside and kicked it shut behind him. One look at his stormy expression told me that if he'd tried to talk his father down, it definitely hadn't worked.

It was easier to make light of the situation than admit how twisted up I felt inside. "Well, you must be happy," I said breezily. "You've been trying to terrorize me out of your house for ages, and now you're finally getting rid of me."

Wylder's green eyes darkened even more. He walked right up to me, hooking his fingers into the belt loops of my jeans and pulling me towards him. The musky smell of him, laced with a hint of the aged whiskey he liked so much, washed over me, and my pussy clenched. I had to hold myself back from swaying even closer.

"You know that's not true," he said.

An eager shiver traveled down my spine. "Isn't it?" I challenged.

"We've talked about why I pushed you away before. And it sure as hell wasn't ever because I didn't *want* you." He dipped his head, letting his breath spill hot down the side of my face. "You belong here with me and my men. You're one of us now."

His words weren't a request but a demand. One I wished I could give in to, especially when he was touching me like this. Wylder Noble was addictive any way you sliced it, but never more than when he got this possessive.

When he slid his hands down over my ass, I swallowed the sound that tried to slip from my throat and forced my voice to stay steady. "Are you really ready to fight your father over this?"

He grimaced, the fire in his eyes dimming for a few seconds. "I will. You can count on it. But I know that's not a battle I can win when we're in the middle of a bigger one. When we've crushed that psychotic jackass..."

I rested my hand on his chest. "I know. That's exactly why *I* didn't fight."

Wylder held my gaze for a moment, a sense of shared understanding passing between us that somehow affected me even more than his touch.

"I'm not letting you set off into the jungle out there completely on your own," he said. "My dad doesn't need to know everything. I'm going to do whatever I can to keep you safe even if you're not inside these walls."

I cocked my head. "What do you mean?"

He lifted his chin toward the backpack. "You look ready to go. Do you know where you're heading?"

The question sent an uneasy twinge through me. I hadn't let myself think that far ahead in much detail yet. Maybe because I knew there were no easy answers. "I'll figure it out. I'm not leaving Paradise Bend, that's for sure. But I know my way around."

"Of course you do. But that doesn't mean we can't lend you a hand." Wylder motioned toward the door.

"Gideon's checking the properties the Nobles own in the county to see which are currently vacant. There's got to be one where we could set you up surreptitiously. At least then you'll have some kind of safe space until the rest is sorted out. When we know where you're going, Rowan and Kaige will follow your cab and make sure no one's tailing you there."

I found myself choking up a bit. It was a team effort, like always, and like always, Wylder was the one calling the shots. He might not be much of one for mushy declarations, but he couldn't have made it more obvious how much I did mean to him now. He was defying Ezra with every gesture he made in my defense.

"You don't have to stick your neck out like that," I had to say. "I'll survive this, like I've survived a hell of a lot before."

"I know you will," he said, moving closer again so his body was pressed right against mine. "I just don't want to take any chances."

"You're beginning to sound like Kaige," I teased.

A faint smile crossed his lips before falling away. "I don't want to see you get hurt. Again." His expression turned pained, and I wondered if he was thinking about Laurel—the high school girlfriend his father had ordered murdered in front of him.

I didn't want that. I didn't want him to be reminded of her when he looked at me.

I cupped his jaw and stroked the edge with my thumb. He gazed down at me unblinking.

"Nothing is going to happen to me," I said. "It'll

take a lot more than Ezra Noble and this Xavier psycho to put Mercy Katz in the ground."

Wylder's lips twitched with an approving smile, and then he was pulling me right to him. I met him halfway. His mouth captured mine, hot and demanding, as he tangled his fingers in my ponytail with a teasing yank that walked the perfect line between pleasure and pain. When a gasp escaped me, he took the opportunity to slip his tongue past my lips.

I kissed him back just as hard, gripping his shirt with one hand and his thick auburn hair with the other. He tilted his head, fusing us together even more closely as if he couldn't get enough of me. His tongue curled while it explored my searing mouth.

He shoved me back against the wall, squeezing my ass and lifting me at the same time. The hard bulge in his jeans pressed against my cunt. I gripped him even harder, arching into him instinctively, and a groan spilled from his mouth into mine.

With obvious reluctance, he eased back. He bit my lower lip softly, and when I hissed, flicked his tongue over the spot, bringing another rush of pleasure. Then he drew away completely, gazing down at me with so much hunger in his gaze I almost melted.

"Fuck," he said in a raw voice. "You have no idea how much I want to bend you over that bed and take you right now, without giving one shit who hears us."

I wet my swollen lips, and his eyes tracked the movement. My pussy was doing more of the thinking than my brain right now, because I was seriously considering encouraging that course of action. But before either of us could do anything momentously stupid, Wylder's phone buzzed in his pocket.

He pulled it out and checked the message. "Gideon. He's found you a perfect spot in the Bend."

Somehow I was both relieved by the news and disappointed to have the moment interrupted. "Are you sure this is a good idea? The property belongs to Ezra, doesn't it? I don't think he'll like it much if I leave the mansion only to start living in one of his apartments."

Wylder gave me a cocky grin. "That's why I'm glad to have Gideon on my side. He can conjure up a rental agreement in the database so it appears the place is already occupied, so no one'll try to show it to prospective renters. Dad doesn't keep very close track of everything he owns around here. Just don't make your presence too obvious."

"I can handle that. Do you have the keys?"

"There's a lock with a code. I'll text it to you. Which reminds me." He held up the phone. "This is a new burner I grabbed that I'm going to use only for communicating with or about you. I'll keep it hidden so my dad doesn't find out. I'll text you the number—if you need to reach out before we check in on you, that's the only one you should use. Got it?"

I arched my eyebrows at his authoritarian tone. "This isn't my first time on the run."

His smile turned a bit sheepish. "You'll go to the apartment?" he asked insistently.

"It sure beats crashing in an abandoned warehouse somewhere."

"Good. You'll need to buy food and whatever else

until we can come see you—take this." He dug out his wallet and handed me a wad of cash. Something in me balked at accepting the charity, but I knew he didn't mean it that way. It was a matter of honor for him to make sure I was taken care of.

And grocery store food sure beat dumpster-diving.

After I'd pocketed it, he paused and then ducked down to kiss me again. His hands came to rest on either side of me, trapping me against the wardrobe. Our scorching breaths mingled with each other.

When he pulled back the second time, he rested his forehead against mine. "I'm going to miss having you around, Kitty Cat," he said. He hadn't called me by the nickname for so long that the mention of it almost startled me.

While I stood there cocooned in his heat and scent, a part of me didn't want to leave. But I didn't have much choice.

I nudged him away from me. "I think my hour is just about up. I'd better get going before I end up with Axel dumping me on the front lawn."

Wylder lingered by the door as I swung the backpack over my shoulder. "Listen," he said abruptly. "I'm not going to tell you to hide away in the apartment all day and night. I know you wouldn't listen to me if I tried to order you to anyway."

I laughed. "I'm glad we've gotten a few things straight."

He shot a half-hearted glower at me. "Just... when you *do* go out into the Bend, be careful about it, all right?"

There was so much concern in those words, I softened. I reached for his hand and squeezed it. "I will be. I'd like to keep breathing too, you know."

We couldn't have more of a send-off than that. I walked down to the foyer alone. A few Noble men were gathered around. Patrolling had been doubled since the incident. All eyes turned to me as I sauntered past them.

Axel was with a few others out on the lawn, smoking a cigarette. He looked almost gleeful to see me leave. The grass glistened wetly, the traces of red finally gone, but a hint of the meaty smell lingered in the air. A sense of foreboding crawled down my spine.

I had one enemy behind me and another in front of me. Was Xavier still lurking nearby, watching me even now?

As I headed down the hill, I called for an Uber. If Kaige and Rowan were following me as Wylder had promised, they were doing a good job of staying discreet. As far as I could tell, I was on my own.

I dragged in a breath and touched my three lucky charms: the bracelet in my pocket, the knife at my other hip, and the pistol tucked in the back of my jeans. Two of those I could thank Wylder for.

Why did I have to be torn away from my guys right after I'd started discovering such a strong connection between us?

When the car finally arrived, I got in and threw one last look at the hill where the Noble mansion stood. Then I glanced down at the backpack on my lap. I'd come to Paradise City's rulers with so little, and in some ways I was leaving with even less... but in other ways, I had so much more.

Of course, that just meant that now I had a lot more to lose.

Mercy

THE BREEZE FLICKED THROUGH MY HAIR, THE SUMMER air cooler now that it was evening. I leaned forward on my rooftop perch, watching passersby come and go on the street of shops below me. With the sky darkening and the streetlamps blinking on, no one would have been able to make out my form where I'd used my parkour skills to clamber onto the top of the bank on the corner.

I'd been roaming around the Bend for the past couple of days since I'd left the Noble mansion—being careful like I'd promised Wylder I would be, but needing to see for myself what was happening out here in the aftermath of Colt's fall. So far I hadn't run into Xavier, which I couldn't say I minded. My explorations had left me unsettled, though.

This was my home. I'd lived here since I was born, but it didn't feel like the same place anymore. There was more tension in the atmosphere than I ever remembered feeling before, a nervousness to the way people moved. Most of these stores would normally have been open until well past dinnertime, but now they were locking their doors at six or seven. By now, coming up on eight, nearly everyone had vanished.

A pang ran through my chest at the thought of how much the ongoing battles for territory had affected the Bend.

Not *quite* everyone had gone home for the night, though. Raucous guitar music echoed through the streets. It grew louder until a car came around a bend, windows down, radio blasting a heavy metal song. The driver swerved back and forth a little as if he was distracted or drunk.

The car jerked to a halt in front of a bar partway down the street, and the music cut out. I frowned, narrowing my eyes.

That bar was the main reason I'd chosen this spot tonight. It was closed, the windows already gathering dust from disuse. The place had used to be one of the Steel Knights' main business fronts, but it didn't look as if anyone had been operating out of it since Colt's death. I'd wanted to keep an eye on it just in case some of his former underlings were still in action.

The five guys who pushed out of the car and swaggered across the sidewalk to the bar weren't Steel Knights though, at least as far as I could tell. It was hard to make out their features in the deepening shadows, but none of them had the typical red bandana wrapped around their upper arms. Three of them carried axes, the other two baseball bats studded with spikes.

Even though they hadn't seemed to be keeping their arrival quiet, they glanced around shiftily as if they were worried about getting caught at whatever they were about to do. One guy flexed his shoulders, and I got the impression he was putting on his swagger to hide his nerves.

"Come on! Let's tear it all down!" he shouted.

He and the other guys went at the bar with their weapons like they wanted to demolish the place. The bats smashed through the front windows, sending broken glass spilling into the bar's interior. A guy with an axe hacked through the door. They barged inside, and more smashing and thwacking sounds reached my ears as they plowed through the furnishings inside. Every now and then, one of them let out a little cheer.

What the hell was going on? Who were these guys? One of the smaller gangs Colt had allied with who'd decided to give him the middle finger after his death? But I couldn't figure out what he'd done that would have pissed them off that much, or what the point would be now that he was gone anyway.

The growl of incoming engines reached me. A few motorcycles and a car roared up the street from the opposite direction. Peering through the dim light, I thought I recognized a mustached man on one of the motorcycles from Colt's crew.

But at the sight of the four men who got out of the car, pulling out guns as they did, a chill ran down my spine. Unlike the bikers, who were wearing tees and jeans, that bunch had on collared shirts and slacks. The air around them reminded me of the mysterious men who'd been hanging around watching Colt's confrontation with the Nobles before—the ones we'd never been able to identify.

Now I had to wonder if they were Xavier's people. If he'd been egging on Colt's quest for power, planning to steal that power for himself once the Steel Knights had done his dirty work, that would fit.

The guys who'd been trashing the bar had emerged at the sound of the new arrivals, their original weapons discarded and their own guns in their hands. They hung back by the broken window, using the walls for cover. "What the fuck do you want?" one snarled.

"Your blood all over that floor," said one of the posher guys, and opened fire.

Guns blasted on both sides, one group taking shelter in the bar and the other around their car. There were grunts and shouts, and I thought at least one guy must have been hit.

Now I was even more confused than before. Why was the first group going up against whatever remained of the Steel Knights and what I assumed to be Xavier's people? I definitely hadn't seen any of them around the Noble mansion. Who else would have dared to take on the guys who'd nearly conquered all of Paradise Bend?

I kept my ears pricked, barely breathing so I could pick up as much of the conversation below as I could. In between shots and muttered curses, the two groups were yelling at each other.

"The Storm has claimed this territory," hollered a

guy I thought was with Xavier's group. "Anyone who crosses us will pay for it."

One of the men inside the bar let out a rough laugh. "I don't think so. The Red Shark is going to take it all. Death to the Storm!"

More gunfire thundered between them. I furrowed my brow. Who the fuck were the Storm and the Red Shark? I'd never heard either of those names before. None of this made any sense.

The Storm side—which seemed to be made up of Xavier's men and former Steel Knights—had the benefit of numbers. There was a thump as another of the men inside the bar fell. The remaining guys on the side that'd talked about the Red Shark made a break for it, running to their car.

Two of them managed to dive inside. The third, trailing behind with a limp from a shot he'd already taken, caught a bullet in the chest. He collapsed on the sidewalk, and his associates didn't even try to help him. Their car peeled away from the curb at top speed, tires screeching.

The Storm people fired a few more shots after them, but then one of the posher men held up his hand, and the others stopped. They took in the wreckage of the bar with grim expressions.

"Fucking Red Shark," one said. "What the hell is that asshole thinking, sending his people in here now?"

So the Red Shark was a person—a he? Did that mean the Storm was too?

I didn't get any more answers. The Storm men took a quick look inside the bar, shaking their heads as they came out, and then drove off without another word.

I stayed in my crouched position for another few minutes, my heart thumping so hard I didn't trust myself to scramble down just yet. No one else turned up. No one ventured into the street at all, the windows in the store-top apartments along the street staying dark, their curtains drawn. The dead body lay there on the sidewalk in a puddle of blood.

My stomach churned. I'd hoped that after Colt's death, most of the violence in the Bend would peter out. It might actually have gotten worse.

The faces had changed, but the cycle remained the same. More groups fighting over the same piece of territory. Why did everyone want Paradise Bend so much?

For the same reason Ezra Noble intended to keep his hold over it, I guessed. I might not like the man, but he'd better hurry up and kick all these assholes back to wherever they'd come from. I'd cheer him on.

There was nothing I could do about the problem on my own. Finally, I peeled myself off the roof and made my way back to the apartment the guys had arranged for me, leaping between buildings and slinking through shadowed alleys.

I hadn't wandered far. I was back at the place in under ten minutes. While I'd memorized the key code for when I needed to use the apartment door, tonight I scrambled up the back of the building with the help of a couple of ridges in the wall and a drain pipe. I'd left the bedroom window just a smidge open so I could squeeze my fingers under the pane and shove it up to slip inside.

Why get myself seen in the building's hallways if I didn't need to?

The apartment was plain but clean and pre-furnished, a modern two-bedroom with tiny bedrooms and an open concept living room/dining room/kitchen about the same size as just the kitchen back in the Noble mansion. I didn't need even that much space, though. I was happy enough still having an actual bed to lay my head down on.

As I reached the bedroom doorway, my instincts prickled. I hesitated, struck by the sense that I wasn't alone here after all. But before I could even pull out my knife or my gun, a wryly amused voice carried from the room outside.

"I should have known you'd come in through a window rather than a door."

I rolled my eyes and stepped out to find Anthea standing by the narrow kitchen island. "And I should have known you'd just let yourself in if you came to visit." Even if she didn't know the code, I didn't imagine there were many locks in the world Anthea Noble couldn't get past.

She hadn't bothered to turn on the lights, so I checked that the blinds were drawn and flicked the switch myself. The stark glow of the pot lights blazed off her bright red hair. She raised a mug of tea she'd made in the dark to her lips, smiling at me over it. "Sorry if I startled you."

"I don't think you really are sorry," I grumbled,

flopping onto the linen sofa that faced her. "What are you doing here?" My pulse hiccupped despite my casual tone. Had something happened to one of the guys?

Anthea didn't look distressed, though. She waved her hand dismissively. "Of course I'd come to check up on a friend. Just because my brother is being even more idiotic than usual, that doesn't mean I've got to follow in his footsteps."

I couldn't help smiling at her breezily insulting description of Ezra. There'd once been a time when Anthea had regularly insulted *me*. I definitely preferred being on her good side. She actually had become a pretty good friend... which wasn't something I'd ever really had before.

A bittersweet twinge passed through my gut. Ezra wouldn't be happy if he found out she was *still* friendly with me. He was doing his best to take that newfound happiness from me too.

"How are the guys doing?" I asked, with an odd surge of urgency. I wasn't used to caring this much about any of the men in my life either.

"They're keeping it together and mostly avoiding trouble." Anthea studied me with those piercing eyes of hers. "How have *you* been getting by, Mercy?"

I shoved my uncomfortable feelings aside and shrugged. I wasn't going to complain, not when I was benefitting from the Nobles' hospitality even now. "I'm fine. Just been taking a look at what's going on in the Bend, but keeping my head low."

"Good. I definitely don't want that Xavier menace sniffing around here." She grimaced. "We can't get rid of him soon enough. I don't know why Ezra can't see that it isn't at all fair to blame you for the havoc some psychotic prick has decided to wreak." She let out a huff and shook her head. "Well, I'll keep working on him. Whatever I can do to get things sorted out so you can stand with the Nobles like you deserve, I'm on it."

My throat constricted. I hadn't really expected her to keep caring that much about what happened to me. "Thank you. I appreciate it a lot. But you don't need to risk pissing off Ezra on my behalf. I really will be okay."

"It's not about whether you'll make it through or not. I already know you will. Women like us always do." She shot me another confident smile. "But you should have a life that's more than just getting by. And I think we'll tackle this new problem faster if we have you working alongside us. I don't like the look of things down here."

That comment had me immediately on the alert. "What do you mean?"

She glanced toward the window. "I know I haven't spent a lot of time in the Bend, but there's much less activity on the streets than I'd expect this early in the night from what I recall. I saw several of the Steel Knights marks that they put up around this neighborhood defaced—scratched up or partly sprayed over. There was a hostile vibe to it that I didn't like."

Trust Anthea to have already picked up on nearly as much as I had. I nodded. "I think it might have something to do with the new guys in town."

Her eyebrows arched. "New guys?" She beckoned

me over, reaching for the kettle to pour me some tea too.

"Yeah," I said as I walked up to the island. I rested my elbows on it, thinking back over the shoot-out I'd just witnessed. "It seems like there's a new gang in town, one I'm not at all familiar with. They broke into one of the old Steel Knights' businesses tonight and started bashing it up. Then some guys I think are with Xavier and former men of Colt's came by, and a fight broke out... They were talking about somebody who goes by 'the Red Shark' and 'the Storm.' I don't know if those are their leaders or what."

Anthea frowned, stirring a little sugar into my tea. "That doesn't ring any bells for me yet. The last thing we need is even more troublemakers in town." She slid the mug across the island to me. "Tell me everything you saw."

Wylder

WE PULLED UP OUTSIDE THE APARTMENT COMPLEX where we'd set up Mercy to live, and I peered out at the gray concrete walls. This was one of the nicer parts of the Bend, but it was still pretty grungy looking. Amateur graffiti marked the side wall, and rust was creeping around some of the window frames.

It was only a few blocks from the official border of Paradise City, but the two places might as well have been worlds apart.

"It was the nicest property I felt we could get away with confiscating unnoticed," Gideon said, taking in my reaction.

Kaige looked out the window and shrugged. "It isn't so bad. I've lived in a lot worse."

So had Gideon. From what I'd gathered, Rowan's family had been comfortably middle-class, but I was the only one here who'd grown up in a mansion.

I shouldn't let that turn me into some kind of snob, but I couldn't help wrinkling my nose as I stepped out of the car. I didn't like the idea of Mercy living here alone. It didn't matter that I knew that she could take care of herself. She deserved better. She should be treated like a fucking princess.

"Do we have everything we need?" I asked.

Rowan nodded to the large rucksack that he then hoisted over his shoulder. "Yep."

I motioned to the side alley. "You know what to do."

Gideon had scoped out strategic places where we could set up surveillance so that we could keep an eye on the building, just in case trouble came calling. It made me feel slightly better when we couldn't be here to personally protect her 24-7.

"If we all stick to the plan, we should be done within the hour," Gideon said, giving Rowan and Kaige a critical glance.

I clapped him on the shoulder. "I'm sure you can keep them in line. I'll go in and see how Mercy's doing. Meet me in the apartment when you're done."

As the three of them scattered, I climbed up the dingy staircase to the third-floor apartment. The low-rise building was five stories total but no elevator. It figured.

I knocked on the door and waited. A minute passed, and there was no sound on the other side. I knocked again, frowning, and then checked the handle, but the door didn't budge. I didn't remember the code off the top of my head.

"Wylder?" said a voice from behind me. I whirled

around to find Mercy just tucking the knife I'd given her back into the pocket of her jeans.

A smile tugged at my lips. God, it was good to see her, cheeks flushed and dark hair in its typical ponytail, looking like her usual impervious self. I had the urge to grab her in a hug, but something in me balked. Just because I was glad to see her didn't mean I was going to go all mushy.

Instead, I turned it into a joke. "Thinking about slicing and dicing me?"

She laughed and nudged me aside to reach for the door. "You did tell me to be careful. Come on, unless you want to shimmy around the building to go in a window."

So that's how she'd snuck up on me. Pride coursed through me. Damn, she was good.

The inside of the apartment was about as drab as the outside, but at least it'd come with all the basics: sofa, table, kitchen appliances. Nothing hung on the walls, but Mercy had added a couple little touches that made the place already feel like it was hers. A few of her silly origami figures stood on the coffee table, and she'd placed a bowl on the kitchen island with some fruit she must have bought with the money I'd given her.

She flopped onto one end of the sofa, totally at home. Well, she'd had five days to get settled in. Which she obviously hadn't forgotten either. She shot me a narrow look. "It took you long enough to come by."

"Things haven't been so smooth back home with Dad," I said. "I didn't want to risk coming here until I was sure we wouldn't be bringing trouble with us."

"I don't suppose the Grand High Noble has changed his opinion of me."

I grimaced. "No, but he's gotten distracted by other things."

"Mostly Xavier, I hope." Mercy straightened up again, her expression instantly alert. "Things are a mess down here. He'd better be ready to step in."

That sounded ominous. I sat down next to her. "What's going on? He's mostly been focused on figuring out where Xavier came from and how big an operation we're up against, not what's going on down here."

"I haven't had a whole lot to do other than keep an eye on things around here," Mercy said. "Carefully, of course," she added dryly when I started to protest. "I haven't figured everything out, but from what I can tell, there are two groups going up against each other right now."

"What? I thought Xavier was out to get *us*, and there haven't been any clashes between him and the Nobles yet."

"I'm a little confused too." She glanced toward the window, maybe thinking about whatever she'd witnessed out there. "There's one group that says they support 'the Storm,' which seems to be a code word for their leader. Maybe that's Xavier. I've seen guys who look like the ones we figured were his in that group as well as some former Steel Knights. I'd guess the remaining Steel Knights threw in their lot with the guy who was backing Colt after Colt died. It'd make sense."

I nodded. "Nowhere else to go. We sure as hell wouldn't welcome them if they knocked on our door."

Mercy smirked and then went on. "Then there's a bunch I haven't recognized at all that are working for someone they call 'the Red Shark.' Another code name, I'm guessing."

"The Storm and the Red Shark," I repeated. "Never heard of either of them."

Mercy sighed. "It's very weird. Anyway, the Storm people I've seen so far look more confident and experienced, but the Red Shark people have been hitting them hard and quick wherever they can. There've been a few run-ins already with bodies dropped on both sides."

I raised my eyebrows, impressed all over again. "You've really been putting the puzzle together." But then, I shouldn't be surprised. This was the woman who'd exposed a murderer none of us had even suspected. When Mercy put her mind to something, she got it done.

That was one of the reasons I liked her so much.

"It's important to me," she said. "There are people here, families who are afraid to step outside after dark. The violence that Colt sparked isn't over yet. I want to see it finished." She paused, giving me a pointed look. "While the Storm people and the Red Shark guys are busy fighting with each other, it seems like it'd be a good time for the Nobles to sweep in and take care of both."

I held up my hands. "Hey, I agree with you. But you know it's not up to me. Dad is pretty pissed off that we didn't realize this Xavier psycho was a factor beforehand. Now he wants to be sure of exactly what and who we're dealing with before he takes any major action. He won't admit it, but I think that whole exploding lackey thing unnerved even him." My own stomach still turned, remembering that bloody scene.

"How long is he going to procrastinate?" Mercy muttered. "What if things take a turn for the worse?"

Seeing the worry etched all over her gorgeous face, something in me softened. "You care about these people."

"This is my home. Of course I care about them."

Caring could be dangerous, though. I knew that, and I made a point of caring about as few people as possible because of it. The fact that Mercy had worked her way into becoming one of that small number still kind of amazed me.

"Do they care about *you*?" I asked.

"They don't know me. Not yet," Mercy said more to herself than me. "But I don't need them to. I just want all of them to have more choice about their lives than I did."

She got up, stepping toward the window. The afternoon sunlight glinted off her dark hair in a sort of halo, and right then, I couldn't tear my eyes off of her. My determined, vengeful princess. She sure hadn't lost *her* spark with Colt's death. If anything, her fire was burning even hotter.

And damn, did I want to burn right with her in all the best ways.

We couldn't get anything else done for the Bend right now, but there were plenty of other things I'd like to do when she looked like that. When it'd been five days since I'd so much as touched her.

I got up and walked over to her, setting my hands on her waist and bowing my head close to hers. "So tell me, Kitty Cat, in between all this prowling, did you ever get lonely here all by yourself?"

Mercy didn't step away. The mood in the air changed, almost crackling with anticipation. I could see the shift as her eyes darkened and her tongue came out to flick across her lower lip.

"I wasn't *totally* alone," she retorted in a teasing tone. "Anthea managed to come by and keep me company."

I dropped my voice lower. "I certainly hope you didn't do with her all the things I'd like to do with you."

Mercy cocked her head. "I guess you're lucky I don't swing that way then, because otherwise she could totally get some."

I let out a little growl and tugged her closer so her breasts brushed my chest. Even with the layers of fabric between us, the sensation sent a flare of heat straight to my groin. "Keep talking like that, and I'll have to find some way to remind you how good you have it with me." I guided her around and eased her backward toward the bedroom door.

Mercy let me direct her steps, but she gazed up at me with mischief as well as desire in her eyes. "*Was* it good? It's been so long, I can't quite—"

I'd been kind of hoping she'd make the first move, but one of us had greater patience, and it sure as hell wasn't me. I grasped her ponytail and yanked her toward me, and our mouths crashed together. It was all heat and teeth and tongues, some kind of battle for dominance I wasn't sure I wanted to win.

I tugged her hips against mine, letting her feel the hard press of my cock. Her breath hitched against my lips. I kissed her harder, walking her farther backward at the same time, pausing on the threshold of the bedroom when I couldn't resist grinding into her. She curled her fingers into my shirt and arched against me. Her needy gasp mingled with my groan.

The bedroom was bare except for a queen-sized bed and a narrow dresser next to it. I lifted her and tossed her onto the bed, climbing over her as she settled onto the covers. Then we were kissing again. Her fingers dug into my hair, tugging gently and then insistently enough to send a prickle of pain through my scalp. I chuckled. "Easy, Kitten."

When she grumbled impatiently, I kissed a trail down her jaw to her collarbone, swirling my tongue around it, tracing the shape of the bone under her warm sun-kissed skin.

She hooked her thighs around my hips and pulled me to her. I had no choice but to oblige. I pinned her hands above her and brought my mouth back to hers, thrusting my hard cock against her pussy through our jeans at the same time.

I was so hungry for her I could have come just like that, but something in me held back. Yes, it would feel fantastic to plunge into her like I had before—but that first and last time we'd fully fucked, I'd made her feel like I'd only been hooking up with her for my own gratification.

I was man enough to rein in my horniness and make this time all about her, wasn't I?

"I'm going to give you loads to remember the next time you're all on your own," I promised darkly, pressing a kiss to her throat and then her sternum, all the way down to her belly over the thin fabric of her shirt. With one flick of my thumb, I opened the fly of her jeans.

Mercy moved to sit up to get closer to me, but I pushed her back on the bed with a firm look she accepted just this once. Maybe because she could sense that what was coming was going to go in her favor anyway. When I gripped the waist of her jeans, she lifted her hips to help me pull them off her. Then I bowed my head to lap my tongue over her cunt through her panties.

They were already damp, the musky flavor of her seeping through. Mercy's breath stuttered, her hips rocking as if to urge me on, and I was more than happy to meet that wordless demand.

I peeled off her panties, almost ripping them off in the process, and nudged her thighs apart so that I could look at her swollen pussy. I leaned closer and took a sniff of her arousal and almost came in my pants. She smelled abso-fucking-lutely incredible.

"Who needs dinner when I've got this," I murmured against her thigh, nipping the soft, warm skin with my teeth. I knelt beside the bed and pulled her to me so that her legs were draped over my shoulders, her pussy right at the edge of the mattress for the taking. "I can't wait to taste you properly."

I lowered my head, swiping my tongue from clit to slit. Mercy moaned, grasping my hair again. Her musk was sweet like honey with just a hint of saltiness to it. Delicious. Grinning at her reaction, I lapped at her slit greedily, all the way to the pucker of her asshole. As I licked, Mercy squirmed so much she almost arched off the bed.

Holding her down, I buried my mouth in her wet, hot cunt before seeking out her engorged clit with the tip of my tongue. I pulled at it slightly with my teeth, teasing the line between pleasure and pain. With a keen, she tensed her thighs on either side of my face to keep me in place, not that I had any intention of stopping.

I devoured her hot pussy, working my fingers inside so that I could simultaneously eat her out while pumping in and out of her. Mercy outright mewled like a kitten, the sound turning me on even more.

I liked doing this to her. I was in absolute control. She didn't owe anything to me, but in this moment I owned her body and owned my own lust. I wanted to see how many times I could possibly get her off without once giving in to my more selfish desires.

I reached up and grabbed one of her breasts, squeezing the nipple while I continued my onslaught on her pussy. Her channel squeezed around my tongue and her legs clamped around my neck, almost shutting off my air supply. And then she came with a scream.

That wasn't enough to satisfy me. I swirled my tongue faster and delved my fingers deeper, seeking out the most sensitive spot inside her. Mercy's legs shook as I propelled her straight into a second orgasm that had her shuddering.

Her head sagged back against the covers. As she panted there, I eased away for a moment. I licked the pussy juice off my lips before giving her a sly grin. "Enjoy yourself?"

"Fuck, yes," she murmured, her eyes at half-mast. She started to sit up, her legs still splayed in front of me with my early dinner on display, and the bedroom door swung open.

"Rowan and Kaige are just finishing up the last installations downstairs, but I wanted to—"

Gideon glanced up from his damned tablet and stopped in his tracks, his eyes widening. He blinked rapidly, otherwise stock-still, his eyes darting as if he wasn't sure where to look. It must have been pretty fucking obvious what we'd been doing.

"I—er—clearly you're busy," he said. "This can wait. Nothing urgent."

He spun to leave, but I hadn't missed the way his gaze had been drawn to Mercy's partial nakedness, the heat that had flushed his cheeks—or the quick adjustment of the crotch of his khakis. My best friend could be so detached sometimes you'd mistake him for a robot, but there was no denying that right now he was turned on.

Mercy sat up, her T-shirt drifting down to partly cover her, but she didn't look bothered that he'd seen her. If anything, *her* eyes had lit up too.

Then it hit me. She didn't look concerned because

he'd seen her before. I'd given Gideon my blessing to go after her, and sometime in the past couple of weeks he had.

Jealousy reared its ugly head inside me. I clamped down on it, resisting its ragged claws. I'd told Gideon it wouldn't change our friendship if he pursued something with Mercy, and I wasn't going to make myself a liar.

It hadn't been so bad working with Kaige to get her off the other night. Why would it be horrible to see her with a guy I trusted even more?

I stood up as Gideon reached for the door, a renewed sense of authority rising inside me. "Who said you have to leave?"

Gideon glanced back at me, hesitant but not unwilling. I looked from him to Mercy, who arched an eyebrow at me, waiting to see what I'd do next. Oh, *she* was game, all right.

I focused on my best friend. "I think you liked what you just saw. You like *her*, don't you?"

Gideon's tongue skimmed over his lips, making the ring there quiver. He considered Mercy in a way that was weirdly analytical and lustful at the same time. Gideon was an intense guy, but I wasn't sure I'd ever seen him quite this intent on anything. The observation only strengthened my resolve.

"She's an impressive woman," he said finally, as if we were talking about a new model of car, but the rasp in his voice hinted at much more emotion than his words.

"No denying that." I dropped my gaze to Mercy and teased my fingers down the side of her face. "Why don't you repay the favor I just did for you by passing it on to my best friend?"

I said it like a suggestion, but my tone made it a command. Mercy let out a little laugh, and I half expected her to tell me off for daring to give her an order like that.

Instead, she got up and walked right past me to Gideon, her luscious hips swaying from side to side. Gideon's gaze stayed locked with hers the entire time, his Adam's apple bobbing in his throat and desire hazing his eyes. He set the tablet down on top of the dresser.

Mercy trailed her fingers down Gideon's chest and glanced over her shoulder at me. I got the impression she was actually enjoying having an audience. Once her fingers reached his pants, she slid down the zipper as she kneeled in front of him. Gideon sucked in a breath, transfixed.

When she delved into his boxers, his cock sprang free, already erect. As Mercy stroked her fingers over it, I focused on my best friend's face. His expression had gone slack, nothing but pleasure written there now. She had him in the palm of her hand, quite literally.

Then she leaned in and wrapped her mouth around his cock.

Gideon's head fell back. He tried to balance himself by putting a hand on Mercy's shoulder as she bobbed up and down over him. She cupped his balls, and he let out a noise from the back of his throat, his eyes rolling back.

Holy shit. I'd thought it would be difficult to watch this, but somehow it was one of the hottest things I'd ever seen: my tightly-laced best friend unraveled by the bold, confident woman we both wanted. My own cock had begun to throb. I rested my hand over the crotch of my jeans, rubbing it lightly to release a little pressure.

Gideon's hands splayed in Mercy's hair, guiding her motions as he fucked her mouth with his dick. His motions were growing erratic. Mercy hummed so eagerly my cock got even harder.

Fuck it. I unzipped my jeans and released my rigid erection. Precum was oozing out of its tip. I smeared it down the length, imagining Mercy taking my cock instead of my best-friend's. But did I even want that? The sight of them going at it hot and heavy set off a fire in me I'd never expected.

My movements didn't go unnoticed. Mercy glanced up, swiveling her tongue around Gideon's dick as she pulled back, the act and the mumbled curse he let out electrifying me even more. She took in my stance with a slow grin and curled her fingers to beckon me over.

Hell, yes. Without a second thought, I walked up to her, feeling as if I were in a trance. This woman could work some kind of magic, that was for sure.

She stroked her hand up and down my cock, slicking more of the pre-cum around and then sucking the head between her lips.

I'd forgotten just how good the wet heat of her mouth could feel, the jolts of pleasure when she worked her tongue over my Prince Albert piercing. A strangled noise escaped me. My balls clenched with the need to unload.

With a hungry but sly glint in her eyes, Mercy eased

back, keeping one hand running up and down my
length, and downed Gideon's cock again. She looked
like she was having the time of her fucking life.

Something about her taking charge of the situation
that I'd begun made it even more erotic. She squeezed
my balls, making me growl, and then turned from
Gideon to me again, teasing him with her fingers this
time. Her tongue circled my piercing and tugged on one
of the metal balls. Then she took me all the way down
so avidly I almost lost it right there. I clutched at her,
pushing my hips toward her so that I could fuck her
face faster.

Her tongue slid all the way down to the base of my
cock as she kept pumping away at Gideon's with her
hand. She drew back, the shaft springing out with an
audible pop, and switched between us. Back and forth
she went, bringing me right to the brink of release and
then stretching out the moment a little longer.

Finally, Gideon's hips started to jerk, his breath
stuttering. Mercy didn't torment him any longer. She
sucked him down hard, and he exhaled raggedly as he
came. He slumped back against the wall next to the
door with a nearly delirious smile.

Mercy swallowed and was on me a second later,
bringing all her tricks to bear. She sucked and lapped
her tongue over me and teased the piercing with the
edges of her teeth. After all that build-up, it took less
than a minute before I careened right to the edge of
that blissful precipice. With one more swirl of her
tongue, I lost it, exploding into the heaven of her
mouth.

"Damn, you're incredible," I said, dropping down on the edge of the bed.

A faint blush colored Mercy's cheeks, but she smirked at me and grabbed her jeans. "I think I've made my repayment in full."

"And then some."

How had a woman this badass walked into my life out of nowhere and turned everything I'd wanted on its head? I'd never felt anywhere near this strongly about another girl, not even Laurel. Every cell in my body screamed to possess her, body and soul.

And maybe that wasn't a good thing.

How could I possibly keep her when I knew that if Dad found out, I'd have signed her death warrant?

Rowan

The apartment we'd arranged for Mercy wasn't anything amazing, but I was glad to see the door looked solid and the interior was clean, none of the furnishings too shabby. The most unusual sight in the place was Wylder at the kitchen counter, prepping sandwiches.

Coming in behind me, Kaige let out a teasing whistle. "Wylder, you really cooking, bro?"

"It's just sandwiches," Wylder said with a roll of his eyes. "Pretty sure even you could manage that."

"Not if you're already making them." Kaige flopped onto the sofa across from Gideon, who was fixated on his tablet as usual.

"Where's Mercy?" I asked.

"In the bathroom," Gideon said abruptly. "She wanted to take a quick shower."

He didn't even glance up, but something about his tone made me study him for a moment. I had the feeling I was missing something, but then, it was hard to tell what was going on in Gideon's head at the best of times.

"Tell her to hurry up," Wylder ordered. "Can't leave a man waiting when he's gone to the trouble of making lunch."

Kaige snorted, and my lips twitched with a smile. I walked to the doorway Wylder had motioned to. The door stood ajar.

It was a bedroom, pretty spartan, the bedcovers a little rumpled. The door to the en-suite bathroom was closed, rustling sounds filtering through it. Mercy must have already finished her shower.

I'd only just thought that when she walked out, dressed and rubbing a towel over her long hair. She stopped in her tracks when she saw me.

Awkwardly, I took a step back. "Hey."

"Hey," she said, lowering the towel and offering a small smile. "I didn't know you were here."

"Kaige too," I said, and then couldn't figure out how to follow that up.

I was supposed to be the smooth-talker, ready to handle any situation, but my mouth never seemed to work quite right when Mercy was around. We hadn't talked all that much in general since the night of the confrontation with the Steel Knights, when I'd apologized for so many things and she'd granted me her forgiveness with a kiss.

I wanted so much more than that. Even standing before me in her typical T-shirt and jeans, she took my breath away. We'd been so close before, and now...

Now I had no idea what *she* wanted or how to even bring up the subject. Especially when it was obvious she'd caught the attention of all three of my brothers-at-arms—and welcomed it too.

As if on cue, Kaige poked his head into the room. Mercy's eyes lit up at the sight of him, and a pang of longing ran through my chest. She hadn't reacted that happily to me.

"Come on, before I eat all of Wylder's hard work," he said, grinning.

"As if I'd let you," Wylder retorted from behind him.

Mercy rolled her eyes, still smiling, and I walked with her into the main room. Wylder had set out plates for all of us on the narrow kitchen island. Mercy grabbed the nearest sandwich and took a big bite. Then she raised her eyebrows at Wylder. "Wow, this is pretty good."

He picked up his own. "Of course it is. I might not be up to Anthea's standards in the kitchen, but a real man knows how to make a proper sandwich."

"Just as long as you don't expect me to make you any," she teased. "My place is definitely not in the kitchen."

He smirked back at her. "Oh, I'm perfectly happy with what you have to offer elsewhere."

Her only response was to aim a playful kick at his shin. The electricity between them crackled in the air, and my skin itched with it. I didn't know just how much had happened between them over the past few weeks, but I was pretty sure it'd gone well beyond one quick kiss.

I swallowed down my jealousy and took one of the other sandwiches. "So what's the plan for the rest of the day?"

As Gideon came over to join us, grabbing a sandwich with one hand while still holding his tablet with the other, Wylder chewed thoughtfully. "Mercy's made some interesting observations about a new power struggle in the Bend. My dad doesn't want to launch a full offensive yet, but I don't think he can object to us cracking a few heads to get some answers."

I nodded, a different sort of electricity prickling through me. The anticipation hyped me up, but it wasn't all a good sensation. With the way the situation in the Bend had escalated, I knew talking wasn't going to get us anywhere. I'd be calling on the other skills I'd built up so that I could stand alongside Wylder Noble. It wasn't how I'd prefer to contribute, but I hadn't earned my place here if I wasn't at his side every time he needed me.

"I'm in," Mercy declared.

Wylder frowned. "You've stuck your neck out investigating these guys enough already."

"I haven't done enough until the Bend is back to the almost-peaceful existence it had before."

"We don't want to paint a target on your back."

Mercy rolled her eyes. "As if I don't already have one? No one's managed to hassle me yet, and I've been out every night."

"You have?" I asked automatically with a twinge of worry.

Mercy looked at me briefly before turning back to

Wylder without answering me. I guessed it had been kind of a stupid question. Had I really expected Mercy Katz to stay cooped up in this place for five days?

"Exactly," Wylder said to her. "You've done your part; now hang back and relax."

Mercy let out a huff of breath. "Wylder Noble, how many times have we had this conversation before? You'd think you'd know better by now."

"She's right, Wylder," Gideon said matter-of-factly. "She's going to come no matter what you say."

"Exactly." Mercy folded her arms over her chest with a triumphant expression.

Wylder sighed. "Fine. But at least let us take the lead. We still have a lot more experience with actual brawls than you do."

My stomach knotted. Mercy had seen me in action before, but I hadn't enjoyed knowing she was witnessing the violence I'd become capable of. Today might be even worse. But I couldn't exactly tell her she shouldn't come for fear it might ruin her impression of me.

I wasn't the same guy she'd dated—the guy she'd loved—five years ago. We both knew that.

We chucked the plates in the sink for later and headed down to the unobtrusive car we'd picked for this trip, not wanting anyone down here to realize who was in it. The hot summer sun blazed over us, but even in the middle of the day, the streets were quieter than I remembered. Only a couple of people ambled by on the sidewalks, their eyes darting nervously when they saw us.

"It's eerie out here," Gideon said.

"Everyone's sticking close to home or work," Mercy said. "Trying to avoid getting caught in any crossfire."

She frowned, but in a way that was better for us. I slid into the driver's seat. "That'll make it easier to find our targets. Who are we looking for exactly?"

Mercy got in the back and stretched out her legs. "We're probably better off looking for the Storm people. The Red Shark guys seem to lay pretty low except when they're on the attack."

Kaige rubbed his forehead as he sat next to her. "Hold on. I feel like I've missed a whole movie. What the hell are you talking about? Shark, Storm, is this the fucking National Geographic Channel?"

Mercy guffawed and explained about the two groups she'd noticed clashing in the Bend over the past week. From Wylder's expression as he got into the front passenger seat, I could tell she'd already filled him in.

"Same cycle, different faces," he said. "Let's look for some of Colt's former men, the ones who seem to have thrown in with the Storm and probably Xavier. I'm very interested to hear what they have to say about all this."

I started the engine and pulled out into the street. I hadn't lived in the Bend for years, but I still had a decent idea of where the tough guys might hang out during the day. We cruised by various bars that hadn't opened yet and other businesses. We were just coming up on one of the smaller parks with a rusted slide-and-swings set when a chemical burning smell reached my nose.

A second later, a plume of smoke came into view farther across the patchy field. Several guys were standing around a big metal trash can that was spouting flames. It looked like they'd set up a grill over the top and were roasting burger patties on it, like some kind of trailer park picnic. A few of them were gulping from beers, and others were smoking what looked like joints —blatantly, as if they didn't care who saw them.

Mercy leaned forward, her eyes narrowing. "At least a couple of them were with the Steel Knights. I recognize that guy with the blond buzz cut and the one with the snake tattoo around his neck. That's got to be a Storm group."

"Perfect," Wylder said, even though we were outnumbered close to two to one. "Park the car. We'll crack some heads until they're down or running, but hold on to those two you're sure were Steel Knights so we can ask them a few questions after."

They weren't expecting a fight, definitely not one as brutal as I knew Wylder wanted to deliver. We could take them. I stopped the car by the curb, and we all got out except Gideon, who hung back with a tense expression.

Instinctively, I tapped my knife in my pocket and my gun at my back, checking the position of my weapons. It was better if it didn't come to blades or guns when we were just trying to send a message, but we had to be ready for anything.

Wylder sauntered right up to the group around the trash can. The humid late-summer air stunk of strong weed and cheap beer. The men looked up at him, a few of them taking on defensive postures.

"Who the fuck are you?" snarled a block-headed guy

near the front, but I could tell a few of them, including the two Mercy had pointed out, recognized the Noble heir. They stiffened more than the others, their fingers tightening around their beer bottles.

Wylder didn't speak. Instead, he nodded to Kaige, who punched the nearest man so hard he went sprawling on the grass.

"What the fuck?" someone shouted. The men leapt in, but in their semi-inebriated state, their reflexes let them down. We tore through them like a bowling ball through a set of pins.

Wylder held one of them by the back of his collar and slammed his face against the makeshift grill with a sizzle of burning flesh. As that guy screamed, a man to my side smashed his beer bottle and lunged at Mercy. I caught his arm first.

With muscle memory trained by years of martial arts classes, I used his own momentum to swing her attacker around and jab the jagged glass right back at him. The shards sank right into his chest through his shirt, blood welling around the spot. He stumbled away, swearing, and ran.

But we still had more to deal with. Kaige was throwing his fists every which way, and Wylder was slamming one guy's head into his knee, breaking his nose. I wasn't as wild as one or as vicious as the other, but I held my own.

I ducked as one of the men swung a plank they'd been using for firewood at me. I gripped the edge of the board and heaved it back at the perp. It hit him square on his forehead and nose, drawing blood. But he came at me again. I pummeled him from one direction and another, dodging around him, until he buckled over, and then I kicked him in the side of the head so hard he slumped on the ground unconscious.

Somewhere to my left, Mercy was ramming her elbow into another guy's temple. I was vaguely aware of her glancing my way, and my stomach balled tighter, but I couldn't let any thought of her judgment distract me.

This was the new Rowan Finlay. I was in control, and I wasn't going to let anybody fuck with my crew.

Kaige sent one more guy reeling to the ground. The only ones left were the two Steel Knights Mercy had pointed out.

The blond man tried to make a break for it, but I snatched the back of his shirt and clocked him in the throat hard enough that he gagged. As I pinned him to the ground, Kaige dropped the guy with the snake tattoo. He hunkered down on the guy's back, and his prisoner groaned.

A couple of their associates lay bleeding and unconscious. The others had taken off. Wylder stalked over, cracking his knuckles, which were flecked with blood. Now that the worst was over, Gideon emerged from the car, carrying his tablet and watching the scene with an analytical glint in his eyes.

"Let's get this over with quickly," Wylder said to our captives. "I'm sure you'd like to go back to your partying and not, say, have your ribs crushed and your skulls bashed in. Answer our questions, and you're free to go."

The guy I was holding swore and tried to squirm out of my grasp, but I gripped him firmly and smacked him across the temple. Mercy knelt by his head with her knife drawn.

"I remember you from the last big fight," she said with a sharp note in her voice that made my pulse skip a beat. "You have no idea how much I'd like to use this. But if you play nice with the Nobles, I'll play nice with you."

She wasn't the same Mercy Katz I'd known either. But I'd always been aware there was a fierceness inside her, always liked it. I just hadn't realized how deep it ran.

Wylder crouched next to the tattooed guy, cocking his gun. "What the lady said goes for me too. The Nobles can show mercy." He winked at her. "We've just run out of patience for upstarts who think they can take over our territory. What's this I hear about someone named the Storm? Is that your new boss?"

"What are you talking about?" the guy under me sputtered. "We don't know anything about him."

Mercy arched an eyebrow. "Who said it's a him?"

He winced, knowing his lie was exposed. Wylder shifted his attention. "We know a lot more than you seem to realize. You were already working with Xavier alongside Colt, weren't you?"

When both men remained silent, he jabbed his pistol against the tattooed guy's temple.

"I don't know," the blond guy said in a panicked tone. "My loyalty was to the Steel Knights. Some other pricks showed up and started talking to Colt like they had an equal say in things, and then after he died that Xavier fuck showed up and said we were his now. He claims Colt made an agreement with him and he's holding us to it."

"And you just went along with that?" Mercy asked, her lip curling with a sneer.

"He shot anyone who argued about it. He's a fucking psycho. I wanted to stay alive... and hell, why wouldn't I want to be on the winning side? It was pretty much the same guys we were working with under Colt."

We'd guessed right about Xavier's involvement with Colt, then. But there was still a lot I didn't understand. "And does Xavier want people to call him the Storm?"

The guy I was holding let out a ragged laugh. "No, he talks about 'the Storm' like it's someone even bigger than him. All I know is, I don't want to ever meet the asshole who's keeping that menace on a leash."

I exchanged a glance with the others, a chill tickling down my spine. Xavier wasn't the leader—he was working for someone even more powerful than him? That wasn't a good sign.

Wylder tapped his gun against the tattooed guy's head again. "What else do you know about the Storm? Has he come into town?"

"Not as far as I know. It's Xavier we've dealt with. I don't think anyone except Xavier's guys has any clue, and maybe not even all of them."

Gideon frowned. "You've got to have at least some idea what Xavier and the Storm want, don't you?"

"Isn't it obvious?" the guy said. "Look around. He wants all of Paradise Bend. Now that Colt's gone, he's going to take everything for himself."

"Not just the Bend but Paradise City too," Wylder said.

"Yeah. The way the Storm's guys talk, they figure once they've got the whole county, it will make the perfect jumping off point to secure the rest of the state. It seems like he wants everything the Nobles have and then some."

Wylder leaned back on his heels. I could see the wheels turning in his head. Xavier might be obsessed with Mercy, but it was clear his interests—or those of his boss—went far beyond her. "And the Red Shark?" he asked after a moment.

"I'd never heard of him—or them, or whatever they are—until a week ago," the blond guy said. "They turned up out of nowhere and started messing with our properties, taking potshots at them. But Xavier's determined to crush them. I definitely wouldn't want to be on *that* side."

Kaige jabbed the tattooed man with his elbow. "What about the drugs?" he demanded. "Where'd that Glory stuff come from?"

Why was he worrying about that? But I guessed it was a reasonable question. The new drug people were calling Glory had only turned up in the city alongside Colt's bid for power.

"Colt was using it to fund our new operations," the man said, with a hiss of pain as Kaige jabbed him again. "Xavier brought more with him, so maybe he was supplying it the whole time. Colt never liked talking about where it came from."

"So basically you don't know a hell of a lot, do you?" Kaige growled.

"Look, the Storm's guys don't like us asking questions. And no one wants to cross Xavier. We just want to stay alive."

"Well, you've accomplished that much. For now, anyway." Wylder motioned for Kaige and I to get up. We released the two former Steel Knights men, easing back with our guns out in case they made any sudden moves. But the guys picked themselves up gingerly, the tattooed one favoring his left shoulder, which looked like it might be dislocated, and the blond one rubbing his hip. They studied Wylder warily.

"Get the fuck out of here," Wylder said, waving his gun. "Storm, Red Sharks, it doesn't matter—you picked the wrong side. The only winners around here are the Nobles, as we just proved. Go tell your friends all about it—and if you know what's good for you, after that you'll get the hell out of the Bend."

Mercy

It was late enough that the night air was getting a bit of a bite to it. I pulled on a thin black hoodie over my tank top and leggings and slipped out the apartment window. The wind nipped at my ponytail as I jumped to land on the roof of the two-story building next door.

Once I was on my feet, I took off running, leaping gaps and climbing trellises and even pipes but not letting my feet touch the ground below. It was safer up here where I could easily melt into the shadows of the city.

Wylder had told me to lay low for a few days after our discovery that Xavier was working under somebody else, somebody who was potentially more powerful than him. And also crazier? I didn't even want to think about that. But I couldn't just wait around doing nothing.

I landed on the terrace of a squat brick building

deeper within the heart of the Bend and scrambled over the bars to drop into the alley below. As I checked my watch, a wry voice carried from farther down the alley. "You're late."

Anthea sauntered over. She'd traded her usual housewife-y dresses for sleek, dark-washed jeans and a black blouse, but even though we'd gone for similar colors, she still looked ten times more professional than me. Well, we each played to our strengths.

I grinned at her. "Only by three minutes."

She harrumphed. "Well, you can't tell me you got stuck in traffic."

"Hey, the pigeons around here can get pretty vicious."

A soft laugh tumbled out of her. She peered past me onto the quiet street. "So, what's the plan?"

"We're going to have a chat with the former Claws members."

Anthea raised her eyebrows at me. "Haven't they all gone into hiding since they turned against the Steel Knights and basically lost that battle for them?"

I shrugged. "I haven't seen them around, no. But I know the usual spots where they'd get together. I'm pretty sure at least a few of them are doing a little business out of a pawn shop a couple of blocks from here."

"Sounds like you've got the situation under control. What do you need me for?"

I tapped her with my elbow. "You're the best person I know at reading people and picking up on subtle clues. I'm going to be asking them some questions they might not really want to answer, about what they found out after they switched sides to join up with the Steel Knights. You can tell me if you think they're being less than truthful. And if I can't convince them to talk, maybe next time we'll come back with some of that truth serum of yours."

Anthea smirked and followed me down the street. We stuck close to the fronts of the buildings, out of the glow of the streetlamps, though half of those were broken or burned out anyway.

The pawn shop's windows were dark and streaked with grime. A very sad looking guitar lay across the display ledge next to a china doll with a chipped nose. The sign on the door was flipped to CLOSED, but I ignored that and headed around to the back.

The back door's paint had mostly flaked off, but the lock held well enough when I tested it. I glanced at Anthea. "This is the other reason I asked you to come. You brought your lock picks?"

She brandished a fabric case. "I'm going to give you a few lessons and my spare set next time I visit so you don't need me for this part."

All it took was a jiggle and a flick of her wrist, and the lock disengaged. As she put her tools away, I took out my gun and eased the door open.

I couldn't be sure exactly how friendly these guys would be. Some of the former Claws men had stood up for me and the Nobles during the shoot-out with Colt, but some of those same men had shot at *us* just a few days before that. And tensions were clearly running high in the Bend these days.

When the door shut behind us, the storage room we'd stepped into was almost totally dark. A faint glow emanated from down a set of concrete stairs that led to the basement.

"Hello?" I called out, not too loudly since I didn't want my voice to carry outside. "Whoever's here, I just want to talk."

The air shifted next to me, and my instincts kicked in before any thought had a chance to. I ducked and punched the body that'd come at me square in the ribcage, sweeping my attacker's legs out from under him at the same time. He went down with an *oof*.

As I turned my gun on my attacker, Anthea illuminated him with the flashlight on her phone. The guy stared up at me, going still as he blinked in shock, and I let my gun hand lower just a little.

It was the man who'd come to warn us about Steel Knights' impending arrival when we'd been setting our trap—who'd stopped us from getting caught in *Colt's* trap. His face had paled beneath his sprinkling of mouse-brown hair.

"Mercy Katz," he said. "What are you doing here?"

"I had a few questions that I thought my father's former associates could help me out with," I said with a crooked smile. "I'm guessing there are at least a few more of the old Claws downstairs."

The man nodded warily, but got up and beckoned to me. "Come on. They won't mind seeing you. I'm sorry —we can't be too careful with the way things have been going. After Jenner and a bunch of the others stood up to the Steel Knights, all of them that are left have been gunning for us."

Funny about that, when their new leader had said he was glad we'd taken down Colt. But then, Xavier wouldn't want the former Claws messing up his plans either. It probably suited him just fine to have some of his new men eager to take down anyone who'd ever challenged their side.

"I never caught your name," I said to the guy as he led us down the stairs.

"Roy," he said, and then called down the stairs, "Everything's okay. Mercy Katz came by to talk to us."

We came around the bend at the bottom of the stairs into a wide, concrete-walled room lit by a couple of bare bulbs. There were four other guys there, all of whom looked at least vaguely familiar, though I didn't know any of their names either.

They were standing in a semi-circle around the doorway, one with a knife in his hand and another just tucking his gun back into his jeans, but the card table in the middle of the room with a pile of chips in the middle suggested I'd interrupted a poker game. I spotted sleeping bags and blankets bunched against the walls. These guys must have been living down here, not just working out of the place.

A pang of guilt hit me. I wasn't the only one who'd lost things in this unexpected war.

"Mercy," said the guy with the gun, giving me a respectful bob of his head. He looked about forty, with a hint of gray just starting to creep through his short moustache, and he held himself with an air of subdued authority. "I'm sorry about your dad. Colt deserved everything you gave him." His gaze slid past me to Anthea. "Who'd you bring with you?"

I touched Anthea's arm. "This is Anthea Noble, a good friend. I couldn't have taken down Colt without her—or without plenty of help from others in the Nobles too. For now, I'm allied with them."

The men eyed both of us but didn't raise any complaints. The Nobles had been standing up to the chaos that Colt—and Xavier—had been instigating, at least as much as Ezra had allowed. Even if these guys had chafed under the Nobles' rule from time to time, we all knew we were on the same side.

"So you came by just to chat?" one of the other guys said, folding his arms over his chest. "What about?"

Roy snorted. "Don't be like that with her, Wheeler. She was the boss's daughter."

Wheeler grimaced at him. "The boss is dead. She's just some chick."

"Shut it," the guy who seemed to be the leader snapped. "If we'd done our job better, maybe he wouldn't be."

"You know *I* didn't have any part in that shit, Kervos," Wheeler retorted, holding up his hands. "I never even knew she was getting married—that's how much anyone bothered to tell me."

Kervos rolled his eyes and turned back to me. "What do you need, Mercy?"

Anthea spoke up. "Why don't you go back to your game while we talk? We don't want to keep you away from it."

The men gave her an odd look, but I assumed she had a good reason for suggesting that. And hey, maybe it'd give me a chance to prove I was more than just some "chick" too. I tipped my head toward the table. "I see there's an extra chair. You want to deal me in next round?"

Wheeler started to make a disgruntled noise, but Kervos swatted him across the head and motioned me over.

The men threw down their last bets, and it turned out Kervos had won. As he scooped up the chips, one of the other guys shuffled the cards and dealt them around the table, including me this time. Roy hung back behind Kervos, and Anthea stood behind me like some kind of guardian angel.

I examined my initial hand and held back a wince. Not looking so great so far. But the key to winning wasn't always in the cards but how you presented yourself. I'd gotten pretty far in this life by acting like the boldest person in the room.

I let a smile creep across my lips and tucked my cards close as if treasuring them, my gaze daring any of the men around the table to challenge me.

"What can you tell me about everything that's going on in the Bend now that Colt's fallen?" I asked. "We've gathered that he started working with this Xavier guy and a group led by the Storm—any idea how that went down?"

The dealer laid down a card that didn't help me at all, but I let my smile widen anyway. "The Steel Knights never told us much even when we joined up with them," he said.

Kervos nodded. "They'd just say things like that they'd made some new connections, brought more power on board. And that they needed the backup after Tyrell had been scheming to take *them* down." He sighed. "I should have pushed harder about that and not bought into their stupid lies."

"Hey, standing up to them put targets on all our backs," Wheeler said. "We might have been dead men if we'd challenged them back then."

"Still," Roy said tightly, "we owed Tyrell more than that."

I glanced at the faces around me. "So none of you saw any actual evidence that my dad meant to betray the alliance with the Steel Knights?"

The next card gave me no favors either, but I tossed a handful of the chips Kervos had offered me at the start into the middle anyway. The men studied the growing pile, Wheeler frowning. "I wasn't around enough to see anything," he said, and set down his cards. "Fold."

The other guys shook their heads. Kervos swiped his thumb across his lips. "Tyrell wanted that alliance more than anything I'd ever seen."

Anthea leaned forward. "I think you saw something. What is it you don't want to tell us?"

God, she was like a wolf about to go for the throat. Yet again, I was glad I could call her a friend now instead of having her as an enemy.

Kervos stared at her, his eyes twitching in a way that

definitely seemed sketchy. "I don't know what you're talking about."

I waggled my hand of cards at him. "I think you do. Whatever it is, just spit it out. Dad's gone, and that means I'm the closest thing you've got to a boss now."

Wheeler snorted at that comment, but I ignored him, totally focused on Kervos. The older man grimaced. "It could be nothing. It was just something that seemed strange to me. And it didn't have anything to do with Colt or the Steel Knights, so I wouldn't have mentioned it."

"Well, I'm asking you to now," I said. "What'll it hurt to tell me? Maybe it could help."

"All right, all right. It was just that a few months ago, before all this went down, Tyrell asked me to bring him a bunch of records and other info on how much money the side-business I'd been handling was taking in and from what sources. He wanted it laid out all organized and shit. I know he made similar requests to some of the other guys."

Anthea chuckled. "And it seemed strange to you that he wanted proper accounting?"

Kervos glowered at her defensively. "Well, yeah. He said he wanted to be more on top of things so everything could be streamlined when the deal with the Steel Knights was fully settled, but that never totally made sense to me. It wasn't how he normally operated, that's all."

"It's true," I said slowly. "That is kind of strange. Dad was never much of one for getting things written down." He'd thought it'd be too easy for someone to find out things he didn't want them to and take advantage of the information.

In my mind's eye, I could see Dad tapping the side of his head with an almost manic gleam in his eyes. *That's why I'm the one on top. Because I can keep track of everything anyone needs to know in here. They all depend on me.*

A sudden desire for concrete data didn't point to any sort of betrayal, though. I mulled it over a little longer and set the knowledge aside in case it meant more to me later. "What about this Red Shark person who's sending his guys into town now? Have you had any run-ins with them?"

Roy barked a laugh. "We've been avoiding running into anyone at all since the Steel Knights started gunning for us."

Kervos took the card dealt to him and considered his hand before adding, "I've never heard of them before. Seems like they came out of nowhere. My best guess is they have some long-standing grudge against Xavier and whoever-all stands with him, and they tracked him down here. Fuck Colt Bryant for dragging us all into this mess."

"You can say that again," I muttered. Suddenly I wished I could stab my ex-fiancé another dozen times. "Well, thank you for telling me what you could, even if it wasn't much."

I accepted a card. My hand was still shit. I cocked my head, sitting up a little straighter, and tossed another handful of chips into the center of the table with a smug smirk.

The other men contemplated me. One folded. I met Kervos's gaze. "How much of your winnings am I going to put in my pocket?"

He muttered a curse and threw his cards aside too. "I'm sure you've got a better hand than I do. Take what you've already gotten."

I couldn't help cackling as I spread out my cards on the table. I didn't even have a pair.

The men all stared as I scooped up the chips. Then Roy started to chuckle. Kervos slapped the table with a loud guffaw. "Holy hell, Katz, you do have some balls on you. More than a lot of my men. I'll give you that."

"I think what you mean to say is that she has a sizable pair of *ovaries*," Anthea said archly, but she was smiling too.

"Look," I said in a more serious tone when I had my little heap in front of me. "I have a lot to thank you for. You stuck out your necks for me and the Nobles, and the people who matter won't forget that. It's getting crazy out there, and I don't like what's happening to the Bend. We're going to take action... but we might not be able to tackle all of these pricks on our own. Can we count on you to stand with us if that's what it takes to get these assholes gone?"

The men exchanged a glance. Wheeler winced, but Kervos squared his shoulders. "It's hard to give a promise when we're not fully sure what's going on out there. All these powerful new groups in play..."

I held up my hands. "I'm not going to force you. Unlike *some* people, I don't want loyalty that only comes under threat."

"If anyone can set things back the way they should be, it's her," Roy piped up, looking a bit nervous. "You saw the way she took on the Steel Knights all on her own."

"She did have a little backing," Kervos said dryly, but his expression was warmer when he turned to me again. "I can see you're not the type to back down easily. Maybe your father should have let you step up more while he was still alive. It's impressive how much you've accomplished in just the past few weeks. If the time comes when we could turn the tide, call on us, and we'll have your back. Just get our home back for us."

I summoned all the conviction I had in me. "You'd better believe I will."

Kaige

I was coming out of the gym when I ran into Gideon—almost literally, since the guy never looked where he was going when he was staring at one of his tech devices. One of these days he'd walk right into a wall.

"Any update about who this Storm prick is?" I asked automatically.

Gideon tore his gaze away from his phone's screen for long enough to raise an eyebrow at me. "Believe me, as soon as I've got anything, you'll be among the first to know. How many times have you asked me in the past twenty-four hours already?"

"I want a go at him," I said with a grumble.

An uncharacteristic smile tugged at Gideon's lips. "I'm sure Wylder will let you at him first."

Electronics aside, I had to admit that in the past couple of weeks, he'd been a little more... relaxed, or cheerful, or some other word I didn't normally associate with the computer guru. I couldn't help suspecting it had something to do with Mercy. She'd had a pretty major effect on all of us, it seemed like.

All the more reason I should get to pummel that X-scarred asshole's head in for threatening her. And killing that cat. Who the hell went around carving up innocent animals just to send a message?

When we reached the foyer, Wylder and Rowan were standing by the door, their heads bent together in conversation. My spirits lifted with the thought that they might be planning another excursion to see Mercy, even though we'd just checked in on her two days ago and we did have to keep a low profile about it. Waiting two days seemed like ages to me.

As we ambled over to join them, Hector stalked past us. A massive bruise was blooming over his right eye, another coloring his left cheek. Damn.

When he'd headed outside, I tipped my head in the direction he'd gone and asked Wylder, "What the hell happened to Hector?"

Wylder sucked a breath through his teeth. "Dad lost his shit on him. He just heard from Jasper Herald that the Demon's Wings don't want to get involved in this shit, which is apparently deeper than Jasper expected, so he's withdrawing from our alliance. It works in our favor, really, since he contributed men already and we haven't done anything for him, but Dad wasn't happy. And he took out his unhappiness on the nearest available face."

I couldn't say hearing that surprised me. Ezra Noble

wasn't exactly known for gentleness. At least Wylder could be glad his dad didn't turn his fists on him... not that Ezra hadn't been plenty hard on Wylder in other ways.

None of our dads were winning Father of the Year awards, to put it mildly.

"News about the Storm is spreading fast, huh?" I said. "We don't even know who he is or why he wants Paradise Bend so bad."

Rowan shrugged. "I don't think it's that complicated. We heard from the Steel Knight guys that he sees the county as a good jumping off point to make more power grabs, and it *is* prime territory. Ezra's been increasing his empire for years. If someone could just grab all of the Nobles' operations and make them their own, they'd be making a lot of profit out of that war."

"It wouldn't be that simple," Gideon said.

"Of course not. But it'd probably be simpler than building the same connections and businesses up on their own from scratch."

"We haven't lost the war yet," Wylder said. "Paradise Bend is and will always be our turf."

I nodded, feeling adrenaline pump through me. Whatever was coming, we were ready for it.

"What are you guys talking about?" a voice said from behind me. I spun around to find Axel there, a cigarette dangling from his lips.

"Have you forgotten the no smoking in the house rule already?" Wylder said with an edge in his voice.

Axel took out the cig with a smirk. "It's not lit, so

technically not a crime. Are you going to answer my question?" He gave us a pointed look.

"Like most people around here, we're talking about the guy who thinks he's going to take the county from us," Rowan said mildly.

Axel made a skeptical sound. "You kids have been busy lately. Always coming and going. I don't remember Ezra giving you any missions."

Wylder grimaced at him. "My dad gives me leeway to make some of my own decisions, you know. We have work to do. We can't sit around while our enemies are already moving against us."

"So you've been going down into the Bend, then?"

"That *is* where this Xavier and his men appear to be operating from," Gideon replied, his voice flat.

"Funny. I'd imagine that's where Mercy scampered off to also. I don't suppose you've run into her at all."

I had to fight the urge to bristle. Who the fuck was he to talk about Mercy when he'd probably egged on Ezra's decision to kick her out? But he obviously suspected we'd stayed in contact with her against Ezra's direct orders. I had to keep my cool.

Which meant keeping my mouth shut and letting the other guys do the talking. I wasn't much good with my words, and I didn't think using my fists to shut Axel up would win us any points with the big boss, as much as I might have enjoyed doing it.

"If she's around, she's been staying out of sight," Wylder said without betraying any emotion. "We obviously haven't gone looking for her, considering my dad's feelings on the subject. Why? Are you worried about her safety, Axel?"

Axel snorted. "Somehow I think you must be."

Wylder gave him a bored look. "As far as I've been able to tell, Mercy's very good at taking care of herself."

Axel eyed the four of us for a moment longer, looking like he was hoping his gaze could dig right into our skulls and read our minds. My hands itched at my sides. I wished so much that punching him on his stupid, smug face was a good alternative to answering his questions. Imagining doing it calmed me down a little.

"Whatever you get up to, I hope you're keeping your loyalties in mind," Axel said finally, and sauntered off.

Gideon waited until he was out of sight and then muttered, "We definitely have to stay careful. I've noticed a couple of the men who report to Axel watching us around the mansion. They're probably keeping track of when we come and go."

I stiffened as an awful thought hit me. "They couldn't track us with one of those fancy thingamajigs you use, could they?"

He rolled his eyes. "I doubt they have enough brain cells to even think of it, but I check our vehicles over carefully before we leave. And the new van I'm having custom-made is almost ready. We won't keep that here at the mansion."

"That fucker, spying on his own people," Wylder muttered. "If he spent half as much energy tracking down Xavier and his boss as trying to screw *me* over..."

His phone rang before he bothered to finish that

sentence. He checked the caller ID and brought it to his ear. "What?"

Whatever the guy on the other end said, it made Wylder's expression darken. "Seriously?" he said, scowling. "The balls on those assholes."

As he hung up and turned back to us, my pulse hiccupped. "Is it Mercy?" I whispered, remembering to keep my voice quiet.

Wylder shook his head, his mouth set in a grim line. "No, a contact of mine in the Bend was calling. He says the Storm's people are handing out free samples of Glory—from *our* waterfront property."

"What the fuck?" I said. No wonder he'd been pissed.

"Exactly. Come on, let's deal with this before my dad has yet another reason to be bashing faces. Maybe Axel will keep his trap shut if we prove we're handling more problems than he's managed to."

———

It was only a half hour later, as we cruised along the highway toward the condo development Ezra had recently bought into that was right near the border of Paradise City and the Bend, that an obvious question occurred to me. "Why the fuck are they giving out free drug samples?"

"Glory is one of the main ways the Storm's people have been funding their operations here," Rowan said from where he was sitting next to me in the back. "They must have brought a new shipment in, and they want to get as many people hooked as possible so they can sell the rest and bring in the cash quick."

Wylder had insisted on driving this time, his knuckles standing out stark white because of how tightly he was gripping the steering wheel. "And they're doing it out of prime Noble territory just in case they can get us in trouble with the cops as a bonus."

"But the project isn't completed yet," I said. "Anyone could have broken in. Even I know it'd be stupid for us to deal right out of a property that's in our name. Who's to say the Nobles are involved?"

"The cops don't care about logic," Gideon said in his know-it-all way. "They like easy targets. If they can pin the blame on us that easily, they'll go for it whether it makes sense or not. We can deal with the attention, but having the cops sniffing around will distract us from the bigger issues."

"So we'll just make sure that doesn't happen," Wylder said, gunning the engine so the car roared along even faster.

"We should take the lay of the land first, see exactly who's there and what they're doing and saying, before we go at them," Rowan put in. "We need to find out everything we can about these guys."

Wylder nodded. "They don't know we're onto them. We go in, scope things out, and then lay down our kind of law."

When the tall, half-finished building came into view up ahead, Wylder pulled off onto a quiet street a few blocks away and parked the car. Gideon stayed there, monitoring whatever traffic cam feeds he could tap into in case he needed to send us a warning, and the rest of us set off on foot.

The waterfront property was being built right on the bank of the river that cut its way through the heart of the Bend before skirting around the city. Work was progressing fast, and the steel frame gleamed against the sky. The lower part of the site was hidden away by a temporary wall of steel and plastic panels.

As we approached, I saw a stream of people ducking in where one of the panels had been wrenched to the side. These must have been the people coming to get the drug, not already high, but I could tell that a lot of them weren't any strangers to the experience. Most had a jittery look to them, their gazes twitching around as they made their way in. The sight made my skin crawl.

The weed I smoked to help me relax and brief highs from party drugs were one thing. You could indulge in those and not fuck yourself up. But these people looked like they'd been into the serious shit, the kind of crap that took over your life and turned everything good in it rotten. If they thought Glory would help them fill that hole, it wasn't anything I wanted a part in.

We joined the line and hung back by the wall after we'd slipped in. I had to reel in my jaw from gaping as I took in the scene.

The Storm's people had gotten the word out pretty widely, and quite a crowd had turned up to take advantage of their offer. A few guys were standing around a couple of crates in the middle of the wide cement slab at the base of the building's frame. As newcomers came over to them, they handed out little squares of white paper. There were a couple dozen people making their way over now, and nearly a hundred meandering around the slab and across the beat-up dirt of the rest of the site.

A few of those who'd just left the distributors were urgently snorting the drugs off the slips of paper in their hands. One guy staggered and then tipped his head back to gaze up at the sky with a loopy smile. Others were stumbling around in various states of chemical euphoria, their eyes glazed. Here and there I spotted some sitting on the ground rocking while they hummed to themselves.

I'd known that crap was strong when I first caught a whiff of it, and the confirmation was right here in front of me.

A man stumbled into me as if he couldn't even see I was there. My arms shot out instinctively, pushing him away from me and recoiling. It was like a fucking zombie apocalypse in here.

"Kaige," Wylder said quietly. "We're trying not to attract attention yet, remember?"

Right. I dragged in a deep breath and stuck close to his side. We circled around the steel frame, gradually getting closer to the guys handing out the drugs. The three of them started chuckling to themselves as if this was some kind of elaborate joke. My stomach churned.

A guy who'd obviously already had a good snort swayed back over to them, making grasping gestures with his hands. "Come on, man. Another hit—you've got lots there."

"One each," the closest dealer said with a sneer.

"You got your sample. You want more, you pay up. Unless you don't want it that bad."

"I do. I do." The guy patted his pockets and winced. "I'll be back. That stuff is fucking amazing."

I gritted my teeth and wrenched my gaze away, only to find myself staring at a couple lying together by a stack of lumber. The woman's shirt was gaping open far enough to expose one of her breasts, but she didn't seem to care, even though a kid who couldn't have been more than eight was standing there next to them, tugging at her shoulder. "Mom, Dad, please, I want to go home."

Neither parent responded to his pleas. My spine went rigid, images I'd buried welling up behind my eyes. My hands clenched at my sides.

That wasn't the only kid here. A man was just going up to the dealers now with a little girl not much more than a toddler clinging to his pant leg. When he held out his hand for his sample, the girl started to cry. He shoved at her with his leg as if she was just an annoyance. "Shut up, Jess. Daddy needs this."

She continued to wail. One of the dealers glared at her and then her father. "Get her the hell out of here. We don't want to have to listen to tantrums."

As if it wasn't their fucking fault she was so upset. They were the ones luring the parents in—they were the ones doping them up so they didn't give a shit about their own kids.

Rage shuddered through my body. My heart pounded in my ears, and my vision flared with red. Suddenly I was marching up to the dealers with only the faintest awareness of Wylder snapping my name from behind me.

When the closest guy turned toward me, my fist was already swinging. My knuckles connected with his cheek, knocking him right off his feet. As he sprawled on his ass, clutching the side of his face, his associates fumbled for their guns.

I slammed one of those guns right into its owner's face hard enough to split his lip. At the sight of the streak of blood, savage satisfaction coursed through me. I whirled to face the last guy, who had his pistol pointed right at me, but I was too keyed up to care. I was going to crush him too.

Two more guns cocked behind me as Wylder and Rowan came up to flank me. The first guy I'd punched staggered to his feet and drew his own gun. "Who the hell are you and what the fuck do you think you're doing?" he demanded.

"I know what *you* are: little pieces of shit," I said. "These people have kids with them, and you're dealing drugs to them?"

"How's that any of your business?" the third one growled.

"I'll show you how exactly." I flung myself at him, trusting Wylder and Rowan to handle the other two.

I punched the man square on his gut before he could pull the trigger, heaved him over my shoulder, and whipped him toward the ground. He hit the concrete with a cracking sound and a groan. I dove onto his chest and punched him across the jaw. "You. Little. Piece. Of. Shit."

My haze of anger was broken by the distant wail of a siren. "Kaige," Wylder called out. "Come on, we need to get the fuck out of here."

My gaze landed on the little girl still standing just a few feet away. Her father was gaping at me, but she was just staring, her eyes round with terror. Terrified of *me*, even though the assholes I'd been smacking down were the real bad guys here.

"Kaige, come on!" Wylder yanked at my arm. The police cars were close—too close. We heard the sound of slamming doors.

"Fuck." At least the dealers would have to make a run for it now too. I might not have done much for the kids, but I couldn't let Wylder down too.

We sprinted to the opening in the wall. Some of the people who hadn't gotten their hit yet were pushing out ahead of us. Others were too high to really register what was happening, the babble of their confused voices carrying through the construction site.

We leapt through the opening and raced across the street, ducking into the alley there just as footsteps pounded around the corner. "Stop!" a voice hollered. "Police!"

Not a fucking chance. We dashed through the alley, my breaths rough in my throat, and burst out onto the next street over. The car was just up ahead. Another siren blared in the distance. I hurtled forward with all the strength I had in me and dove into the backseat behind Gideon.

"I tried to warn you as soon as I saw them coming,"

he said as Wylder dropped into the driver's seat, Rowan scrambling in beside me. The engine roared.

"I know," Wylder said. "Kaige flew off the handle, and we had to rein him in before we could get out of there."

His voice was flat, but I could hear the anger coursing through it. As he yanked the steering wheel and sped off toward home, my stomach sank.

We'd almost been caught by the fucking cops, and it was my fault.

Mercy

SOMEHOW I WAS STANDING AT THE BANQUET TABLE for my rehearsal dinner all over again. Gunshots thundered all around me.

Grandma fell, blood gushing down her dress. One bullet and another caught my father in the chest—but it wasn't Colt firing them. His face had been replaced by Xavier's, while an even larger shadowy figure loomed behind the scarred giant.

Another bang—and I jolted out of sleep, the sheets tangling around my limbs. My heart was thumping hard. It took me a second to realize that I really was awake in the bedroom of the Nobles' apartment, but for some reason the banging sound hadn't stopped.

It was coming from the apartment's front door: an insistent heavy knocking.

"Open up!" a muffled voice hollered. "Police!"

Shit. My heart practically lurched right out of my chest. I vaguely registered the glowing numbers on the clock perched on the dresser: 2:06 a.m. What the fuck were the cops doing here in the middle of the night?

What were they doing here, period?

Another bellow cut through my confusion. "If the door isn't open within thirty seconds, we're busting it down. This is your final warning."

I scrambled off the bed and grabbed a hoodie off the floor. I'd gone to bed in just a tank-top and pajama shorts, no bra. Tugging the hoodie on, I checked that I hadn't left anything incriminating lying in view. My gun was on the mattress lying next to my pillow—I shoved it between the headboard and the wall, grabbed my knife, and shoved that into the pocket of my hoodie on the way to the door.

After fumbling with the lock and yanking the door open, I found two cops standing in the hall outside. They gave me a once-over, their eyes lingering on my bare legs. I had the urge to see if they wanted an even closer look, like if I slammed my knee into their smug faces, but I wasn't quite annoyed enough to be that suicidal despite my interrupted sleep.

I hadn't seen much of the police in the two decades that I'd lived in the Bend. They mostly focused on civil disputes and personal crimes, looking the other way when it came to all the gang activity in the area. Most of them were getting payoffs from one organization or another.

"Are you alone in here, ma'am?" the shorter cop asked, saying the last word with a bit of a sneer. The suspicion in his eyes convinced me that he knew who I was—or more importantly, who my father had been.

I didn't like to admit to being on my own, but if I said someone else was here, they'd probably demand I bring them out. "Yep, just lil ol' me," I drawled. "Is there some reason you woke me up at two in the morning, officers?"

The tall one glowered at me and barged right past me into the living room. "We got a complaint about a disturbance, some sort of ruckus that had people concerned. We'll need to check the place out and make sure everything's in order here."

That was total bullshit. If there'd been a "ruckus" in or around the apartment, *that* would have woken me up instead of these bozos. It was just an excuse to get them inside without a warrant.

So what did they actually want?

The tall cop started prowling through the apartment. A prickle of apprehension ran down my spine, but it was hard to keep an eye on both him and the short dude who stepped inside and planted himself in front of me.

Shortie narrowed his eyes. "Miss Katz, isn't it? You've been a difficult woman to find."

I folded my arms over my chest. "Who's been looking for me?"

"An awful lot of people, I suspect, after the massacre we found in that restaurant downtown. Whoever was responsible took out your whole family... but somehow missed you. Very interesting."

My stomach tightened. "'Interesting' isn't the word I'd use."

"You couldn't be that torn up about it," Tall Guy tossed out from where he was opening and closing the kitchen cupboards. Did he think the "ruckus" had been started by a cereal box and a stack of plates? "Isn't it strange that nobody came forward to receive the bodies, especially the last remaining member of the family?"

"I didn't have much choice about that," I snapped, and then clamped my mouth shut. I'd had to steer clear to save my own life. No way would Colt have stood back and just let me claim the bodies, arrange funerals —I'd have been lucky to make it through the doorway of the coroner's office alive. But what did these assholes care about that?

Guilt twisted through my gut anyway. I'd assumed that by now it was too late to do anything for my family, but maybe I'd dismissed the possibility too quickly. "Are the bodies still in... custody, or whatever?"

Shortie snorted. "They were cremated a couple of weeks back. We don't have room to hold onto a pile of corpses for ages, especially with how many of 'em have been turning up lately." He shot me another narrow look. "I believe the coroner holds onto the ashes for a while, if it actually matters to you."

"That's good to know," I said, stiffly grateful. I could still do something for them then. There were a few places Grandma and my aunts might like their ashes scattered. Dad... He'd be lucky if I didn't drop his down a sewer drain.

But right now I had nowhere safe to keep the ashes. Even this apartment didn't really belong to me. I couldn't take a stash of urns with me while I was on the run.

"And what exactly are you doing *here* right now?" Shortie asked, raising an eyebrow.

I glanced around. "In the Bend? This is my home."

"No, I mean in this apartment."

The prickle of apprehension came back. "Is there some reason I shouldn't be?"

He gave a disbelieving cough. "It's also interesting that we find the sole survivor of the Katz family in a place owned by Ezra Noble."

I kept my expression carefully blank. "Should that mean something to me?"

Tall Guy let out a scoffing sound as he bent to check under the sink. What the fuck did he expect to find anyway?

Shortie kept glowering at me. "I can't imagine your dear old dad kept you that much out of the loop about how things work in the Bend. What are you doing for the Nobles, Miss Katz? Why have they set you up in this nice place? They must have you on the payroll."

I shook my head, ignoring the growing knot in my stomach. "I have no idea what you're talking about."

"I guess we'll see about that," Tall Guy remarked, coming around the kitchen island and glancing under the stools.

I frowned, stepping to the side as if I could block him from coming any farther into the apartment.

"You're not supposed to just randomly search people's homes, are you?"

He sneered at me. "We told you, we got a report. If someone was hurt in here or there was a violent incident, we need to check to make sure you're not covering it up."

In the kitchen cupboards? I bit back the urge to let loose my snark out loud. Instead, I turned slowly on my heel, letting my eyes dart around the room.

They were here for a reason. They expected to find something... because someone must have pointed them my way. Someone who was confident that the cops wouldn't leave with empty hands.

Nothing in the living room looked out of place to me... Except the little pillow on the sofa. I hadn't paid much attention to it when I'd come in last night, but I had a distinct memory of eating my breakfast yesterday morning with the TV on and my feet propped on top of that pillow. It was straightened up against the arm of the sofa now.

If it hadn't been for the cops' presence, I'd have assumed Anthea had stopped by and instinctively done some tidying up. But suddenly the discrepancy seemed much more ominous.

As casually as I could, I ambled over to the sofa and plopped myself down on it as if I were bored with the proceedings. Then I slid my hand past my hip as if to scratch my back. Instead, I tucked it behind the pillow, feeling quickly for anything other than the fabric of the cushions.

My fingertips brushed the corner of what felt like a plastic baggie wedged next to the seat cushion. At the same moment, Short glanced over at me. My pulse hiccupped. I raised my hand and scratched the back of my neck next.

Tall Guy had gone into the bathroom. Shortie was stalking through the living room, examining the bookcase around the TV. Any second now, he'd want to check over the couch.

When he glanced my way again, I stared up at the top shelf and frowned as if I'd just noticed something there I wouldn't want him seeing. His gaze jerked away from me in an instant. I restrained a smirk.

The second his attention was back on the shelves, I dipped my fingers behind the cushion again, snagged the baggie, and tugged it out. I managed to stuff it in the back of my hoodie and set my hand back on my lap just as Shortie shot me another suspicious look. I leaned back on the couch and muffled a yawn, kicking my foot impatiently in the air.

What the hell was in that baggie? I couldn't check it in front of him. At least the bottom of the hoodie was fitted enough that the bag should stay in there as long as I kept it zipped up.

Shortie left the bookcase and started toward me, just as Tall Guy came out of the bathroom. There was my opportunity.

I leapt up before Shortie had to insist and pressed my thighs together as if I were about to wet myself.

"Sorry," I said. "I've got to dash to the bathroom."

"Wait a second," Shortie said, scowling.

I bobbed on my feet. "Please. I had to run to answer the door when you woke me up—I didn't have a chance then."

Tall Guy looked me over, and I smiled innocently at him while continuing to jitter on my feet. He sighed and motioned for me to get on with it.

I wasn't going to get much time before they figured out something was up. I hustled into the bathroom, shut the door firmly, and sat down on the toilet to actually pee in case the jerks decided to listen in. While I did my business, I pulled out the baggie and examined it.

It held maybe a quarter of a pound of a fine gray powder that looked very familiar. I took a quick sniff and grimaced.

Yep. This was the same drug we'd stolen a huge shipment of from Colt—the stuff they were calling Glory.

I sure as hell hadn't brought it into the apartment. So who had? How had they even gotten in here? And why had they wanted to get me arrested?

The apartment had never really felt like a home, but now the walls around me didn't offer the slightest sense of security. An enemy had breached them, and I hadn't even realized until it was almost too late.

If I lingered any longer in the bathroom, the cops would get suspicious. I emptied the drugs into the toilet and flushed them away along with my piss. Then I folded the baggie as small as it'd go and squeezed it behind the window frame. Even if they checked the bathroom again after I came out, they weren't going to find anything.

I washed my hands and walked back out to find Tall Guy shaking his head at Shortie. "—a bad tip," he was just saying. He shut his mouth at the sight of me.

Shortie glared at me as if blaming me for wasting their time, when they were the ones who'd gotten me up at two in the morning. "It seems everything's in order here after all, Miss Katz. If you have any reason for concern, I'm sure you'll notify the PBPD."

"Absolutely," I said with forced brightness that I doubted they believed.

They marched out, and I shut the door firmly behind them, pushing the deadbolt into place. But the thunk of the heavy metal lock didn't reassure me as much as it used to. Someone had gotten past it once already.

At least once. How many times had the intruder come in here before? Planting the drugs might not have been the first time.

The thought made my skin crawl. I glanced toward the bedroom, but my nerves were too jittery for me to get back to sleep. Something was very, very wrong here.

And if they'd come for me, who else might they be coming for?

I grabbed my phone, taking a small bit of satisfaction in knowing that now I wouldn't be alone in getting woken up to bad news in the middle of the night.

Wylder picked up his new burner phone after a few

rings, his voice tired but tense. "What's going on?" he asked without preamble.

I swallowed thickly, resisting the urge to hug myself even though he couldn't see me anyway. "We've got another problem."

Gideon

I CONTAINED MY THIRD YAWN AS I TAPPED AWAY ON my tablet. Wylder had woken me up way too early in the morning with three simple words that had effectively dissipated any annoyance I might have felt: "Mercy's in trouble."

The swaying of the van made me hit the wrong digital key. I muttered a curse to myself and bit back a sharp comment toward Kaige, who was driving the van I'd just finished setting up to my satisfaction yesterday. I didn't actually want him to slow down when who knew what might be happening to Mercy while we rushed into the Bend, and hurrying never made for a smooth ride.

Beside me on the padded bench that lined one side of the van's large cargo area, Rowan stared at the flat-screen monitors I'd mounted all along the opposite wall. Various surveillance feeds from the cameras we'd set up around Mercy's apartment and footage from traffic cams I was in the process of hacking into flickered across their glowing surfaces. He let out a low whistle. "You really outdid yourself."

"And yet some bastard managed to get into Mercy's apartment anyway," I said, unable to keep the edge out of my voice even though it wasn't Rowan's fault. If anyone was to blame for a flaw in the security system, it was clearly the guy who'd set it up, a.k.a., me. I gritted my teeth and frowned at the footage before me.

As far as I could tell, no one except the cops and Mercy herself had gone into Mercy's apartment tonight. Now I was scanning back through the earlier footage. I'd been skimming through it regularly since we'd set it up, but I could only keep so close an eye on it without Ezra or one of his men noticing that I was even more glued to my devices than usual. I must have missed something.

Damn it. I knew exactly who'd been able to circumvent my security efforts before, and it was the last person I wanted anywhere near Mercy. The image of Xavier's X-scarred face and ominous grin flashed through my memory.

Wylder swiveled in the passenger seat to peer back at us. "Anything?"

"I'll tell you as soon as I find something," I said, my stance tensing even more. I hadn't been able to defend the Noble mansion effectively, and now I'd fucked up somehow when Mercy needed me more than ever. What good were all the skills I'd built up if they didn't fucking *work* when they were supposed to?

Kaige swung around another turn. Through the small, tinted windows on the van's back doors, which allowed us to see out but no one else to see in, the darkened streets looked just as deserted as they did on my screens. The rumble of the van's engine sounded almost blaring in the stillness. I hoped that was just my nerves talking and that we weren't drawing every creep in a ten mile radius to our meeting spot.

The van jerked to a halt. To give Kaige a little credit, the tires only screeched a tiny bit. Almost immediately, there was a knock on the back door.

Rowan leapt up to pull it open and stepped back so Mercy could scramble inside.

She was wearing an oversized hoodie and sweatpants, and her hair was pulled into a messier ponytail than usual, several stray strands falling around her face. She flashed a smile at us as if this were an ordinary get-together, but her gaze darted behind her before she yanked the door closed.

As soon as she did, Kaige hit the gas again. The van lurched away from the curb.

"Thank you for coming so early in the morning," Mercy said, swiping her hand over eyes that looked slightly bleary. Of course, she'd gotten even less sleep than the rest of us. Her gaze twitched to the back windows and the view behind us again, and I could tell that as nonchalant as she was trying to be about this situation, she was nervous.

Who the hell wouldn't be? We'd promised her a safe haven, and it'd been violated by a total psycho.

I flicked my fingers across my tablet to switch the

focus of a few of the screens to the cameras mounted on the outside of the van and footage from the streets around us. "I'll make sure no one's following us. So far we haven't seen anything."

She took in the array of screens and let out an awed laugh. "You've obviously got every possible angle covered."

"That was the idea. Doesn't seem like it worked out so well after all."

Mercy sat down on the carpeted floor and leaned against the bench next to me. She reached up to give my knee a quick but affectionate squeeze that sent a flare of heat straight to my cock despite my distraction.

"Hey, I'm fine," she said. "We'll figure it out like we always do."

She might not have been fine, though. The jackass had decided he wanted to frame her rather than kill her —this time. For all we knew, he *could* have killed her any time in the past week and just hadn't bothered to. I jabbed at the tablet with more force, as if that would change anything.

"Here," Wylder said to Kaige. There was a rattle of gravel against the undercarriage as the van pulled off the road.

When the engine cut out, the two guys squeezed past the front seats into the cargo area with the rest of us. The space was big enough to fit us all fairly comfortably, but I wouldn't have wanted to hold a party in here.

Wylder crouched down across from Mercy while Kaige hovered next to him, looking like he wished he'd gotten there first. Wylder's gaze took her in, and he met her eyes with an intensity I didn't often see from my best friend. "You're sure you're okay?"

"Tired and irritated, but I've been a lot worse," she said, offering another smile. I couldn't help thinking it looked a bit stiff around the edges. This woman knew how to hold herself together, but even she had limits.

"What exactly happened?" Kaige demanded. "These cops showed up—they were looking for drugs someone had planted?" Wylder had given us a hurried secondhand explanation as we'd hustled to the van, but no doubt it'd been missing some details.

"A little more than an hour ago, a couple of cops started banging on my door," Mercy said. "As an excuse to search the apartment, they claimed there'd been a call about a disturbance. I had a bad feeling about it, obviously, so I looked around too, and managed to find a baggie of what I'm pretty sure was Glory tucked in the couch cushions."

Kaige let out a growl. "Fucking Glory."

"You got rid of it?" Rowan asked.

Mercy nodded. "I got a chance to flush it down the toilet. The cops left empty-handed. But I have no idea how the baggie got there in the first place... I'm pretty sure it must have been during the afternoon when I was out of the apartment yesterday, but maybe I'm wrong. And why set me up like that?"

The rest of us exchanged a glance. We hadn't had a chance to fill her in about the incident at the waterfront property yet.

"It seems to be Xavier's new strategy of choice,"

Wylder said tightly. "Get drugs on our property and then sic the police on us. A few of the Storm's people had a whole Glory party at the new waterfront property yesterday. The cops got there before we could break it up. They almost caught *us*."

"What?" Mercy's eyes widened. "Why didn't you tell me anything?"

"It just happened, and it didn't seem like something you needed to know about urgently. I figured I'd bring it up the next time we dropped in." He ran his hand through his auburn hair and grimaced. "Those Storm assholes. Using our own fucking strategy against us. *We* were going to sic the cops on *them* with the truck we stole, and now they've stolen our plan and spun it around on us." He smacked his fist against the floor.

I'd have pointed out that we had bigger problems than copyrighting our schemes, except just then I caught a blurred shape on one of the screens. Sucking a breath through my teeth, I tapped the controls to pause that one and cycled back through the frames to the right spot.

Mercy caught my reaction, looking from me to the screens. "Did you see something?" Her whole posture had gone rigid.

"Not anything happening right now," I assured her, and her shoulders relaxed just a bit. "It's footage from one of the cameras around the apartment building— from yesterday afternoon, like you thought..."

There. He was only on the screen for half a second, but I recognized Xavier's burly form. He hadn't come right up to Mercy's building, though. He was heading into the run-down office building next door.

Everyone around me had fallen silent, clearly recognizing him too. Wylder swore a few times. "How'd he get from there into Mercy's apartment? There's no sign of him going to her building?"

I shook my head, my stomach twisting. "He must have used similar tricks to what she has in the past—gone from a window or the rooftops to one of her windows." I had a camera in the hall outside her front door, so he definitely hadn't gotten in that way. None of the feeds had been covered or cut out even briefly—I'd come up with a way to program the system to alert me if either happened.

But he'd found a way around it anyway. My hands clenched on my lap. "I'm sorry," I said, my strained voice rasping in my throat. I couldn't hold my own in a fight, couldn't physically protect her, so I was supposed to manage it this way. And this prick had shown me up yet again.

Mercy looked up at me with concern in her dark eyes—concern for *me*, when she was the one who'd been in danger—which knotted me up inside even more. She reached for me again, grabbing my hand this time. "It's not your fault. He's beyond anything any of us have had to deal with before. But we're not going to let them win."

I had to figure out how to stop him from winning before we could be sure of our victory.

"I get why they came at us through the waterfront property," Kaige said. "But why target Mercy?"

Mercy's brow knit. "Yeah, it's not as if I'm such a huge threat."

"You're selling yourself short," Wylder said. "I'm sure Xavier found out how big a role you played in taking down Colt. He might be happy with the result, but that doesn't mean he wouldn't realize you could cause problems for him too."

"And he's seemed to have some vendetta against you for a while now," Rowan pointed out. "Leaving that crap at the mansion for you to find... For whatever reason, he's fixated on you."

But he was still playing with her, terrorizing her without following through—yet. It probably amused him to know he could get under her skin. Like a game of chess he was playing with us, and he kept catching us off-guard no matter how many moves ahead I tried to see.

"He was obviously in your apartment," I said abruptly. "You can't go back there. It's compromised."

Wylder nodded. "We'll find another safe location to move you to."

But what location would actually be safe? What place could I *keep* safe for her? I stared down at my tablet, and a wave of anger and despair washed over me.

If I didn't step away from this conversation, I might hurl the device at the screens I'd put so much work into setting up, and that wouldn't help anyone.

I pushed to my feet. "I need fresh air to think properly. Give me a minute."

The other guys blinked at me, but I walked right

past them and hopped out of the van into the cool early morning air.

A hazy greenish glow was just touching the distant sky as dawn crept closer. The narrow alley we'd pulled into stank of urine, but I didn't dare walk farther than the end of it several paces away. What if I screwed us over again by letting someone catch a glimpse of me?

The van door thumped behind me. Mercy walked over. "Hey, are you okay?"

"I just... have a lot to think about," I said. The last thing she needed was to be burdened with my worries along with her own.

She nudged her shoulder against mine. "Nowhere to get acceptable coffee around here. It's definitely too early to go without caffeine."

I cracked a smile despite myself. It'd only been a couple of months since she'd barged into our lives like a whirlwind, and she already knew me so well. Better than anyone except maybe Wylder, really. She was the first person I'd willingly shown my scars to. The first person I'd *wanted* to open up to.

I didn't know how it'd happened. I barely knew what to do with the emotions that rushed through me whenever she was near. They were exhilarating but also unsettling.

I grappled with my words. "I don't like how he keeps upping the ante. I feel like they're backing us into a corner."

"You always get us out of any corners we end up in." She touched my cheek to turn my face so I'd meet her eyes. "You're beating yourself up like you did over the shit Xavier pulled before, I can tell. But did you ever think that you did *more* than anyone else here managed? You're the one who got him on camera to confirm it was him. You're the one who figured out which apartment I should stay in so I wasn't out on the streets where he'd have gotten to me that much easier."

Whether it was her touch or her words, warmth flowed through me, melting a little of my sense of failure. She wasn't wrong. It just didn't seem like enough.

"I hadn't looked at it that way," I admitted.

"Well, I'm not going to forget it."

She bobbed up to plant a gentle kiss on my lips, fleeting but sweet. Somehow the simple gesture squeezed my heart more than when that mouth had been wrapped around my cock. Not that I hadn't enjoyed the latter a whole lot too.

When she drew back, she flashed me a conspiratorial smile—like we'd already figured out the answer together.

Resolve solidified in my chest. Mercy saw me, right through to my core, without pity or judgment. So what if I wasn't sure how to handle the emotions she stirred in me? All that mattered was that I wanted to kill anyone who messed with her, preferably slowly and painfully. If Xavier had been in front of me, I'd have gotten started on it right now.

But he wasn't. It was just me, empty-handed.

Maybe that was the problem. I'd spent all my time trying to be prepared for him to come to us instead of aiming to take him down before he even had a chance.

"Okay," I said. "Let's go back and get on with the planning."

Wylder and the others were in the middle of a conversation when we climbed into the van. "We're going to have to deal with the cop problem before we can focus on getting the Bend back," Wylder said, and nodded to me. "We can't fight a war with them breathing down our necks."

"How are we going to do that?" Kaige asked.

"We could lay low for a few days and let them make the next move," Rowan said. "See what they're planning next."

"No," I said. Every eye turned to me. I drew myself up into as firm a posture as I could manage. "I'm tired of waiting around for them to make their moves. They're too unpredictable for us to learn much like that anyway—and they're getting too close to making major damage. We need to squash Xavier and everyone who stands with him as quickly as we can."

Mercy cocked her head. "What exactly are you suggesting, Gideon?"

"We take the fight to them," I said. "If the Storm is going to set us up, we can just as easily do the same damn thing to them."

Mercy

When we pulled up around the back of the apartment building where I'd been staying, Gideon was deeply immersed in the real estate listings he'd pulled up on his laptop. "By the time you finish checking the place over, I'll have a new spot picked out," he said without looking up. "More secure this time."

Part of me was a little worried there wasn't any place that'd be totally secure from the psycho stalker I seemed to have picked up, but I didn't want to say that out loud. I curled my fingers around my childhood bracelet in my pocket.

The other guys escorted me to the building's back door and up the stairs to the apartment. The thought of stepping back into that space now that I knew my privacy there had been violated made my skin crawl, but Wylder had understandably wanted to take a look around just in case the intruder had messed with something I hadn't noticed. I'd already packed up my meager belongings before I'd gone to meet the guys.

"Never liked cops," Kaige muttered as we climbed the stairs. "They're never on the right side."

He made it sound somehow personal. "Wasn't your Dad in the army?" I asked, remembering his dog tags. Their chain gleamed around Kaige's neck. Like my bracelet, he always kept them on him.

Kaige touched them self-consciously. "Yeah," he said, and then fell silent. I was about to push him to go on when we came out into the hall near my apartment. I stopped in my tracks.

The door to the apartment was slightly ajar. Wylder glanced at me. "Didn't you lock it when you left?"

"Of course."

The hairs on the back of my neck stood on end. Was *he* in there now, behind the door, waiting for us to show up? Xavier. The image of him from the video recording flashed through my mind, and dread curdled in my stomach. I reached for the knife at my hip.

Wylder and Rowan both drew their guns. Kaige's hands squeezed into fists. He stepped forward first, storming up to the door and kicking it open as if he figured he'd just pummel whoever was on the other side.

He barged right in with no sounds of struggle. The rest of us hurried after him. As we stepped inside, I noticed the curtains billowing around the living room window. The window that'd been closed when I'd left the apartment. I ran to it.

"Mercy, wait!" Kaige called from behind me, but I

ignored him. I leaned over the narrow ledge into the dim dawn light to look below.

I couldn't make out anyone or anything moving in the shadows below. My heart thumping, I pulled back inside just as Rowan reached my bedroom doorway. His hand whipped to his mouth, muffling a curse.

"What now?" Wylder snapped. He marched over, reaching the doorway just as I did.

Rowan stepped inside and over to make room for us, careful to avoid the walls. For good reason, I realized as soon as I peered inside.

A cloying, metallic smell filled my nose—not rancid like when Xavier had tossed a chopped up corpse into the Noble mansion, but equally unnerving. Even more unnerving were the dark red streaks that had been smeared across the walls all around the bed where I'd been sleeping just a few hours ago. A pool of it was soaking into the blanket.

Some of the streaks were just random splatter, but others formed letters. *The cat's running scared now*, one wall said. And beside the door, *Next time I'll paint with yours.*

Kaige had come up behind us. He stared at the mess, his jaw dropping. "Is that blood?"

My nose had wrinkled. "Sure smells like it," I said, trying to keep a jaunty tone despite the horror swelling inside me.

"Probably from some kind of animal," Rowan said, his mouth twisted at a queasy angle. "We know he has no problem killing random innocent creatures."

Like the cat he'd slaughtered and left gutted on the

lawn outside my window. I closed my eyes for a moment, gathering myself.

Wylder gripped my shoulders and forced me to back out of the room—but to be fair, I didn't really fight him. I'd seen enough.

"He came back," I said. "He must have been here less than an hour ago." But then he'd left again before we got here. He could have stayed and attacked us.

But that'd never been his goal before. "He's toying with me," I went on, opening my eyes again to glare at the window. "He wants to scare me. Well, fuck him."

Okay, so I was scared. But that didn't mean I was going to run off with my tail between my legs.

Wylder let out a growl. "The bastard is taunting all of us."

Kaige paced the living room, his fists clenched so tight the veins stood out in his forearms. "Let me get my hands on him, and we'll see who's laughing then. He's a fucking coward."

"Let's move quickly," Rowan said. "We don't want to hang around here any longer than we have to." He shot a worried glance at me, and I knew he mostly wanted to get me away from the threats painted in blood all around my bedroom. Despite my efforts, a shiver crept down my spine at the memory.

"He's not putting one finger on you," Wylder assured me, his eyes blazing with unrestrained fury.

They stalked through the apartment, checking around all the furniture. Wylder grabbed the baggie that'd held the drugs from where I'd stashed it in the bathroom when I pointed it out. None of them turned up anything that concerned them—as if the bloody walls weren't a big enough problem.

"I'll figure out someone we can call on to clean the mess up who won't mention it to my dad," Wylder said as we headed back to the van. "Worst comes to worst, we'll wash it off and repaint ourselves." He clambered into the back of the van, where Gideon was still hunched over his tablet. "Got anything yet?"

Gideon's tongue flicked over his lip ring the way he often did when he was deep in thought. "I think so. It's not the best spot but not awful. It takes a key rather than a lock code, though. It'll take me a little while to get a copy of that."

"What do we do until then?" Kaige asked.

"We could take her back into the city," Wylder said stubbornly, as if it'd be easier to hide me from his dad there.

"Guys, I'm right here," I said. "You can't decide for me. I say I stay in the Bend. Xavier's come right to the Noble mansion before—it's not like he stays away from the city. It'll be easier to hide where people are used to looking the other way and questionable stuff is going down all the time."

"She does have a point," Rowan said, and turned to Gideon. "I'd like to know how Xavier found out about this place to begin with. You were really careful, weren't you?"

"I've gone over the records I set up," Gideon said. "There's nothing in them that should have tipped anyone off—and they'd have needed to get into the

Nobles' servers to look in the first place. I haven't seen any breaches."

I grimaced. "It's probably my fault. I've been going out so much. The Storm's people have probably been able to get access to the traffic cams like Gideon can. All it'd take is catching one glimpse of me and they could have pieced together the footage to get an idea of where I was staying."

"That means we have to be even more careful this time," Wylder said.

The tension on his face made something clench inside me, but as much as I appreciated his concern for me, I couldn't simply accept it. "I don't know if that's possible. I can't stay cooped up in some apartment day in and day out while the Bend is falling apart around me. If Gideon can point out all the cameras to me, I'll avoid them as much as possible, but... this guy is good, and he has a lot of men on the streets. I've just got to make sure he never catches me unprepared again."

"So do we." Wylder motioned to the other guys. "I say one of us needs to be with Mercy at all times." I opened my mouth to protest, and he cut me off with a glare. "You'll be safer that way than on your own. This isn't up for discussion."

"I don't need a babysitter," I huffed, not knowing whether I wanted to kill him for his over-protectiveness or kiss him. I didn't like him bossing me around, but when it was because he couldn't stand the thought of anything happening to me, it was kind of a turn-on at the same time. Fucking hell.

"Of course you don't," Gideon said matter-of-factly. "Safety in numbers is just a logical strategy."

I found it harder to argue with that. As I sighed, Kaige perked up. "I volunteer for the first shift!"

Wylder rolled his eyes at him. "Big surprise there. Fine, you can stay with Mercy in the van while Gideon gets her new apartment sorted out. I'd imagine she'd like to get some more sleep."

Kaige waggled his eyebrows at me. "And I'm sure I'll enjoy getting you ready for that sleep."

I swatted him, but my lips twitched into a smile. "All right. It's a plan."

We cruised along several streets until Wylder found a discreet place to park. It was a small lot around the back of a pawn shop that was boarded up, not big enough to fit more than five cars and with a high picket fence surrounding it. Kaige got out and used a stray board to smash a rusty-looking security camera mounted on the fence.

"Was it even still working?" I asked when he came back.

He shrugged. "Better safe than sorry."

Gideon had pulled a couple of sleeping bags out from under the seats up front. "I thought it was best to be prepared for a longer stint in here, even if I wasn't prepared specifically for this situation," he said, setting them on the floor. "There's a storage box with various snacks when you're ready for breakfast."

"Jackpot," Kaige declared, and started unrolling the first sleeping bag.

Rowan had sat down on the bench, the pen in his hand flying over a scrap of paper.

Wylder took one last glance around. "We'll come back to switch off and hopefully get you to a proper home as soon as we can. Don't call us unless it's absolutely necessary. We don't know who else is tracking us."

I nodded, shaking off a fresh shiver.

Wylder walked right up to me. He grasped my shoulders, holding my gaze, and the heat of his body washed over mine. "For once in your life, be fucking careful, Kitten. The Bend isn't going to burn down in the next seven hours. Stay in the van until we get back."

"Fine," I said, swaying toward him instinctively. I was probably going to be sleeping most of that time anyway. After the late-night waking and all the shocks of the night, I was exhausted.

He kissed me fast but hard and kept his hand on my arm as he looked at Kaige. "Keep your head on straight and make sure she stays safe, or I'll take that head right off you."

Kaige just grinned, unoffended by his friend's domineering act. "Got it, boss. I'll keep her way too busy to even think of setting foot outside these doors."

Wylder's grip tightened just a smidgeon, but whatever jealousy he might still have over my connection with the other guys, it wasn't much. He released me and motioned to the others.

Gideon grasped my hand and squeezed just for a second, a show of affection that was unusual enough coming from him to startle me. "I'll get everything worked out—better this time."

"It wasn't your fault," I said, but he didn't reply to that.

Rowan stopped in front of me, holding out the piece of paper he'd been doodling on. "Just... a reminder that there were better days before, and there'll be better days again," he said awkwardly. The second I took the paper, he hurried out after the other guys, shutting the van's back doors behind him.

I unfolded the paper, and a softer smile crossed my face. It was a cartoon drawing of a sun and a cute little kitten lying on its belly under its rays. Yeah, someday, maybe I could be that relaxed.

I turned to Kaige and noticed he'd laid out the sleeping bags not beside each other but fully unzipped with one on top of the other, like a single mattress topped by a blanket. I raised my eyebrows at him. "You just assumed we're sharing a bed?"

He aimed one of his cocky grins at me, as if nothing in the world could be all that wrong. "Don't go telling me I was wrong now. You'll break my heart."

I snorted, but I didn't actually mind anyway. Being in this small space so close to him, feeling the heat of his gaze on me, a little of my tiredness fell away behind a flare of desire. Maybe a little of his bedroom skill was just what I'd need to put all the craziness of the night behind me.

I slipped under the top sleeping bag, and Kaige scooted over beside me. He slipped his arm behind my head. His fingers stroked over my shoulder, but his voice softened. "You know, it's okay to be scared once in a while. *I'm* fucking scared of this Xavier dude every now and then. It keeps us humble."

I tipped my head toward him, letting my forehead rest against his cheek. "Since when are you humble?"

"Oh, all the time. I'm just very quiet about it," he teased.

His other hand drifted over my thigh, drawing more heat over my skin through my jeans. But I couldn't quite settle into the moment. Too many worries were niggling at me.

"How big of a problem do you think the whole thing with the waterfront property is going to be?" I asked.

Kaige shrugged, but I felt his body tense beside me. "Beats me." The casualness of his tone sounded forced.

I turned over so that I was lying on my side, my gaze focused on him. Kaige looked down at me. Though adorable was not a word I'd normally associate with Kaige, that's exactly how he looked tucked beside me in the van's cramped space.

"Something about what happened there bothers you," I said. "And don't you dare say I'm wrong. I can tell."

He made a dismissive sound, but his gaze flicked away from me. "It's nothing."

"Kaige," I said warningly.

"Fine," he grumbled. "It's all in the past anyway. I just don't like being around druggies or the people who turn them into druggies. My parents were... deep into some pretty hard stuff, and I saw how it changed them.

I hate seeing other people pissing their lives away like that."

My throat constricted. "I'm sorry."

"That's why I didn't want to tell you. Why're you sorry? You didn't do anything."

But it obviously affected him a lot. "I know," I said, struggling to find the right words. "But I'm sorry you had to deal with that. Tell me more about them. You know you can talk to me about anything."

His voice turned teasing again. "Why would I want to talk when I can just do this?"

His fingers trailed downwards to my pussy. My breath caught at the sudden contact. I knew he was trying to distract me, but it was awfully hard to remember why I should mind when he was stroking all kinds of sparks through my nerves with his fingers running over my slit through my jeans. I wanted those fingers inside me.

He obviously wasn't ready to talk. I could respect that. I'd get him to open up to me eventually.

I nudged my head up to kiss him and he met me halfway, pulling my body on top of his. He moved my hips up and down so that his crotch was lined up to mine, taking charge like he always did, and just like that I had no interest in talking anymore either.

Mercy

As the engine idled, Kaige drummed his fingers on the steering wheel. "Are you sure this is a good idea?"

"Definitely," I said, scanning the street through the windshield. The mid-day sun blazed over the row of run-down shops, making me grateful for the blast of air conditioning washing over us. "Wylder said I shouldn't leave the van, and I won't. He didn't say anything about the *van* going places."

Kaige snorted and glanced at me sideways. "Somehow I don't think that's because he wanted you driving all over town."

"Well, I'm not driving. You are." I sank back in my seat and checked my phone for any new texts from the people we were supposed to meet. "If Xavier is closing in on me, then it's even more important we find out everything we can about his operations as soon as possible. These guys helped me before—trust me on this."

To my relief, Kaige nodded. It'd taken some coaxing to get him behind the wheel in the first place, but he was committed to my little side-mission now.

Thankfully, his patience didn't need to be tested any longer. Two figures sauntered out of the shadows of an alleyway and headed straight for the van. They climbed in through the back door I'd left unlocked. I twisted in my seat.

"Hey, Kervos," I said, nodding to the bigger guy and then the slimmer one. "Hey, Roy. Thanks for coming out."

The two former Claws members I'd played cards with the other night came over to lean against the back of our seats. "You remembered my name," Roy said with a little laugh. "I got introduced to your dad at least half a dozen times, and he always acted like it was the first."

"Tyrell had a lot more people to keep track of," Kervos grumbled, but he gave me a nod that seemed approving before taking a closer look at the space behind him with its wall of screens and other tech. "Quite the setup you've got here."

"It's not really my van," I admitted. "I don't know how to use all that stuff. We're just relying on our eyes today. You said you know a few businesses the Steel Knights were operating that might still be active?"

"Even in hiding, we hear things," Kervos said.

Roy rubbed his angular chin, darkened with a few days' old scruff. "What do you want to check those out for anyway?"

"If we're going to strike back at the Storm's people most of the Steel Knights seem to have joined up with, we've got to hit them where it'll hurt," I said. "Whatever they're doing to make money, wherever they're stashing supplies."

"Makes sense." Kervos pointed down the street. "The nearest place we can try is a few blocks south and then take a right on Maple Avenue."

Kaige pulled away from the curb and headed south.

Most of the businesses we passed looked like normal stores and restaurants, but that didn't mean they weren't fronts to hide gang activity. Even in the middle of the day, barely anyone was out walking the streets. It was so quiet it made my stomach ache.

How long was it going to take for the Bend to recover, even if we crushed these Storm assholes tomorrow?

A moment after we'd turned the corner, Kervos motioned to a building just down the street. "There. That salon. The Steel Knights had some hookers using the rooms overtop, and they sold stolen merch out of the back sometimes."

Kaige slowed as we cruised by. I spotted the remains of a Steel Knights symbol spray painted in red beside the door, but someone had scrubbed most of it off.

We parked down the street and watched for several minutes. A woman went in through the front doors who was probably just a regular client. Then a couple of guys who didn't look as if they'd had a haircut in at least a year ambled out from the alley that led around back, one of them with a duffel bag slung over his shoulder.

The bulge at the back of the other's jeans told me he was carrying a gun.

"There you go," Kervos said, following my gaze.

"They're not wearing the Steel Knights bandanas on their arms," Kaige pointed out.

"Neither were the ones I've seen with the Storm's people before." I frowned. "I guess that makes it even more likely the ones using the salon have gone over to the Storm. Drive around the block so I can get a closer look at it."

Kaige did as I asked, and I jotted some notes about potential access points and the activity we'd seen. I wasn't sure the salon was seeing enough action that cracking down on it would make much impact, but we had to keep our options open.

Next Kervos directed us to a convenience store that turned out to be closed. We watched it for a half an hour without anyone coming or going. That didn't guarantee they were no longer using it, but it obviously wasn't a happening spot.

The butcher shop we checked out next was similarly deserted. Finally, we ended up parked near an old arcade that I remembered had gotten popular with my high school peers a few years back when retro gaming had become cool again.

We'd only been there for a couple of minutes when a truck stopped outside and some men hauled several boxes in through the front door. None of them were wearing bandanas either, but I expected as much now. They had an air about them that told me whatever was in those boxes, it had nothing to do with video games. I caught a flash of a pistol when one guy lifted his arms to close the back of the truck.

"I think any Steel Knight who didn't want to stick around with the Storm's people got shot for their trouble," Roy said. "They're all or nothing, those guys."

We'd just have to show them what we were capable of when we put all our might into this war.

A few more guys went in and out of the arcade, and I saw movement by one of the upper windows. This place was definitely the most active out of the bunch, which made it the most promising target.

"We'll see what else Gideon can dig up on that spot," I told Kaige as I jotted down a few more notes. "Let's get out of here before they notice us."

"You're really going after these pricks?" Roy asked.

"Somebody's got to. The Bend doesn't belong to them." I shot him a look. "Do you want to stay in hiding for the rest of your life?"

He grimaced. "Okay, I get your point. Well, I hope we helped."

"It's a start. Any news about the Storm himself?" I asked. "Has anyone seen him—or someone they think is him—in the Bend?"

Kervos shook his head. "No sign of him. He seems to operate his entire business through that crazy one, Xavier."

"Keep your eyes and ears peeled for any news about him. He's the one calling the shots. Him and this Red Shark dude."

"Haven't gotten any reports about him either,"

Kervos said. "They obviously like to hang back while their lackeys do the work."

"There's one more place which we haven't checked out yet," Roy said suddenly.

Kervos glared at him. "We're not going there."

"Going where?" I asked curiously.

"The Storm's people are rumored to have set up their headquarters close to the factory that you blew up a few weeks ago," Roy explained, ignoring Kervos's scowl. There was an awkward pause following his words. Back then, the former Claws members had been fighting for Colt, actively trying to kill me and the Nobles.

"They have their own headquarters here now?" Kaige asked. "The fucker's moving fast."

I gritted my teeth against the sudden wave of anger. Xavier was trying to take the Bend over, hook, line and sinker. "Where is this place?"

"I haven't looked into it myself, but from what I heard, not too far from here," Roy said. "There'll be a lot of Storm people around, though."

Maybe even Xavier himself. I sucked my lower lip under my teeth to worry at it and glanced at Kaige. He caught my expression and glowered at me. "I don't think this is a good idea."

He might be right. But if the Storm's people had established themselves that deeply, I wanted to know what we were up against.

"We'll drive carefully in that general direction," I told Kaige. "If we see too many people on the streets, we can always turn around."

Kaige let out a wordless mutter of protest, but he started the engine. But we'd only made it a few blocks when my gaze caught on a figure on a corner up ahead, and I grabbed Kaige's shoulder. "Stop!"

He swerved over to the curb and parked with a jolt. Kervos and Roy swore where they must have jostled on the bench.

"What's wrong?" Kaige asked, staring at me wide-eyed.

I leaned toward my window, squinting. I definitely hadn't seen wrong. "Axel's up there. A couple of guys are coming over to him. It looks like they're talking."

"Axel?" Kaige bared his teeth and bobbed up in his seat to peer over the parked car in front of us. "What's he doing skulking around here?"

"Who's Axel?" Roy asked from the back.

"One of Ezra Noble's top guys," I said. "He... doesn't like me very much. Maybe he's doing some business for Ezra in the Bend." We couldn't let him see me and Kaige together, that was for sure.

"He might be keeping an eye out for us," Kaige said as if he'd had the same thought. "Or just for you, Mercy. He was asking a lot of questions about whether we'd seen you since you left the mansion."

I watched Axel for a minute longer. He nodded at something one of the guys had said and clapped another on the back. I thought I'd seen those two around the Noble mansion before—lower underlings. One of them had a lightning bolt shaved into his buzz cut on the back of his head.

The three of them definitely weren't a big enough

force to be taking on the other gangs. Kaige might be right about his reasons for being here. Axel could have assigned a few of the lesser Noble guys to lurk around hoping to catch us out. Asshole.

"Let's get out of here," I said. "We should probably let Gideon do his magic to find out more about the possible Storm headquarters before we go barging in there anyway."

Kaige gave a relieved sigh and gunned the engine to pull back into the road. But he was distracted enough by Axel that he didn't notice he nearly cut off another driver zipping past us right then.

The other car's horn blared. Kaige hit the gas, and the car swerved around us, but Axel and his two companions had all jerked around to stare in our direction.

Shit. "Go, go, go!" I said, sliding down in my seat so I wouldn't be visible through the windshield.

Kaige jammed on the gas pedal again and spun the wheel. The van lurched forward and spun around. We roared off down the street in the opposite direction.

"Do you think they saw you?" I asked Kaige.

"With all the special stuff Gideon got on these windows, I don't think they'd be able to make out much of anything, and they were still pretty far away," Kaige said. Then he glanced at the rearview mirror. "Fuck, he's jumped into a car to come after us."

"He must have figured anyone who took off like that is up to something," Roy remarked.

My pulse hiccupped. If Axel caught me and Kaige

together, all our lives were going to get a hell of a lot harder. "Can you lose him?" I asked Kaige.

"I'll do my best. Hang on!"

Kaige rammed his foot down, and the van roared, throwing me back in my seat. I grabbed the door to steady myself.

The van wasn't built for racing. The engine groaned in protest as we tore down the streets, turning corner after corner. But the white sedan we'd seen Axel get into was matching us turn for turn.

As we sped toward the next turn, a low, grassy embankment came into view ahead of us. A narrow road below it ran parallel with the adjacent street. The embankment was steep, but Kaige made no sign of slowing down or turning. Instead, he pushed the engine even harder, staring straight ahead.

"Kaige," I said. "What are you doing?"

He flashed me a grin. "Losing him. Just trust me and brace yourself."

"Man, you're crazy," Roy said from behind us, but he sounded at least as impressed as he was worried.

"I know," Kaige said just as we hit the curb of the embankment.

The van jerked forward violently. For one instant, we were suspended in the air. I closed my eyes, bracing for the impact.

When it came, the sudden jolt wasn't half as bad as I'd been expecting. My eyes popped open to check the rearview mirror. We were speeding away, leaving all sign of Axel's white sedan in our dust.

Relief coursed through me. Kaige gave a triumphant

cheer, and I grinned back at him. Sometimes, a little bit of crazy was good.

After a couple more turns, I realized we'd ended up in a particularly familiar neighborhood. "We're near my old house," I said. "The Steel Knights might still be hanging around there."

Kaige's expression darkened. "Maybe we should give them a run for their money, then."

"Hey, we're not here to get into any fights, remember? Wylder definitely wouldn't forgive me for that."

Something flickered across Kaige's face and vanished. He nodded.

As we cruised by the house, I couldn't help peering out the window at it. I didn't see any men standing guard on the sidewalk nearby, but a couple of guys were standing on the porch. As we passed, two more came out, swaggering like they owned the place.

My teeth gritted. "I guess the Storm's people have totally taken it over now."

Kervos shifted on the bench to get a better view out the back windows. "I don't think those are Storm men. Look at the graffiti outside."

I jerked around in my seat, craning my neck to stare through the tinted glass as the view of my father's house dwindled behind me.

Someone had marked a different red logo on the telephone pole outside the house—a gaping mouth full of pointed teeth.

"Pretty sure that's the Red Shark's guys," Kervos added.

One of the men had looked kind of familiar, hadn't he? Was he one of the Red Shark's people I'd watched fighting with the Storm's forces?

"What would the Red Shark's men be doing at your house?" Kaige asked, his forehead furrowing.

As I settled back into my seat, my stomach sank. "I don't know. Maybe it's one of their wins over the Steel Knights?" But I was pretty sure the Steel Knights had only been watching the house because Colt had hoped to catch me coming there. What possible value could it have to these newcomers?

I wasn't totally sure I wanted to find out the answer to that question.

Mercy

Wylder was scowling at me, but by now I'd perfected the art of ignoring his bad moods. "Going off like that was totally reckless," he said. "I told you to stay put."

"Oh, get over it already," I said, and Anthea tried to muffle a snicker. I motioned to the supplies on the floor of the van by our feet. "We wouldn't have been able to pull off this plan if I hadn't done some scouting."

Anthea fanned herself. "Why don't we go over the last stages of that plan before I melt in here?" We'd turned off the air conditioning while the van was parked so we didn't run down the battery, and it was already getting sweltering inside.

Kaige rolled his shoulders, his expression momentarily tensing as he looked at the bags of Glory that were among our other equipment. "Right. We go in, leave the drugs, get out, and sic the cops on the Storm's people. No big deal."

"It's a little more complicated than that," Gideon said, glancing up from his tablet. We'd already gone over a blueprint of the arcade building, figuring out the best room to target and how we'd enter.

Kaige waved him off. "Details, details."

"We also need to plant the drugs carefully," Rowan said. "It won't do us any good if the Storm's people find the baggies like Mercy did in her apartment and dispose of them before the cops get there. But we don't want them so well-hidden that even the cops can't find them."

Anthea nodded. "I was just getting to that." She motioned to the smallest of the bags. "You want to leave a trail. Just a very light dusting, nothing you can even see. The cops will bring K9 units, and they don't need much to sniff it out. Stash the larger bags somewhere really out of the way, where no human is likely to spot it, and lay down the trail to ensure the dogs will find it. Even better, put the larger bags in different places, each with their own trail, so even if one gets found, you still have a chance."

I clapped my hands. "That's fucking brilliant."

Anthea grinned. "That's what you brought me in on this operation for, isn't it?"

"All right," Gideon said, setting his tablet aside. "We've covered everything. I should get on with my part before the next shift change."

He stood up, his expression typically cool and unfazed, but the flick of his tongue over his lip ring made me suspect he was more nervous than he was letting on. He didn't normally go out to face our enemies so close up.

And he obviously wasn't the only one concerned. Wylder got up too, frowning. "Are you absolutely sure you need to do this on foot? We could park closer to the building—"

Gideon shook his head. "I've taken a careful look at their security system. The device I can use to hack into the alarms only works at a very close range." He cracked a rare smile. "Let's just be glad I don't have to go right inside. Through the wall should work just fine."

It still put him awfully close to all the Storm's men on the other side of that wall. A twinge of my own worry ran through my gut. "You've got your gun?"

He patted the back of his jeans. "I'll be fine. It's about time that I stepped up more and took one for the team like the rest of you do on a regular basis." Determination hardened his voice.

Wylder folded his arms over his chest. "You've done plenty for the team already. You do all kinds of shit we don't know how to."

"You're definitely the brains of this group," Kaige said with a chuckle.

"Well, I'm going to use those brains in closer proximity than usual, that's all." Gideon stepped toward the back doors.

Wylder didn't stop him, even though he still looked tense. He nodded to his best friend. "Give us the signal when you're done and get the hell back here as fast as you can. We'll take care of the rest."

Gideon hopped out into the back alley where we'd stashed the van. It led all the way to the other end of the block and the back of the arcade building. With luck, we wouldn't have to set foot on the street where we could be spotted at all.

As Wylder pulled the door shut, Kaige turned to me. "I'm more worried about Mercy. You're the one who's going to be leaping off of buildings."

I rolled my eyes at him, adding an affectionate nudge of my shoulder. "I've done it a gazillion times. You've *watched* me do it plenty of times. I'll be fine." I'd been using my parkour skills since I was ten, and at this point, I could make the necessary leap with my eyes closed. I checked the knife at my hip and the gun at my back, and refastened the laces of my shoes to make sure they were secure, finally adding a pat of my childhood bracelet for luck.

"*You* need to actually stay put this time," Wylder reminded Kaige. "No charging into the fray unless we get into a real fight. Otherwise, you're just keeping watch."

Kaige brought his fist to his chest in a salute. "Got it."

We popped the buds into our ears so we'd be able to hear any warning Kaige gave us, and he put on the inobtrusive mic Gideon had fixed to look like a wristwatch. Just as I was tightening my ponytail, a message flashed across the screen in the center of the array of displays. ALL CLEAR.

Rowan reached for the door. "That's our cue."

The four of us other than Anthea spilled out into

the evening shadows and set off in different directions, other than Wylder and Rowan heading down the alley toward the back of the arcade together. Kaige ambled over to where he could see down the street from the mouth of one lane, and I scrambled up onto a dumpster that put me in jumping reach of a fire escape. I clambered up the metal rungs onto the rooftop of a building on the opposite side of the alley.

Most of the stores were right next to each other with no gap in between, giving me an easy jog across the roof tiles and shingles. I had to make a couple of sprints to hurl myself over laneways, but I landed easily both times, the impact radiating through my legs and exhilarating me. Parkour was the closest I'd ever get to flying.

As I came up parallel with the arcade building, the warm breeze played with my ponytail. I eyed the open window we'd already spotted and the ridges on the wall around it, and rubbed my hands together. The room on the other side was dark, which meant it was probably empty. No problem.

I took a running start and launched myself off the roof toward the window. The air whipped past me, and I heard a faint sound below me that was probably one of my guys, watching. My fingers caught on the top of the protruding window frame, and I automatically shifted my position so my feet hit the window ledge with more of a light thump than a heavy smack.

I held myself there for several seconds, listening for any disturbance inside. When nothing reached my ears, I bent down and slipped through the opening. My sneakers made only a faint scuffling sound on the floor inside.

I'd come into a room some of the men must have been crashing in overnight. Sleeping bags and a few cots stood around the space, and the smell of sweat in the air made me wrinkle my nose. There was no sign of any of the Storm's people around right now.

I crept to the door and eased it open. Voices carried faintly from a room at the other end of the second floor, but no one was in the hall. The stairs we'd seen on the blueprint stood just to my right. I slunk down them as quickly as I could.

At the base of the stairs, I had to pause, flattening myself against the wall with my heart thudding, as footsteps traveled by in a nearby hall. When they'd faded away, I darted to the storage room we'd identified and ducked inside.

It was dark too, but I didn't want to risk discovery by turning on the main lights. I got out my phone and flicked on its flashlight to cast a thin illumination over the space.

Several dusty defunct arcade machines stood in a couple of rows against one wall. The others held shelves stuffed with boxes, and a few large crates had been pushed up against the arcade machines. I'd be willing to bet at least some of them held stolen property. Maybe we'd get the Storm's people on charges other than drug possession.

I made my way to the back door and unlocked it. Wylder and Rowan hustled inside. Wylder gave my arm a quick squeeze. "You're a fucking superhero, Kitty Cat," he whispered.

"How many men are inside?" Rowan asked, pulling the baggies of Glory out of the rucksack he was carrying.

"At least a few upstairs and several down here," I said. "I managed to avoid all of them. Hard to be sure when there's a bit of a racket from the actual arcade too."

"Well, let's stash this stuff." Wylder glanced around in the dimness. "I'll wedge one behind those machines over there. They don't look like they've been touched in years."

I grabbed a baggie from Rowan. "I'll do one of the crates."

Rowan hefted his own. "Under the shelves seems out of the way enough."

We split up again to put our contraband in place. Then Rowan opened up the smaller baggie and we each took a small handful. I smeared the powder on the concrete floor so it disappeared into the rough surface in a line leading to the crate I'd picked and up the wooden side. We brought our trails together in the middle of the room and left a wider trail leading to the back door. Wylder wiped traces around the door frame for good measure.

"No dog's going to miss that unless it's lost its nose."

Just then, Kaige's voice crackled through my earphones. "A car just pulled up out front—a bunch of guys are getting out, carrying some stuff. They might be heading back to where you are."

"Good thing we're already done," Wylder murmured. We hustled out the door and shut it firmly behind us. If the Storm's guys noticed it was unlocked, hopefully they'd blame each other's carelessness. They had no reason to assume anyone had been inside.

At least, they wouldn't have had any. We'd only just stepped away from the door when a couple of figures appeared from a laneway a few buildings away. In the light of a security lamp over them, I immediately recognized one of them from the Steel Knights.

Unfortunately, he recognized us too. "It's the Katz girl!" he snapped, yanking at his partner. "And the Noble heir. They were fucking with our stuff!"

I glanced wildly at Wylder and Rowan and knew we'd all come to the same conclusion in an instant. There was no way we could let these guys live, or they'd give away our plan. We had to take them down before they alerted the Storm's people inside the building.

"What the hell were you doing in there?" the Steel Knight guy demanded, raising his gun as he marched toward us.

None of us bothered to answer. We threw ourselves at them, aiming to get all the advantage we could out of a little bit of surprise.

I drew my knife as I charged, more comfortable with the blade than my gun in close combat. Wylder pulled one of his own out of his pocket. "No shots fired," he hissed—the sound might bring their colleagues running. Then he slammed his knife straight at the guy with the gun.

He only managed to slash the guy's wrist, but deep

enough that the Steel Knight dropped his gun. I kicked it away and then aimed a roundhouse at his partner, who'd grabbed at me. My kick to his gut sent him stumbling backward into Rowan, who clocked him in the temple with a swift fist.

Wylder tried to knock the first guy to the ground, but the Steel Knight fought back savagely. He landed a punch to Wylder's face that split the Noble heir's lip and clipped his shoulder when Wylder ducked. I threw myself in behind him, knocking the legs out from under the Steel Knight. As he stumbled, Wylder was on him, plunging his knife straight into the guy's heart.

Rowan had been facing off with the other guy. I turned to see him aiming several quick, vicious strikes at his opponent's head. His eyes were bright with a sort of wildness I'd never seen in him before.

It distracted me for just a moment, so I wasn't totally ready when the guy he was fighting flung himself away from Rowan and straight into me. His fist rammed into my ribs, and his greater weight sent me tumbling to the ground with him on top.

He groped for his own gun. I squirmed against him, flinging elbows and knees, and he slammed my head back so hard that stars of pain exploded behind my eyes.

My attacker wrenched his gun around, aiming it right at my face—and then his head jerked to the side with a gush of hot blood all over me.

I gasped and gagged, whipping my head away even as the metallic taste seeped into my mouth. The man slumped over me. The ragged end of a broken plywood board dug halfway through his neck, practically decapitating him. What the—

My gaze focused on the figure standing over us. Rowan was breathing hard, his mouth set in a grim smile. As I watched, he jabbed the board even deeper into the guy's neck. Any lingering struggle went out of the body as it collapsed completely. On me.

Wylder yanked at the guy's arm, and I scrambled out from under the body. The Noble heir gave the scene a softly approving whistle and nodded at Rowan. "Make use of whatever you can get your hands on. Very creative. I like it."

A glint of triumph lit in Rowan's eyes for just a second before they caught mine. His gaze darted away, his expression turning suddenly uncomfortable.

I swiped at my face with my hands. My fingers were already sticky with blood. My shirt wasn't going to be much help either, since it was practically drenched with the stuff. I restrained a shudder.

"You okay?" Rowan asked, his voice oddly stiff.

"Yeah. Just... bloody." I pulled my soaked shirt away from my torso and grimaced. "At least none of it's mine."

We looked down at the two bodies sprawled in the alley.

"We can't leave this mess behind," Wylder said. "We'll drag them to the dumpster and get them out of the way until my contacts can dispose of them completely."

He clapped Rowan on the shoulder. "Nice work. I've always been able to count on you to do whatever it takes." Wylder shot a grin at me. "You should have seen him when a bunch of assholes thought they'd get one over on me back in high school. Finlay here practically tore them apart, didn't stop even when they'd nearly gutted him. That's why I took him on."

"You know I've got your back," Rowan said, but he was still avoiding my gaze. This obviously wasn't the time to find out what was bothering him, though. We had a couple of dead jerks to take care of.

I bent down and grabbed the thinner one's wrists. "Let's get moving before anyone else shows up to join the party."

13

Mercy

THE VAN PULLED UP JUST AS WE REACHED THE END OF the laneway where Wylder had texted the others to meet us. The back door swung open to reveal Anthea's grim smile. "Need a ride?"

We clambered in to meet her and Gideon. Kaige craned his neck from where he'd taken the driver's seat, and his jaw dropped. "What the hell happened to you, Mercy?"

I glanced down at my blood-drenched clothes, feeling the tacky sensation of the smeared splatters drying on my face, and grimaced. "We ran into a little trouble. Somehow that seems to end with me covered in blood a whole lot more often than I'd prefer."

"Me too," Kaige muttered darkly. "You took care of the bastards?"

"It's all under control." Wylder waved him back toward the wheel. "Now let's get out of here."

Rowan turned to Gideon, who was taking me in with a tight expression. "Has there been any sign that the guys in the arcade realized something was up?"

Gideon's gaze jerked back to his tablet and then the screens on the van's wall, some of which were showing traffic and security cam feeds. "No unusual activity. I think we're good."

I let out my breath in a huff. "I guess we'll find out when we sic the police on them."

"Let's just take a look with our own eyes," Kaige said, turning the van toward the arcade.

"Kaige!" Wylder protested.

The other guy shot him a defiant look. "I'll cruise by quickly. We should be sure this isn't going to backfire on us, right?"

Our attempts to trick our enemies had gone sideways before. Wylder scowled, but he made a gesture for his friend to keep going.

The van turned the corner and headed along the street with the arcade. Kaige slowed just a tad as we approached the building. Gideon held up his tablet to record the scene. All of us held our breaths, but to my relief, everything seemed quiet, no noticeable activity.

"I imagine there would be quite a ruckus if they found the drugs or any of us meddling with their business," Anthea murmured.

Just as we passed by, three men came out of the arcade. Two of them I recognized as Storm men from my past observations, but the other one—

"That's one of Axel's guys," I said, frowning as we left them behind.

Wylder's head jerked around. "What?"

"You remember Kaige and I told you that we crossed paths with Axel and a couple of his men yesterday. One of those guys was with the Storm's people at the arcade." The young dude with the lightning bolt in his buzz cut—it wasn't exactly a common hairstyle.

"What would he be doing with those assholes?" Kaige demanded.

"Keep driving," Wylder told him. "To the new apartment. We'll sort it out." He beckoned Gideon over to the bench and sat down on it hard. "You got them on camera, right?"

Gideon nodded. I sank down at his other side as he brought up the footage. The three guys ambled out, and I pointed to the one I'd seen with Axel. When he turned his head, the shaved lightning bolt was clearly visible at the back of his head. "Him."

Wylder paused the video and studied the screen. "I have seen him around the mansion at least a few times. He must be one of the newer recruits mostly working under Axel."

"Why would he be hanging out with the Storm's people, then?" I asked.

Anthea rubbed her mouth. "I suppose there are a few different explanations."

"My father vets people pretty carefully," Wylder said. "This is probably part of one of his operations— send the guy in undercover to dig up information on the Storm's resources before the Nobles launch a full attack."

That did make sense, but my sense of uneasiness didn't leave me. "Well... keep a close eye on him if you see him around again, just in case."

Wylder tugged on my ponytail, which had managed to escape the bloody spray. "We'll take care of anything that needs taking care of, Kitty Cat. Now let's get you to your new apartment so you can get cleaned up."

Kaige drove us deeper into the Bend. The three-story building he pulled around back of was more run-down than the first place they'd stashed me, but I didn't need anything posh.

"Sorry," Wylder said, wrinkling his nose as we tramped up the steps in a stairwell that smelled like stale beer.

"It's fine," I said. "If it wasn't for you guys, I'd be sleeping in an abandoned warehouse or something."

"It was the best I could find where I was sure no one would notice the sudden occupation," Gideon said, scanning the hall we came out into.

The apartment itself was a bachelor, the whole thing about the same size as just the living room and kitchen in the other place. A plain bed stood at one end—"I changed the sheets for you," Anthea murmured to me. A shabby love seat squatted in the middle, and a table that'd only seat two stood in front of a short stretch of counter, fridge, and stove that looked like they'd been transported out of the '70s.

I glanced into the bathroom and found that it held only a cramped shower stall squeezed next to the toilet. At least the showerhead emitted decently warm water. I grabbed soap and shampoo out of my bag and headed in. "Time to get all traces of this dead asshole off me."

Rowan took out his phone. "I'll leave the anonymous tip to the cops about the arcade. If we're lucky, they'll get it taken care of tonight."

As I scrubbed myself off in the shower stall, scarlet swirled into the water around my feet. I worked shampoo through my thick hair two times and even gargled with soapy water a few times. The I rubbed more soap all over me again and again until the water ran totally clear. I stepped out to grab a fresh change of clothes in a much better mood that wasn't at all dampened by the mildew creeping along the grout between the tiles.

When I came back out, Anthea was just finishing unloading a couple of bags of groceries into the kitchen cupboards. Gideon glanced at me over the top of his tablet. "I've got the new cameras up and running. I'm trying an experimental program that will hopefully alert me if a form similar to Xavier's moves past them. I'll probably get a lot of false alarms, but better that than missing him."

I went over and gave him a quick kiss on the cheek. "I already feel better knowing you'll be watching over me."

Rowan ran his hand through his hair, meeting my gaze and then jerking his away. "Everything's set up with the cops," he said.

Something was definitely bugging him. I didn't think he was likely to tell me in front of the other guys, though. Rowan had worked very hard to present a certain kind of image in his new role. I wasn't going to try to undermine that, not when I understood where he was coming from so well now.

Gideon cleared his throat. "Are we going to continue having someone with Mercy at all times? I could take this shift."

I grinned at him. "As much fun as I'm sure we'd have, I think it's actually Rowan's turn."

Rowan startled, but he quickly caught himself. "All right," he said, looking solemn. "I didn't have anything to take care of back at the mansion tonight."

Wylder looked from him to me with a speculative expression, but thankfully he didn't let his possessive prick do the talking. "Sounds like everything's settled. The rest of us had better move out before anyone starts wondering too much about where we've been." He leaned in to claim a quick but demanding kiss. "We'll be seeing you soon."

"I'm counting on it," I said, swatting him.

As she headed out with the guys, Anthea squeezed my shoulder. "Rest up. You need it after today."

No kidding. All the running around from the last couple of days was beginning to catch up with me. My body ached from being constantly on the alert.

Anthea had left a bottle of what looked like nice wine along with the food, I couldn't help noticing. When everyone had left, I grabbed that and a glass out of the cupboard. I was going to need a little help relaxing.

"Do you want anything?" I called over my shoulder to Rowan.

"No," he said, his voice oddly tight. "I'm fine."

When I looked over at him, he was pacing the room, his gaze averted. I took a sip of the wine I'd poured and went over to join him. He stopped when I reached him, but his posture stayed tensed.

Whatever was bothering him, it'd started with the fight in the alley. I cocked my head, waiting until he met my eyes. "You know, you were pretty impressive out there tonight."

He raised his eyebrows. "You think so?"

"Yeah. I mean, it's not how I'd have pictured you when I knew you before, but that's understandable. You've changed a lot since then."

Rowan's mouth twisted. "I have. More than you've even seen yet. You know as well as anyone that you can't get into this kind of life—can't survive it—without a certain amount of ruthlessness."

"Well, maybe that's not totally different," I said. "You let the ruthless side of you come out to protect me. I know you'd have done whatever you could to defend me back when we were teenagers too."

A new intensity came into his deep blue eyes. "I'd have done anything for you, Mercy. You're right. That one thing hasn't changed."

Something in his tone sent an eager quiver right down to my pussy, but I didn't think we'd gotten to the heart of the matter yet.

"Not just that," I said, and went to my bag to dig out the little sketch of the kitten he'd drawn for me. "There's a lot of the Rowan I fell in love with in this too."

But when I held it up, he shook his head, tearing his gaze away from me again. "You can't go by that. Everything went to hell the night Carina's friend was murdered in our house. I brought the threat to our family. I knew I had to do something—make myself into someone—who could protect them too." He let out a rough laugh. "But my family fell apart anyway, and the guy you knew might as well be dead."

I grasped his arm. "I don't think that's true, Rowan. Going through shit like that hardens you, but it doesn't have to take you over completely—and I can tell that it hasn't. I know I was harsh on you when I first came to the Nobles, but that was only because I didn't understand why you vanished on me. There's nothing *wrong* with who you are now. And that guy can still make me smile with some pen on paper." I waggled the sketch.

Rowan winced. "That's the most I've really drawn in years," he admitted. "I still get the urge, but... It doesn't feel like it fits with the life I'm living now. How can I even deserve to enjoy trying to make something... something beautiful or whatever when I'm also the kind of person who'll destroy a person's life by hacking his neck in half with a piece of plywood?"

Now we were getting somewhere. "You did what you had to do," I said. "You can't blame yourself for that."

"I know. I don't. That's the point. They were the enemy, and we needed to take them down by whatever means necessary. I can't apologize for it, because I'd do it over again if I had to."

I ran my thumb up and down his forearm. "I'm not asking you to apologize."

"But maybe you should." He raised his head, his eyes somehow fierce and sad at the same time. "The guy you loved is gone. Something... something's broken in me. I thought I was protecting my little sister by joining up with the Nobles, but I've become someone I don't even trust around her anymore in case I scare her somehow. That's just how it is, but that doesn't mean—" He cut himself off and exhaled sharply. "That doesn't mean I like you seeing it."

A sudden rush of affection hit me. That was the most Rowan-like sentiment I'd ever heard, even if he didn't recognize it.

I tugged him closer to me, gazing up at him. "You know what? Seeing you like that doesn't make me like you any less. Maybe I even like you more. I'm sure I'm broken in all kinds of ways most people wouldn't understand. But you can now. I don't have to hide anything from you—and you don't have to hide anything from me."

"Mercy," Rowan said roughly. Heat lit in his eyes, but he held himself still as if he was afraid of what would happen if he let himself move.

I reached up to touch his cheek. "You were a total badass out there tonight, as brutal as you needed to be. But I think—I *know*—you can still be tender. If you can still find beauty in things, then of course you deserve to let your other talents shine. You can be more than one thing, and I'll enjoy all of them."

I eased up on my toes, giving him enough time to

move away if he didn't want this after all. My body was already burning with just a few inches between us. Rowan let out a strangled sound and dropped his head to meet my kiss.

Despite everything he'd been telling me, our kiss was pure honey, sweet but intoxicating. His hands came up to cradle my face. His tongue traced the seam of my lips and coaxed them apart, and I melted into him.

I tugged him over to the loveseat. Rowan moved with me without breaking the kiss, lowering himself with me and lining his body above me as if we were picking up exactly where we'd left off five years ago.

I liked his weight on me. I ran my fingers over his short-cropped hair, enjoying the softness of the tufts. Rowan grazed his teeth over my bottom lip before sucking on it. I groaned, and he slipped his hot tongue back into my mouth.

Making out with him was so familiar but at the same time a rush of a new experience. I could sense the new confidence and fierceness in him.

But like I'd assured him, that ferocity didn't take away his capacity for gentleness. He left my mouth to kiss a slow trail down the side of my neck, soft and reverent, as if he were worshipping my body. I found myself flashing back to the first time we'd slept together, when he'd worked over my cunt with his mouth until I'd come and then entered me when I was so slick and eager I didn't feel more than a pinch of pain.

In the present, I yanked his collared shirt, impatient

for the feel of his newly hardened muscles against me. Why the hell had we waited so long to get back to this?

When I traced my hands over Rowan's bare chest, he groaned. "I missed you so much. No one else could ever compare to you. It feels like a miracle to have you back."

"I missed you too," I murmured, my throat tightening as I realized just how much I had. He'd been the only gentle thing I'd had in my life, and maybe I'd needed that. Needed someone *I* could be tender with, not always putting on a tough front. Rowan had given me room to discover a side of myself that wasn't always on the defensive.

He drew my T-shirt over my head and gazed down at me. The bra I was wearing was plain, but he looked at me as if I was the most amazing sight he'd ever seen.

"You're so beautiful," he whispered. "You always were, but somehow you've gotten even more gorgeous."

Emotion swept through me. I pulled him close again, tucking my legs around his hips so he had no choice but to lean into me. He rocked against me with a rhythm that brought a moan to my lips that he caught with a kiss. His deft artist's hands removed my bra with a few tugs and closed over my breasts.

He caressed them until pleasure was flowing all across my chest and then dipped his head to catch one of the peaks between his lips. He twisted the other nipple, provoking a sharper jolt of bliss. I gasped, arching into him.

"Fuck," Rowan muttered. His hand dropped to the fly of my jeans. We squirmed against each other as he peeled those off and I undid his. When he pulled back to kick them off completely, I made a disgruntled sound at the loss of contact.

Rowan chuckled and lowered himself back over me, but not before I noted the outline of his rigid cock straining against his boxers. My mouth watered. I wanted him so bad.

I sat up, meaning to devour him in the best possible way, but Rowan shook his head and eased me back down with a sweetly sly smile. "I don't know if I can make up for the five years I left you on your own, but I'm going to give it my best shot. Tonight is all about you, Mercy."

He tugged my panties down. Before I could argue, he'd curled his finger inside me. My head tipped back with a moan. He pumped the finger in and out of me slowly at first before adding another and another, gradually filling me, stroking my clit with his thumb.

Did I deserve this kind of sweet devotion? It was kind of hard to believe it, but I couldn't see stopping him either. If Rowan thought I deserved it, if it made him this happy to cherish me like this, it couldn't be *wrong*, could it?

"So wet for me," Rowan said, his voice rough. He brought his fingers, now coated in my pussy juices, to his lips and licked them off one by one. "I've missed your taste too, Mer."

At his words, something unraveled in me. I was hungry for him, the kind of hunger I had buried deep inside me for years. But no longer.

I pulled him down, and our mouths met again, open

with teeth and tongues. Reaching beneath the waist of his boxers, I curled my fingers around his swollen cock. With a guttural sound, he grabbed at his pants and retrieved a condom from his wallet. As he stared down at me, his eyes growing hooded with lust, something shifted in his pose and his expression.

"Put it on me," he said, his voice quiet but commanding at the same time, so passionate it sent a giddy jolt straight to my pussy.

I peered at him through my eyelashes and gave his dick a few more forceful strokes. I did love the darker side of him too, just as much as his sweetness. "Let me have it then," I murmured, holding out my hand.

I tore open the packet and rolled the condom over him. Rowan's eyes closed for a moment at the sensation, and then he nudged my thighs apart to settle his hips between them. There was barely space for the both of us on the loveseat, but neither of us cared.

He gave me a finger to suck on which I did obediently. When I was done, he slid that inside me. I gasped quietly, my hips rising as his fingers explored my wet pussy. He watched me carefully, his eyes transfixed by my reactions.

As Rowan brought me close to my peak, he hesitated for just an instant with a hint of a question in his gaze. I gave him the smallest of nods, and just like that he withdrew his fingers and thrust his cock into me all the way to the hilt. Pleasure rushed through my body.

I clutched him, rocking my hips to meet his powerful rhythm. Our sexual exploits before had never felt quite this intense. My pussy clenched around his dick as he continued to stroke in and out of me. Every nerve in my body seemed to be quaking, ready to embrace my release alongside him.

He put his arms around my head as if to cocoon me in his embrace. "You have me, and I have you," he said, breathless but determined. "I'm never leaving you again, Mercy."

The words, both possessive and loving, sent me spiraling closer to the edge. I wrapped my legs around his waist to pull him even closer, needing all of him that I could get.

Rowan circled his hips to hit a sweet spot inside of me that made me gasp in turn. Sensing that I was close to exploding, he increased his pace, his thrusts becoming erratic as he pumped in and out of me. A groan reverberated from deep in his lungs.

The feel of it where our chests met made us jerk against each other harder, our naked bodies slapping together, and a blazing orgasm tore through me. Rowan followed me right after, bucking into his release, and his last thrust tipped me over the edge once more.

Our bodies collided and melded together. We lay panting in each other's arms, his weight almost crushing me, but I didn't want to move. I wanted to stay like this for weeks on end, tucked in the heat of his embrace.

Maybe this moment had been inevitable. I was totally tangled up with all four of my guys now. And they *were* mine. I couldn't imagine ever giving this up, no matter what Ezra Noble had to say about it.

14

Mercy

Wᴇʏʟᴅᴇʀ ᴄᴀᴍᴇ ɪɴᴛᴏ ᴛʜᴇ ᴀᴘᴀʀᴛᴍᴇɴᴛ ᴡɪᴛʜ ᴀ ꜱᴄᴏᴡʟ I was starting to think had become permanently plastered to his face. "Hey," he said gruffly, tugging me to him for a quick kiss, so I didn't think his bad mood was anything to do with me this time. But as he flopped down on the loveseat, his expression didn't lighten.

I glanced toward Kaige and Gideon, who'd come in after him. "What's up with him?"

Gideon sat down at the little table, setting his laptop on it. "Wylder's convinced Axel saw us leave."

"He's getting too hard to avoid, the way he's keeping an eye on us," Wylder grumbled. "Like he hasn't got better things to do."

"Even if he did notice us heading out, he can't know where we've gone," Gideon said in a matter-of-fact voice. "I checked carefully across our entire—very roundabout—route. There's no way he could have followed us all the way without me noticing."

"Right," Kaige said, slinging his brawny arm around my waist. "And Axel's being Axel. He's all talk, no action."

"I'm not so sure this time," Wylder said. Agitation was clear on his face. He sprang off the loveseat again to peer out the window, but I already knew it offered nothing but an up-close view of the brick wall of the office building next door.

Rowan came out of the shower, rubbing a towel over his hair, which was even spikier when damp. I smiled at him, resisting the urge to go over and run my fingers through it, and he grinned back. Whatever tension that'd remained between us had completely vanished. A flare of heat shot through me at the memory of his cock buried deep inside me.

But I wasn't going to be led around by my pussy when we had bigger issues at hand. "What happened with the arcade? Did the cops crack down on the Storm's people?"

Gideon grimaced. "There's good news and bad news. Police followed up on the tip and raided the business. They confiscated the drugs and took the men on site in."

"And the bad news?"

"The Storm's overall drug operation doesn't seem to have been significantly affected. They're still dealing it out on the streets—we saw people on a few corners when we were driving in today, blatant as ever."

Kaige grunted. "At least it should get the cops off *our*

backs about Glory now that they've got clear proof of these other guys dealing."

"And we weren't going to topple the Storm overnight." I rubbed my hand over my mouth. "What about the Red Shark's people? Have they been up to anything new?" The image floated up in the back of my mind of the gaping jaws spray-painted on the telephone pole outside my old house.

"I actually wanted to talk to you about that," Gideon said, his fingers flying over the laptop's keyboard. "A few days ago, I was able to place bugs near a couple of places where we've seen the Red Shark's people getting together. I've recorded several conversations since then. None of them have revealed anything we could use against them, but I did hear something that gave me pause. Since you know the Bend best, I'd like to hear what you make of it."

I squeezed Kaige's arm and stepped away from him to sit down at the table across from Gideon. He ramped up the volume and hit play.

There was a faint scratching noise, followed by static. Then a man's voice filtered through the tiny speakers. "Quiet night, huh?"

"Color me relieved. Maybe we won't have to risk our guts being blown out for once," said a second guy. They obviously had no idea anyone was recording them.

"Damn right, man. This place...it's not as quiet as it looks. I definitely didn't expect us to get this kind of pushback."

"Neither did the boss, I think," another one said. "He would have thought twice before coming in."

"Hell, yeah. The invitation we got might as well have been torn to pieces before we even showed up. I don't know why we even bothered coming when the people who sent it have been taken out of the picture. What's the point in sticking around? Especially when we're dealing with that psycho the Storm has on his payroll."

The other guy made a derisive sound, but I could hear the nervousness in his voice. "Yeah, his own fucking men are afraid of him."

"I say we should get the hell out of here before things get worse, but who the hell will listen to me?"

Gideon paused the recording and glanced at me. "What do you think?"

I shook my head, reeling from what I'd just heard. "Someone invited the Red Shark into the Bend? Why would anyone do that?"

"Colt invited the Storm, as far as we can tell," Wylder pointed out from where he was still staked out by the window. "Maybe someone didn't like how much he was taking over and wanted to balance the scales."

By turning this place into a full-out bloodbath? I winced. "I'm not sure I agree with their strategy."

"But whoever called them in, they're gone now," Rowan said, frowning. "Who's been 'taken out' who was a major player here other than Colt and your father?"

"No one I can think of." It couldn't have been Dad, right? He hadn't even known what Colt was planning before he'd died, or he'd never have walked into that restaurant for the rehearsal dinner in the first place. "Maybe... Maybe Colt brought them in too? He figured he and Xavier would have crushed the Nobles by now, and he could get the Red Shark's people to clash with the Storm and they'd destroy each other, leaving everything for him?"

Gideon ran his thumb over his lip ring. "It's possible, but I'm not sure I can see him planning anything that risky and complex."

Me neither. But then, Colt had gotten pretty crazed in the last few weeks before his death. Who knew what all had been going on in his head?

"Or could it have been someone lower down in the Steel Knights—or the Claws?" Kaige asked. "Someone who was pissed off about what Colt was doing?"

"They wouldn't have had much authority to orchestrate some kind of invasion," Wylder said.

Rowan cocked his head. "They wouldn't necessarily have needed it if they put on a good enough front. They might even have pretended to be someone else, and they're not dead after all."

"Yeah." A shiver ran down my back. If people had been working behind the scenes to bring in not just one but two different gangs we'd never heard of, who else might turn up next? "I guess it doesn't matter all that much now."

"That's what I said." Wylder marched back toward us and slapped his hand on the back of the loveseat. "It sounds like the Red Shark's people are already considering leaving. The Storm is obviously the bigger threat. I figure we should go out and mess with them some more today."

Yes. At the thought of taking some kind of action, as vague as it was right now, my back straightened and my resolve steadied me. It didn't matter where these assholes had come from or why—we were going to kick their butts right back to where they belonged. "Sounds good to me. Where are we headed?"

He tossed his car key in his hand. "Like Gideon said, we spotted a few of them out on the streets on our way in. Let's drive around a bit, find the biggest fish, and see if they can lead us to someone even bigger. We want to hit them where it'll hurt even more next time."

We tramped down the steps and into the fresh evening air. Wylder got into the driver's seat of the van. Kaige followed him, and Gideon sat down on the bench to scan the video feeds, Rowan joining him. I stood behind the front seats, peering through the windshield as Wylder pulled out of the alley where he'd parked.

"There's a skatepark about ten blocks that way," I said, pointing. "It's always been a popular spot for dealing."

"We'll check that out first, then," Wylder said.

We cruised by the concrete ramps and stopped where we had a decent view of the park. The streetlamps had flickered on to cut through the deepening shadows with a yellow glow.

A couple of guys were standing at the edge of one of those pools of light, their hands in their pockets, looking shifty. No skateboards, either. I peered around and spotted the edge of a duffle bag poking from where they'd tucked it away behind a nearby bench.

"That's probably where their stash is," I said, motioning to it. "Looks like they brought a lot. They must be planning on doing a lot of business tonight."

"We should keep an eye on things," Wylder said. "Once they start bringing in a decent amount of cash, they'll be handing it off to someone. When that happens, we follow those guys to wherever the money's going. Get closer to the heart of their operations."

"Right," Kaige said, leaning forward in his seat, his gaze intent on the dealers.

Wylder nudged him. "We're *only* watching. Not engaging. At least not until I give the word."

Kaige nodded, but it was hard to tell how much he was really listening.

Wylder tuned the radio to a rock station, and wailing guitars filled the van's interior. As Gideon tapped away on his laptop, the screens mounted around us wavered to show views from traffic and surveillance cameras from around the neighborhood. "I'll give you a shout if I see anyone who looks likely heading this way."

But the only people who turned up during the next half hour were customers. As I'd suspected, the dealers knew they'd picked a good spot. Several people on their own or in pairs wandered by as if they just happened to be taking a walk that way, but stopped briefly to chat with the sketchy-looking men. Cash and baggies of pale gray powder changed hands.

"It's definitely Glory," Kaige muttered. "Fucking Xavier."

"I've been hearing more and more reports from people I know on the streets," Rowan said. "It's getting increasingly popular. Unfortunately, I think their stunt at the waterfront property paid off."

Kaige just growled at that.

I was just rolling the tension out of my shoulders when a few kids who looked around eleven or twelve showed up with skateboards at the far end of the park. They pushed off, the wheels of their boards rattling loud enough that I could hear it through the walls of the van when the next song petered out. The kids laughed and cheered each other on as one and then another hurtled across the curved surface, turning a few tricks that weren't too far off from my parkour skills.

"They're pretty good," I said, just as Kaige snarled, "What the fuck?"

The dealers were sauntering closer to where the kids were riding. When one of the boys stepped off to the side to catch his breath, the men sidled even closer and started speaking to him. The kid looked a bit taken aback, his shoulders coming up, but he raised his chin, putting on a tough front like everyone learned to pretty early on in the Bend.

His friends came over to see what was going on. One of the dealers fished a small baggie out of his pocket and dangled it briefly before closing his fingers to hide it against his palm. My stomach twisted.

Wylder had tensed in his seat. "Pricks," he hissed, but he stayed in his seat. "When we're ready, they're going to regret coming into our city so fucking much."

"What do you mean, 'when we're ready'?" Kaige demanded. The veins on his neck looked ready to pop. "Don't you see what they're doing? Those monsters are trying to give drugs to literal babies."

"The kids don't look all that impressed," Rowan said reasonably. "They'll probably turn it down."

Kaige smacked the dashboard. "How smart were you at that age, huh?"

He had a point. Curiosity might get the better of them, and who knew what other bad choices that could lead to. That was exactly what the dealers were counting on. Get them hooked before they had enough experience to know better. My fingers tightened around the back of the seat, my knuckles whitening.

"It's not our problem," Wylder said in a strained voice.

Then one of the kids stretched out his arm, and the dealer moved to put the baggie in his hand.

"Fuck this!" Kaige shouted, and threw the door open. Before any of us could stop him, he was charging into the skate park.

"Shit," Wylder mumbled, fumbling for his own door.

"Kaige!" I yelled after him, but he didn't even slow down.

Rowan and I scrambled out the back. Kaige was bearing down on the drug dealers, who'd jerked apart from each other, staring at him.

"Fucking cowards, what do you think you're doing giving drugs to kids?" Kaige yelled. "I'm going to break every bone in your bodies one by one."

The men must have been able to tell they didn't stand a chance against Kaige's hulking form, even two against one. Their eyes widened, and they took off in opposite directions. The preteens gaped as Kaige barged through their midst, chasing down the guy who'd offered the baggie to the kids.

"Get back here, you fucking animal," he hollered.

"You're a big enough man to ruin people's lives, but not to get what you deserve?"

We raced after him. "Kaige!" Wylder snapped. "Let him go. You're going to ruin what we're trying to do here. This isn't how we stop them."

Kaige just pounded on across the park in pursuit of the dealer. I sucked in a ragged breath, pushing my legs harder, and added my own voice. "Kaige, please, listen to me. It's over. The kids are okay. Just—stop. Please."

My final plea penetrated whatever haze of rage was gripping him. Kaige slowed and came to a stop. He stared after the dealer, who'd vanished around the side of one of the ramps, and then back at us, his expression almost bewildered.

I caught up with him and grabbed his arm. "Thank you. It's okay. It's over."

He peered down at me, and his voice came out choked up. "He was going to—"

"I know," I said. "But he didn't, and he's gone now."

"And now we've got to get out of here before he brings a ton of his friends down on us," Wylder added from beside me.

I tugged Kaige's arm, and he came with us back to the van. The kids had fled, leaving us alone. Kaige's jaw worked, but Wylder raised his hand. "Don't say anything. You fucked up our whole plan."

"I couldn't just sit there and do nothing!"

"Yes, you fucking could. For once in your life—"

Wylder cut himself off, stopping in his tracks. As Kaige and I followed his gaze, Kaige froze too. My heart stuttered.

We'd almost reached the sidewalk, but down the street, half a block from the van, an all-too-familiar car had just come to a stop. I recognized Axel's tattooed scalp through the windshield before he climbed out.

"Hello, boys," he sneered, his gaze fixing on me. "What do we have here?"

Wylder grasped my elbow and yanked me close. "Mercy," he said, low and more urgent than I'd ever heard him. "Get the fuck out of here. *Now*."

I stared at him, every particle of my body protesting the idea of leaving them to face the music alone. "But—"

"*Go!*" he repeated as Axel strode toward us. A couple more guys were getting out of the car behind him. "I don't know what will happen if Axel manages to take you back to Dad."

I couldn't mistake the fear in his voice. He knew his father and Axel way better than I did. Maybe it should be his call.

My hands clenched at my sides, but *I* was afraid of what Wylder might do if I stayed and he felt he had to defend me right here and now. Shit.

I gave him and Kaige one last, apologetic glance, and just this once, followed Wylder's orders. Spinning around, I took off in the opposite direction as fast as my feet would carry me, regret burning a hole in my gut.

15

Wylder

Axel was glowering at me as if I'd gone against *his* authority somehow. As if he had any real authority over me.

"I thought the instructions couldn't be any clearer," he said. "No contact with the Katz girl after she leaves the mansion."

Instead of answering, I glared back at him. We'd arrived back at the mansion half an hour ago, and Axel had insisted on marching me straight to my father's office after barking at one of the lower lackeys to find the man in charge. Dad hadn't shown up yet.

"What do you think you're going to get out of tattling on us?" I asked. "No one likes a rat, Axel."

"I was doing my job, unlike you," Axel retorted. "Maybe you've forgotten who you owe your loyalty to."

"Don't fucking talk to me about loyalty. Everything

I've done so far, every difficult decision I've made, and every bullet I've nearly taken has been for this family."

My father's cold voice carried from the doorway. "And yet you're willing to throw all of that away for the princess of the Claws."

He strode inside, his face an impenetrable mask, but I could tell he was angry. The chilliness of his tone was a dead giveaway.

He closed the door behind him and walked to his desk. I got up from the leather sofa and approached him. "Dad, you have to hear me on this."

"Hear what exactly?" he said. "You went behind my back and met with Mercy Katz. Several times, I'm guessing, since I highly doubt Axel just happened to catch you on the first occasion. He's said he's noticed you and your inner circle vanishing on unexplained missions quite often."

"I have every reason to believe that they've been helping her from the moment she left the mansion," Axel jumped in, like the brownnosing prick he was. "I wouldn't be surprised if they've been using Noble resources to help her get by."

What a fucking dickhead. He *wanted* that to be true so he could look even better to Dad for having caught us, as if spying on me and my men was what our resources should be focused on instead. No one had been using those apartments anyway.

My fingers itched to close into a fist, one I longed to drive into the wall—or, even better, Axel's self-satisfied face next to me. Hell, I wanted to punch Dad too, just to see some reaction, to catch him off-guard enough that he might think beyond the box he'd already put my disobedience into.

But I knew that wouldn't actually work. My father believed in self-control. I had to play this situation strategically. God knew what would happen if I really pissed him off and he took it out on Mercy.

"What do you have to say about that, Wylder?" he asked, his gaze boring into me.

"I haven't touched the Noble accounts or anything earmarked for other purposes," I said stiffly. I wasn't sure I could say the same for Anthea, but I wasn't going to drag my aunt into this after everything she'd done to help us. "What I do with my personal money and time shouldn't be relevant."

Dad made a scoffing sound. "I think it is if you've been focused on that girl rather than the real problems we're facing here. We sent her away for a reason. She's no longer a part of our organization. Why are you and your inner circle still associating with her?"

I took a deep breath before I finally answered, the sense prickling over me that more than one life might hang in the balance here. "With all due respect, Dad, I didn't agree with cutting ties with her in the first place. She left the mansion as you ordered. She hasn't been involved in any larger operations the Nobles have been working on. But she's been instrumental in my own continued efforts to get these intruding gangs out of Paradise Bend."

His tone turned even icier. "Are you suggesting I made a mistake?"

There was no good answer to that question. I

squared my shoulders. "No, only that we had a minor difference of opinion. Mercy knows the Bend better than any of us do—she's given us intel that my men and I have been able to use to strike at this Storm guy's operations. You wanted her to leave because Xavier was targeting her, didn't you? Now that she's gone, he hasn't come near the mansion. Why shouldn't I take what she can offer while she's someplace else?"

"And just how much of what she's 'offering' are you taking?"

The insinuation in his voice was clear. My stomach knotted, but I kept my tone even. "Anything we could use to tackle Xavier and the rest of the assholes trying to usurp us. That's all. And we've made a lot of headway into disrupting their presence here thanks to her."

Axel snorted in disbelief, but I kept my attention focused on Dad. He skimmed his hands over the top of his desk and then folded them in his lap.

"Xavier appears to have gotten distracted by the other new presence in the Bend," he said. "I don't think we can judge how much of a thorn in our side he'll be until they've settled that conflict—at which point, it seems likely he'll focus his attention back on us. And who drew that attention to us in the first place?"

It took all my willpower not to snap at him. My voice came out rough despite my best efforts. "Not Mercy. The whole reason he and the rest of the Storm's people came here was obviously to take over Paradise Bend. We'd have been in their way regardless of what happened with Mercy. It doesn't make any sense to blame her."

Dad's eyes narrowed. "So now you're questioning my mental faculties."

Shit. "No," I said, scrambling for another argument, but Dad leaned back in his chair with an air of finality.

"It's clear to me that this girl has warped your priorities in dangerous ways, Wylder. You've gotten too close to her to see the full problem she presents."

"What's that supposed to mean?" I demanded.

"Your interest in her clearly goes far beyond ensuring the success of our organization. I think it's personal now. Perhaps it has been all along." He pinned me with his stare, as if he thought he could read the truth from my mind straight through my skull.

I did my best imitation of his hardened expression, shoving down my apprehension. The last thing we needed was him realizing just how much Mercy meant to me—and not just me but my friends as well.

"That's not true," I insisted. "All I care about is getting the Nobles through this unexpected war. I'll use whatever I can, and she's nothing but a means to an end."

"That's not how it looked to me when you told her to take off on us," Axel muttered, and turned to my father. "He got awfully up close and personal with her, murmuring in her ear. Protecting her from us mattered more to him than facing up to how he went against your orders."

My jaw set on edge. "No one asked your opinion."

"But I'm glad to hear it, especially considering it supports my suspicions." Dad pushed back his chair and stood up, bringing the full impact of his height to bear.

We stood equally tall, but he had a little more heft to his shoulders and a weight to his presence that always made me feel smaller.

I remembered abruptly Mercy's comments outside the arcade the other night—how she'd noticed one of Axel's men there. I hadn't really figured he was acting outside of Axel's orders, but if I could use it to deflect even a little attention from this line of conversation, I'd take it.

"Maybe you should be aiming some of those suspicions at your right-hand man," I said to Dad, motioning toward Axel. "He doesn't seem to be keeping very good track of *his* people."

Axel's head jerked around. "What the fuck are you talking about?"

I met his gaze with my own accusing one. "We've seen one of the guys who reports to you in deep with the Storm's people, acting all chummy with them. What's *that* all about?"

To my surprise, rather than shooting back a quick retort, Axel's expression twitched with what looked like surprise. Had he not actually known about his underling's activities? But a second later, he was glowering at me again. "I've told my men to take the lay of the land and find out what we're up against. They're following *their* orders."

"And what have they managed to uncover so far?" I asked.

"Enough with the interrogation," Dad snapped. "I brought you here to get an explanation for your behavior, not put one of my most trusted men on trial."

I spun back to face him. "This is what you've been training me for, isn't it? To develop my judgment and trust my instincts. I'm telling you that Mercy is doing a lot more good than harm to our interests—yours and mine—and I wouldn't have anything to do with her if that wasn't true."

"That's not what I see," Dad said, staring me down. "I see a child taking on decisions bigger than himself and putting us all in harm's way just to satisfy his own ego and urges."

How the hell did I get through to him? "You have to trust me on this," I started, knowing I was losing the argument but refusing to give up.

Before I could go on, Dad stepped around the desk to loom right over me. "And why the fuck would I do that when you went behind my back and did the exact thing I asked you not to?"

"He's still a boy," Axel sneered. "Me and my men will clean up the mess in the Bend a lot faster than they've managed with all their running around with the girl."

"Yes. I think if Wylder wants to prove what he's really made of, he'll need to start by cleaning up *his* mess." Dad turned to Axel. "Where did Mercy go?"

"She took off running—I didn't want to go after her when I knew it was more important we deal with our own." Axel shot an accusing look at me. "I'd bet he knows."

I didn't, though. Mercy was smart enough not to go back to the new apartment, one that was in the Nobles' name. I had no idea where she'd have fled to, and that realization made my heart sink.

Of course, it wouldn't be that hard to find out. She'd still have her phone. I could reach out to her in an instant. No way in hell was I telling the men in front of me that.

"How should I know?" I said. "We met up at agreed spots. I have no clue what she was up to the rest of the time."

"We'll track her down quickly enough," Axel said.

Dad made a dismissive gesture. "No need for that. Like I said, my son needs to clean up his own mess." He lifted his chin toward me. "I want *you* to track her down."

If my heart had sunk before, now it dropped all the way to my shoes. "What for? I thought you didn't want me to have anything to do with her."

Dad gave me a sardonic smile. "Oh, there's one thing I'd like you to do with her, just to ensure that we're still clear that family comes first. The girl has served her purpose. We can no longer allow her to undermine our standing in Paradise Bend. The sooner she's out of the way, the less our association with her will injure us in the long run. Before she can become any more of a threat than she already is, you're going to get rid of her."

My throat constricted. "You want me to kill Mercy," I repeated, with the faint hope that I'd somehow misunderstood his meaning.

No such luck.

"You heard me," Ezra said. "Your defiance has put you on thin ice. Do this, and you'll have *started* to earn my trust back. I need my heir to be ruthless and focused. I need to know that when the time comes for you to lead the Nobles, you won't be taken off course by petty little distractions."

He spoke as if Mercy's life meant nothing at all. I couldn't help arguing, even as a wave of hopelessness crashed over me. Once Ezra Noble set down a decree, his mind wasn't going to be changed. "But if you just—"

He held up his hand to stop me, his expression as foreboding as I'd ever seen it. "I don't want to hear another word about it. You say she's just a means to an end to you? Then make her a means to getting back into my good graces. Kill her, and bring me the proof. You have five days."

16

Mercy

FROM A SAFE DISTANCE, I OBSERVED THE FRONT LAWN of my old house. A couple of guys were standing at the edge by the sidewalk just beyond a streetlamp's glow, sipping beers. No lights shone in the windows, and in the hour I'd been watching, I hadn't seen anyone moving inside or going in or out.

Now or never. With Wylder and the other guys dealing with whatever the fallout was with his dad, I couldn't just sit around twiddling my thumbs. I needed to know why these Red Shark jackasses had set up shop in the house. Had Dad been keeping more secrets than I'd guessed?

My heart skipped a beat at the thought of how I'd run off on the guys, but I'd only done it because Wylder had insisted. I just hoped he found a way to get through to his own dad—or to stand up to him in a way that wouldn't get him hurt for his trouble.

I forced myself to push those thoughts aside and crept through the night's shadows to the back of the house. After ducking through the neighbor's yard, I scaled the sturdy fence between our properties with a leap and a quick scramble, and sprang from there into the oak tree in my old back yard.

The leaves rustled. I crouched on the branch in the darkness for the space of a few breaths, listening hard. When no sound of alarm was raised, I clambered across the tree and made my way through one of the second floor windows, just like I had when I'd gone to retrieve my bracelet weeks ago.

Inside the house, I stood completely still for another minute, confirming there were no sounds of movement around me. My fingers drifted over the outline of the *Little Angel* bracelet in my pocket. When no noise reached me except faint laughter from the men outside, I slipped down the darkened hall.

Maybe it was a risk coming here right now. But something had been niggling at me ever since Gideon had played that recording of the Red Sharks guys talking. If I was going to find any answers to the questions I couldn't get out of my head, it'd be here.

Back when everything was... well, as normal as my life had ever been, Dad's home office had always been locked, even when he was inside. He hadn't allowed me to set foot in there since I'd been around seven or eight, but I'd understood more than he'd realized when I'd been a little kid.

I'd come equipped with the lock picks that Anthea had given me a brief tutorial on during one of her recent visits, but it turned out I didn't even need them. The door was standing ajar, the knob completely removed. One of the past intruders had broken in. I picked up my pace, setting my feet quickly but silently on the floor as I hurried over.

At the doorway, I scanned the room quickly. The intruders had gone through the contents on Dad's desk. Papers were strewn all over the room. Chairs had been overturned, books had been pulled off the bookcase, small trinkets that Dad had collected over the years as mementos of particularly big jobs lay smashed on the floor. Whoever had gone through the place, they'd been thorough.

Had they figured out his secret stash?

My heart thumping wildly in my chest, I walked to the corner of the room and knelt. The thick curtain over the window gave me the confidence to get out my phone and use it for a light. I felt along the baseboard with my other hand. There. I pressed down on the wobbly spot and pried open the loose section before flashing the beam of light inside.

A sigh of relief rushed out of me. It didn't look like anything in Dad's favorite hiding place had been discovered.

I pulled out a wad of cash first and pocketed it. That could come in handy now that I was relying completely on myself for housing and food. Next I found a couple of notebooks, a phone, and a United States passport.

I shook the last item open. The picture was Dad's, but the name was fake. He'd never used this one—none of the pages were stamped.

Sitting down on the floor, I turned to the notebooks next. He must have written some pretty important stuff in them if he'd kept them in there. By the dim glow of my phone, I flipped through the pages.

Unfortunately, whatever illicit business Dad had written about, he'd been more careful than just hiding it behind the baseboard. The notebooks were full of a mix of recognizable words and what looked like random strings of jumbled letters and numbers. He'd written it in partial code. I'd known he'd used one sometimes, but he'd never shared it with me. Or anyone else, as far as I knew. He'd meant the information in here to be for his eyes only.

I snapped pictures of the pages in case I lost the notebooks. Maybe Gideon would be able to crack the code and make something of the information. Then I stuffed them into my bag and picked up the phone. It was my last chance of figuring anything out myself tonight.

The screen was smudged and a crack ran across one corner. I was afraid it might have died with all that time in storage. But Dad had obviously charged it regularly, and he'd shut it off completely between uses so that it kept some power. It turned on when I pressed the button, the screen flashing to show 15% power remaining.

It asked for a passcode, but I'd been able to pick up Dad's typical one from careful observations over the years. There were a few benefits to being constantly underestimated. I tapped it in.

There were no apps on the phone other than the

standard ones that came with installation. I checked the text messages. The most recent conversation was with a contact Dad had labeled "Teeth."

I frowned at the screen. I couldn't think of any of the business associates I knew of who'd gone by that nickname.

The moment I tapped through to the conversation, a chill washed over me. I skimmed back through the messages to make sure I wasn't missing anything.

The text conversation had started about five months ago and gone on for several weeks after that—pretty much right up until Dad's death. Here and there, messages had been deleted as if they'd contained particularly sensitive information, but what remained told a clear story.

I think this alliance could benefit both of us, Dad said at one point. *You'll take over some of my territory here, and share some of yours with the Claws, and we'll expand our reach together.*

We definitely see the reasoning behind your proposal, the contact he'd named Teeth had answered. *We're just working out the logistics. This isn't the kind of thing we'd want to move quickly on.*

And later, from Dad, *Is everything going forward as you hoped? If you need more specifics on my businesses here, I can give you that.*

The response: *Everything looks good. I believe we can get started within the next few months. You're ready for our arrival?*

You'll be welcomed with open arms. We're going to do great things together.

The more I read, the more my dread grew, until my eyes started to blur. I swiped at them and forced myself to read all the way to the end.

It wasn't hard to guess who Dad would have given a code name like "Teeth" to. I'd seen the shark-jaws logo on the post outside, and the content of the messages brought all the other pieces together.

Dad had been talking to someone from the Red Shark's organization for months. *Dad* had invited them into the Bend, offered them an alliance and territory to expand his own power. That must have been why he'd asked Kervos and others for documentation on their business activities—so he could show these guys how profitable associating with him would be.

My father was the reason the Red Shark's people were here, causing so much more violence than the Bend had already faced.

I slumped back against the wall, dropping the phone to my side. An ache spread through my chest. I didn't want to believe it, but how could I deny what I'd just seen?

Dad hadn't said anything in the texts about taking out Colt or about needing to go up against the Steel Knights. I had to assume he'd meant to bring Colt in on the arrangement once we were married. Obviously he hadn't discussed the newcomers he was encouraging to take a stake in our territory with my former fiancé beforehand, though.

But somehow Colt had caught wind of the negotiations and assumed Dad meant to betray him with the new alliance. He'd lashed out first... and now here we were, a whole lot of pain and blood later. Most of it from innocent people who'd had no idea about any of this mess.

"For fuck's sake, Dad," I murmured in a choked voice. It figured he'd set a complete catastrophe in motion and manage to get taken out of the picture before he had to deal with any of the consequences.

No, that fell on *me*.

What the hell was I supposed to do? How could I look anyone in the Bend in the eye, all these people who'd had their homes, businesses, and loved ones destroyed because of Dad's stupid decision...?

I stayed crouched there in his office for longer than I'd meant to, my head spinning. I just couldn't get a grip on myself.

I needed to hear someone else's voice, to talk it through with someone who could help me see where the fuck I went from here. And I only had one person I could reach out to, risky as it might be.

Desperately hoping that Ezra hadn't discovered Wylder's extra phone, I got out my own and tapped out a text to him with shaky fingers. *I need to see you. ASAP. Please tell me you're okay.*

My chest constricted more with every passing minute while I waited for a response. Then a new text appeared. *All important parts still intact. What's going on?*

I just need to talk to you face to face, if you can manage it. Is there somewhere safe we can meet?

The next answer came much faster. *The picnic table near the fountain in Calliver Park. I've got something to talk to you about too. Give me an hour.*

Thank God. I dragged in a breath and managed to push myself off the floor now that I had a destination in mind.

I left the house the same way I'd come in, feeling like a zombie. Each beat of my heart drove the knowledge I'd just discovered in deeper like a knife in my gut.

It was Dad's fault I'd lost my entire family. Dad's fault my whole life had been ruined—not that I regretted missing out on marrying Colt, but everything else... Dad's fault the Bend was in chaos, ordinary people afraid to even walk down the street. Dad's fault those streets were being painted with blood.

And with Dad gone, who could anyone point the finger at but his heir?

I slunk across rooftops and through alleys, making my way to the park, which lay near the border where the Bend turned into Paradise City proper. It was surrounded by a wrought-iron fence with a gate that was locked at night, but a few metal bars weren't enough to keep me out. I climbed inside, wove through the trees until I spotted the picnic bench by the limestone fountain with its sculpture of a trio of leaping dolphins, and melted into the shadows to wait.

It didn't take long before the soft rasp of careful footsteps reached my ears. Wylder stopped right by the tree I'd hidden behind. "You can come out now, Mercy."

I stepped out, raising an eyebrow at him. "How did you know I was here?"

"Intuition?" Wylder said.

I smiled. "Or just pure luck."

"It's weird, but I can always tell where you are," Wylder said, taking a step towards me. He looked me over. "Are you all right, Kitty Cat?"

My heart raced at the concern in his words. "Kind of. Not really. Everything's..." I made a vague gesture, unsure of how to put all the turmoil inside me into words. All I wanted to do was run my fingers through his soft auburn hair and pull him closer for a kiss.

But even though he smiled back at me, it didn't quite reach his eyes. My own smile faltered. "Are *you* all right? What happened with your dad? You said there was something you had to talk to me about."

Wylder stiffened a tiny bit, but only for a moment. Then he shook his head. "We can get to that later. Something's obviously wrong. What's going on, Mercy?"

I swallowed hard. "Are you sure? Your dad must have been furious. Are the other guys okay?"

"He was mostly angry with me, and I handled it." Something in his tone made me think that hadn't been too easy. "Don't try to dodge the subject. You said you needed me here. Tell me what happened."

He gazed into my eyes so intently that I found I couldn't hold his gaze. My head drooped. "I went back to my old house. I knew—my dad kept some secret documents and things in a hidey hole in his office. I just wanted to make sure there wasn't anything I was missing. But there was."

Wylder gripped my shoulder. "You went back there? Aren't the Red Shark's people using it in their operations?"

"Yes, but I was careful. No one saw me. That's not

what matters." There was no point in putting it off. I had to just spit it out. "They're using the house because my dad's the one who invited them into the Bend. That's what the guys Gideon caught in his recording meant."

Shock rippled across Wylder's face. "Are you serious? How do you know?"

I explained everything I'd found out from the text conversation with the contact named Teeth. "They were talking about joining forces. Dad wanted to expand his territory, and he figured an alliance with a bigger power was the way to do it. Expanding by sharing their territories or something... I don't know what was going on in his head."

"Why the fuck would he want to do that? He had plenty already without bringing a bunch of strangers into it."

"I know!" I threw my hands into the air. "But he did, for whatever stupid reason, and now— I've been defending myself and him all along, refusing to believe Colt's claims about Dad, saying the Steel Knights were the real problem, but— Maybe *your* dad is right. My family is the biggest threat Paradise Bend has faced. We're where we are now because of the Claws."

"But not because of you," Wylder said. "Are you even listening to yourself? Your father didn't make you a part of his plan. You didn't know about any of this until just now. *You're* not responsible."

"I was right there. Maybe he thought he was doing it for me, so Colt and I would inherit more— It doesn't make any difference. I'm the leader of the Claws now, and there's no one else who can take responsibility. Everything—the violence on the streets, and the deaths —it might as well be my fault."

My vision blurred with a sudden welling of tears. "Fuck," I muttered, pressing my palms to my face. I didn't want him to see me crying.

"Mercy." Wylder's grasp on my shoulder tightened. He gave me a little shake. "Get a grip on yourself. You're in shock."

Despite my best efforts, tears rolled down my cheeks. "If I'd found out sooner—if I'd managed to stop him—if I'd been able to say something before the Red Shark's people showed up—"

Wylder's voice hardened. He sounded almost angry. "Listen to me. You're not to blame for your Dad's shitty actions—or Colt's either, for that matter. From what you said, the real problem was Colt making assumptions instead of talking to your dad to find out what was going on like a sane person would have. All he had to do was mention what he'd heard, and it would have all been sorted out. He's the one who flew off the handle instead."

His forceful tone brought up my hackles, pissing me off enough that my tears dried up. "If my father hadn't gone after more power in the first place—"

"You're not him, something I'm very glad for. Why the hell do you think you owe him anything?"

"I don't," I snapped back. "It's about what I owe the Bend."

"There," Wylder said, jabbing his finger at me. "There's a little of the Mercy I thought I knew. Are you really going to run away because of what you wish you'd done, Princess? Or are you going to stay and fight? Where's the cat with the claws, with enough fire to burn down the world around you? You're not going to let this one thing break your spirit, are you?"

His fingers dug into my shoulder painfully. I pushed his hand off me and shoved him back.

"No," I said, my voice almost echoing in the thick foliage of trees around us. I was more than this. I was more than my father's actions, more than the men who had tried to put me under their thumbs.

Wylder nodded in appreciation, his stance starting to relax. "I didn't think so. The woman I know always fights back."

I glared at him, my emotions even more jumbled up than before—but he'd stirred up a defiance in me that seared away the most hopeless parts. "You wanted me gone not too long ago," I couldn't help reminding him. "I never did then, did I?"

Something in his face softened. "No, you didn't. And I never really *wanted* you out of my life. I thought I was protecting you. Obviously that didn't work out very well for either of us."

"You don't think so?"

Wylder stepped up to me again and put his hand under my chin, slowly stroking it with his thumb. I relaxed into his touch automatically. Even with all the history behind us, he was the first person I'd turned to when I was in trouble. And he had come for me in more ways than one.

"I don't want you to go even though I know you'll be

safer that way," he murmured. "You're stuck with me now, Kitty Cat."

He didn't kiss me. Instead he touched his forehead to mine. We stayed there for a few moments as my mind cleared and the last of the helplessness I'd been feeling dissipated.

I wasn't alone. I had Wylder and Kaige and Rowan and Gideon. And I had the Bend. No matter what had led us here, I couldn't back down now.

"I'm not going anywhere," I said, easing back so that I could meet Wylder's gaze. "The Bend is still my home. It's broken, but I'll do everything I can to fix it. I'll rebuild it better than it ever was, and at the same time I'll rebuild my family's legacy. The Katz name doesn't end with my dad."

Wylder nodded, affection shining in his eyes. "So what comes next?"

I raised my chin. "I *am* the head of the Claws now. That means it's time to take some responsibility and see if I can undo what the leader before me set in motion. Let's find out if I can convince the Red Shark that his invitation's been revoked."

Mercy

IT FELT WEIRD TO BE STANDING IN FRONT OF MY house again, this time in daylight and facing the front door, as if I hadn't snuck inside just last night. In the guise of darkness, I'd been able to pretend that I was in a different reality, one in which my house belonged to me. Now I had armed strangers eyeing me from what was technically *my* porch.

I dragged in a breath and fidgeted with the collar of the button-up shirt Anthea had lent me so I looked more professional than I felt. Then I marched up the front walk.

The men on the porch straightened up, but they didn't draw the guns I could see at the waists of their jeans. They were expecting me. I'd called this meeting with the Red Shark's people as the current leader of the Claws and the daughter of the man who'd called them into my world.

A couple of the men—younger ones—shifted restlessly on their feet. I didn't think they liked my arrival. Well, too bad for them.

As I climbed up the steps, refusing to let my nerves show, the front door opened. A man in a polo shirt motioned me in. "Mercy Katz. You came."

I fixed him with my best Claws Princess look. "I said I would."

He gave me a tight, sharp-edged smile. "Some of us thought it was a prank. But we made sure we were prepared anyway. Come in."

As if it was his house and not mine. I bit back the snarky remarks I wanted to make and stepped over the threshold.

The family pictures that had been hung in the foyer were missing, leaving pale marks on the striped wallpaper where they'd been. The only one left was of Dad alone, and it'd been disfigured with streaks of red and black paint. Had these pricks defaced it, or had that been the Steel Knights who'd staked a claim on this house before?

The man saw me watching the picture. "Like that?"

I ignored his bait. "I'd like to get on with our meeting. Are you in charge of the Red Shark's presence in Paradise Bend?"

Several men had come down the stairs and stepped into the hall to watch, a couple of them with guns in hand. More than one gaze lingered on my chest. I restrained a shudder of disgust.

"Don't go by appearances, boys," said the man who'd greeted me. "This one bites. Hard." He nodded to me.

"Your reputation precedes you. We've heard that you took on the Steel Knights and killed their leader yourself. We'd just like to make sure you don't get any of the same ideas here. My boss is this way."

He led me into the dining room. Someone had smashed the crystal chandelier that hung over the broad oak table. My teeth set on edge as I took in the man sitting at the head of the table.

He was middle aged, with a creased forehead and a graying goatee, dressed in a suit I could tell was expensive. He glanced up from his newspaper with a bored look as if I'd disturbed his reading, but I didn't let that faze me. I knew the Red Shark's contingent was on the losing side of the battle with the Storm so far. I'd seen the edginess of his men. They wouldn't be so worried about little old me if they'd been sure of their foothold here.

"So you're Mercy Katz," he said, setting the newspaper aside. "You have ten minutes to tell me exactly why you're here, or my men will put a bullet in your head." He smiled thinly as if he hadn't just threatened my life.

I echoed his expression. He wasn't going to intimidate me. I'd faced much worse. "I don't even need ten minutes. It's very simple. I know that my father's the one who suggested you come here and take a stake in Paradise Bend. He never told me about that deal or why he made it, but he's dead now, so I don't see how it matters. What matters is you don't have any deal at all with anyone alive here."

"Are you looking to make a new one, Miss Katz?"

I folded my arms over my chest. "No. I'm telling you I think you should leave. You don't have any alliances here. You've lost men to the Storm's forces, and they're obviously not letting up their attacks. What's the point in staying?"

He cocked his head. "Why do you care? Just want us to make things easier for you when you try to reclaim your territory."

"No," I said. "I want to stop seeing blood all over the streets and the people I grew up with living in terror. But I'll point out that this territory was never really my father's to bargain away anyway. The whole county belongs to the Nobles, and they're not interested in giving it up."

The man snorted as if I'd said something ridiculous. Then he tapped the tabletop. "Yes, your father is gone —and thanks to you, I understand, so is Colt Bryant and the Steel Knights. The two most powerful gangs in this part of the county. That leaves quite the power vacuum. You can't expect us to walk away and leave it all to the Storm."

"So you're willing to kill whoever stands in your way out of greed?" I asked.

His eyes glittered coldly. "We've already killed plenty, and we have no shortage of weapons coming in to take down more. And the one good thing the Storm's troops have done is prove just what an avid customer base exists here for certain types of products. We have our own merchandise we'll be moving in."

Nausea gripped my stomach. "More drugs?"

"Among other things. So if you don't have any better

argument than you've already presented..." He raised his eyebrows.

I resisted the urge to punch him right in his haughty face. "If the Storm's people don't crush you, then the Nobles will. You're fighting a losing battle here."

His shoulders stiffened, but he waved me off. "We'll see about that. I think we're done here." He pointed at the guy who'd escorted me in. "Send her off."

The guy stepped toward me, but I jerked away before he could touch my arm. There obviously wasn't any way these men would listen to reason. They were too caught up in their egos and greed.

"This is my house," I couldn't help reminding them. "I can get out on my own. Thank you very much for your hospitality."

I strode down the hall and out the door. I could barely breathe until I was halfway down the block. Sweat had broken out on my forehead. I stopped to swipe at it, and a van rolled to a halt next to me. Kaige leaned his elbow out the driver's side window and grinned. "You look like you could use a ride."

Rowan and Gideon were waiting in the back. As I dropped onto the bench next to them, Wylder pushed past the seats from the passenger-side one to join us. Kaige started driving again, taking us farther from the Red Shark's men and that uncomfortable conversation.

"It didn't go so well, huh," Wylder said, nodding to the screen where our voices were being recorded in erratic wave patterns.

I reached inside my shirt and pulled out the bug

that had been pinned against my collarbone. "I don't think they even considered my suggestion."

"Well, it was worth a try," Rowan said.

I gave him a crooked smile and turned to Gideon. "Do you think the bug picked up anything in the conversation that we could use against them?"

"We got a few tidbits we might be able to spin the right way to get the cops focused on them, if we want to go that route," Gideon said. "He confessed to bringing weapons into the Bend and to multiple killings, if in a vague way. And intending to get in on the drug trade."

"Okay." I sagged back against the wall of the van. We hadn't figured there was all that much hope of convincing the Red Shark to back off, but we'd at least hoped to get some ammunition we could use as leverage to force them out.

"The Storm's people are still the bigger problem," Rowan pointed out.

Wylder nodded. "We'll sit on this recording for now. We'll have it in our back pocket when we really need it. Mercy did good."

He tugged my ponytail in his usual affectionate way, but his expression stayed tense, and his gaze only held mine for a second. Uneasiness prickled over my skin.

He'd said last night that he needed to talk to *me*, but he'd never gotten around to telling me what that was about. Something was obviously bothering him.

But it was something he didn't want to discuss in front of the other guys, I had to assume. He wasn't likely to tell me much if I undermined his authority by badgering him about it with them around. The next time we were alone, though, I'd have to drag it out of him.

Gideon had gone back to tapping on his tablet. "Hey," he called over to Kaige, "take a right up here and then stop at the end of the block."

As Kaige followed his instructions, Wylder gave his best friend a curious look. "Where are you leading us now, oh tech genius?"

A sparkle came into Gideon's eyes at the compliment, but his jaw tensed too. "I've got plans for a few more ways we can screw with both the Storm's and the Red Shark's guys, but I need to pick up supplies. There's a store near here where I can pick up a few... unusual items."

The building he had Kaige park outside looked practically abandoned, the windows dim and the sign over the doorway cracked. Spray-painted graffiti marked the outer walls. But Gideon sauntered inside with more confidence than he usually showed when we were out on a mission, enough that I enjoyed admiring the view of his ass before he vanished through the doorway.

The rest of us got out too, stretching our legs and scanning the rest of the street. We ambled to the corner and glanced around, but there was no sign of any activity in the area. Both nothing dangerous and nothing simply normal. It was only just coming up on the evening, and the Bend was way too quiet.

But the Red Shark, the Storm, and all their lackeys didn't give a shit about how their war was killing this place, did they?

Kaige's stomach let out an audible growl.

Rowan shook his head. "Are you hungry already? We had dinner before we left."

"All the running around makes me super hungry," Kaige said. "And I'm not going to apologize for my appetite. It's how I got these guns." He flexed his massive biceps, and all three of us laughed.

"Guys." Wylder hadn't been taking part in our banter. When I glanced at him, he was gazing intently down the street. A black SUV was cruising toward us.

Beside me, Kaige stiffened. "That isn't Axel again, is it? That fucker—"

Before he could finish his sentence, the SUV jerked to a stop and four men poured out. The three in front had guns at the ready. In their wake, the fourth stomped out onto the sidewalk in heavy combat boots, his form looming over the others, and I got my first in-person look at the man who'd been haunting me for weeks.

Xavier was a hulking figure, towering no less than six-five, with corded shoulders. He might even be wider than Kaige, if that was possible. The angry scars on his cheeks must have become less pronounced with age, but it was still unnerving seeing how the ominous Xs drilled into his skin took over most of his face.

But that wasn't even the worst part. His eyes had a manic glint in them, and his toothy smile widened when he saw us. Every nerve in my body clanged in warning: this man was unhinged. An involuntary shiver passed down my spine.

"Hello, my cat," he said, addressing me directly. "We finally meet."

Wylder pushed in front of me, his stance rigid, his

hand leaping to his gun. Xavier's gaze fixed on him, and he let out a low, rolling laugh. "Do you think that little toy is going to stop me? Do you really think a bitch like her is worth protecting?"

"I think I didn't fucking ask you," Wylder said. "Back off."

"Oh, no." Xavier strolled toward us, his men flanking him. He didn't bother to draw his own weapon, as if he thought he was bulletproof. "But if you want to make me toss you aside to get to her, that'll just make it more fun."

I didn't have any weapons of my own on me—I'd left them behind to go into the parlay with the Red Shark's men. My hands balled into fists. I wasn't going down easy anyway. "I've never done anything to you. I don't even *know* you. Leave me alone, asshole."

Xavier clucked his tongue. "Sorry, but it's time to collar the cat. I've given you free run for too long."

Just then the door to the shop opened, and Gideon strode out. "I couldn't—"

His words died when he saw Xavier, his feet skidding to a halt.

Xavier cocked his head at Gideon, and an expression came over his face that turned it even uglier. "And you must be the kid who's been messing with my people's security systems."

Gideon didn't speak, standing rigidly still. I wasn't sure he had a weapon on him either, and Xavier was closer to him than we were.

Xavier sneered. "You know what happens when you piss off the lion? I will tear you limb from limb until you beg for death. It's payment time." He nodded to his men.

The three guys charged at Gideon. Xavier barreled toward me, his teeth bared.

Kaige threw himself into the fray, tackling one of the men before they'd even reached Gideon. Rowan took a shot at one of the others, who slowed, ducking. Wylder stayed between me and Xavier, firing his own gun, but Xavier dove to the side at the last second.

We spun around, Wylder shooting again and hitting Xavier in the chest—but the impact barely seemed to shake the beast of a man. He thumped his stomach, and I heard a thud that told me he was wearing a Kevlar vest under his shirt.

Before Wylder could take aim at Xavier's head, the other man launched himself at us with a roar. He managed to knock the gun right out of Wylder's hand, his shot going wild. Wylder whipped out a knife and slashed it across Xavier's arm, and I aimed a kick at his gut that from the looks of things hurt my foot more than it did our attacker.

Xavier cracked his knuckles, circling us for a second, considering Wylder's knife. From the corner of my eye, I saw Rowan and Kaige shielding Gideon as they wrestled with Xavier's other two men.

One of the lackeys punched Rowan hard enough that blood flew from his mouth. He landed with a thump on the ground and rolled back onto his feet. The guy was already swinging his gun hand up to shoot Kaige while the last attacker had him distracted.

Rowan sprang in the way so fast he was almost a

blur. He wrenched at the man's arm with a snap of breaking bone and pulled the trigger right at the guy's face for good measure. The front of the attacker's skull burst apart.

Kaige threw the last guy to the ground so hard that he lay there, stunned. As they hurried Gideon to the van, Xavier made another grab at me. At the same time, he slammed his elbow into Wylder's ribs to force him to the side. Wylder let out a pained huff of breath, staggering. Xavier's meaty hand snagged on my wrist.

Acting purely on instinct, I karate-chopped his forearm with all the desperate strength I had in me. Xavier just yanked me closer to him, his other hand reaching for my throat—

And then Wylder rammed his knife into the monster's shoulder.

Xavier's grip shook, and I pulled free.

"Come on!" Rowan yelled from the van. Another car was just screeching to a halt behind the one that had brought Xavier, and the guy Kaige had toppled was starting to push himself upright.

I hated turning tail and running, but sometimes that was what you had to do to survive.

Wylder and I dashed for the van. The second we'd thrown ourselves past the back doors, Kaige hit the gas as hard as he could. The tires screamed in protest, leaving marks on the pavement. Shots boomed after us as we heaved the doors shut.

Then the gunfire stopped. I looked through the back windows to see Xavier staring at us, several men around him, his smile back in place. Even with the tint on the windows hiding my face, it felt like he could see right into my eyes. Then he threw back his head. The last thing I heard before we raced around a corner was a cold laugh spilling out into the dusk.

The sound chilled the blood in my veins. I rubbed my bruised wrist. "He wasn't even trying that hard. He's still toying with us."

What the hell were we going to do when he decided to really get serious?

Rowan

My hand moved rapidly over the paper. With every stroke of my pencil, the harsh lines of the man's face became pronounced. His X-like scars took over both of his cheeks, extending all the way to his jaw.

A shudder ran through me, but I couldn't stop myself. After yesterday's run-in with Xavier, I hadn't been able to get the image of him, of the savagery in his eyes, out of my head. This seemed like the only way to get it out.

"What are you doing?" said a voice from behind me.

I snapped back to attention at the kitchen island, flipping over the paper automatically as my head jerked around. Ezra Noble had come up behind me so quietly I hadn't realized I was no longer alone.

He studied me from where he'd come to a halt a few feet away. "What do you have there, son?"

"Er, it's nothing important," I said. "I was just sketching a little."

"All the same, I'd like to see it." Before I could protest, if I'd even have thought that was wise, he stepped up to the island and lifted the paper. As he studied my rendition of our greatest known enemy's face, his expression revealed nothing. "That's quite an interesting drawing."

"We had a run in with him yesterday. It was... unnerving. Drawing him felt like a way of taking control, even if that sounds silly."

"It's not silly at all if it works." Ezra pushed the paper back to me. "You've got talent. I didn't know you liked to draw."

"I haven't much lately," I admitted, wondering why the big boss was in here making casual conversation with me. Other than our relatively brief discussions about the few projects he'd taken me on directly for, like the negotiations for the waterfront property, we'd rarely talked. He definitely hadn't ever expressed interest in my hobbies. "Is there something you needed me for, sir?"

Ezra leaned against the counter, offering me a mild smile. "You can call me Ezra. I think you've earned it."

Even stranger. I kept my stance looking relaxed on the outside, but inside every part of me went on the alert. "Thank you."

"You haven't had quite the amount of support you deserve in our ranks lately, have you, Rowan," he said.

I had no idea where he was going with this. "I'm not sure what you mean," I said cautiously.

"Well, my son was your original supporter, but it's hard to say where his mind is lately, isn't it? So focused on that Katz girl, and making odd decisions on the fly. He hasn't always been quite so erratic."

Apprehension wrapped around my stomach. I didn't think Wylder had been behaving all that oddly, but that obviously wasn't what his father wanted to hear. I settled for a noncommittal response. "I think a certain amount of unpredictability is expected given the unpredictable situation we've found ourselves in."

Ezra nodded. "Very generous of you. That's the kind of loyalty we should be rewarding. But he still sees you as less than those other two of his, the computer fanatic and the meathead, just because he's known them longer. That's not how *his* loyalties should work."

I still wasn't sure what his goal was here, but he was obviously trying to drive a wedge between me and Wylder. Did he think I'd agree with his assessment of the other guys, that I was bitter about my place in Wylder's inner circle? Maybe he was hoping for that— that I'd be easier to manipulate because *I* had less history with his son.

An eerie calm settled over me. I needed to know what Ezra had up his sleeve, and I was just the man to figure it out, wasn't I? In the past week, I'd mostly been called on to use my combat skills and the viciousness I only let out when I had to. It was nice to have a chance to put my preferred talents to use, working with my words rather than my fists.

I'd rather I didn't have to use them against the man who held all our livelihoods—and our lives—in his hands, but beggars couldn't be choosers. If my position in the Nobles was at stake here, I intended to hold onto it every way I could.

"I guess he is a little closer with the other guys," I said, keeping the same unconcerned tone and watching Ezra's body language carefully. "That's understandable too."

"Not in a man who's meant to become a true leader. I have no idea what's going through his head these days. How will any of the men respect him if he's willing to be led around by his dick by some girl?"

Ezra shook his head, and I resisted the urge to clench my jaw in anger. He clearly had no idea about my and Mercy's shared history or about how those feelings had been reignited. He was probably hoping I'd let something slip about her relationship with Wylder.

But then Ezra went on in a different direction. "While he's busy chasing a piece of ass, you could enjoy much more authority if you reported directly to me. You've done good work for me in the past. I'd like to see that rewarded."

Report directly to him? He wanted to take me into *his* inner circle, alongside Axel and the few others Ezra totally trusted? Technically that'd put me on almost equal footing with Wylder rather than beneath him.

A little thrill shot through me. Even though I couldn't say I had any interest in the offer, I still recognized it as an honor.

If it was even about me and not about undermining Wylder, that was.

"What exactly would that look like?" I hedged,

fiddling with the corner of my paper. In what other ways was he planning to disrupt Wylder's operations?

Ezra gave a casual shrug as if it was no big deal. "You would no longer be answerable to Wylder. Consider it a promotion. You'd come to me for your marching orders, and I'd assign men who'd report to you and follow your own orders in turn. You'd essentially be on the same level as Wylder himself."

"But not quite, because he's your son," I had to say, nudging him just a little.

"Blood isn't everything," Ezra said. "Power should be earned. I wouldn't consider the position of heir certain just yet."

Was he really saying what I thought he was? My pulse stuttered, but I made myself look awed instead. "You can't really mean you think I could fill those shoes..."

He patted my shoulder, leaving my skin crawling. "You sell yourself short, Rowan. If you play your cards right, who knows, the rulership of the Nobles might be up for grabs. Think my proposition over and let me know when you're ready to start."

He ambled out of the kitchen without any indication that he'd even considered I might refuse. I stayed frozen on the stool by the island, chilled through to the bone, with that fake smile still plastered on my face.

He wanted to replace Wylder—to wrench everything Wylder had worked for away from him over a few disagreements that frankly I thought Ezra had the wrong idea on. And he was trying to lure me away with that promise. Not that I'd have trusted anything the snake said after he'd revealed how little respect he had for the son he'd raised.

What was he going to think if I turned him down, though? Fuck.

"I need a drink," I muttered to myself, and headed over to the lounge room with the home bar.

I poured myself a double shot of vodka and downed most of it in one go. It burned down my throat. The sour taste made me grimace, but I threw back the rest to chase it.

"What's gotten into you?" Wylder said from the doorway. "I thought day-drinking was my domain."

He grinned at me as he came over to the bar. I motioned to the bottle. "You could have some too if you're feeling left out. I'll pour."

Wylder shook his head. "I'm not much for vodka, and I've already been hitting the brandy as much as I think is wise." He rubbed his temple. "It's been a shitty couple of days, hasn't it?"

"You can say that again." I eyed the bottle of vodka, debating whether I could stomach another shot. Whether I might say something stupid if I did.

"Thanks for looking out for Gideon when we were up against Xavier and his pricks," Wylder said. "All the power in that brain of his, but he definitely isn't going to take down three thugs in a fist fight. I'd have jumped in there, but..." He grimaced.

He'd had to protect Mercy from Xavier himself. I'd have liked to take a few swings at that prick too.

But even as my frustration with her psycho stalker

flared up, most of my nerves settled, the uneasiness in my gut fading. Wylder *did* appreciate how I contributed to the team, and he wasn't afraid to say so. I'd sure as hell rather be working under him than a treacherous bastard like Ezra.

Which meant I knew exactly what I had to do now with my loyalties.

"Of course," I said. "Gideon's practically family. And so are you. And speaking of family... Your dad and I just had a very unusual conversation."

Wylder frowned. "About what?"

"About you, actually."

"Ugh, I'm not surprised. What did he say?"

I hesitated for a moment, not because I had any doubts about telling Wylder, but because I didn't want to make the revelation more painful than it had to be. But who was I kidding? Hearing it was going to suck no matter what.

"He was feeling me out, trying to see if I've been unhappy working under you," I said. "Making comments about your competence. He's encouraging me to come over and answer directly to him." I paused and swallowed thickly. "And he hinted that you might not inherit the Noble empire after all."

To my surprise, Wylder started laughing. Then I heard the harshness of the sound. There was no humor in it.

"It figures," he said with unconcealed bitterness. "He lays down the law and doesn't even wait to see if I'll step in line. Gee, thanks, Dad."

I could tell I was missing something. "Step in line

about what? Did something else happen between you two after Axel caught us with Mercy?"

Wylder's face turned serious, and his green eyes cut to mine. The silent anger in them was unmistakable. "He... He ordered me to kill Mercy. And he gave me five days—three now—to actually execute that order." The glass in his hand cracked. Wylder looked down at it but didn't even flinch.

A rush of panic and rage nearly overwhelmed me. I grappled with my emotions, fighting for control. "Excuse me?"

"There's nothing more to it. He wants Mercy out of the way, and he wants me to prove I'll fall in line by being the one to do it."

A sudden chill broke through every other feeling in me. "Why didn't you say anything? You aren't really—?"

Wylder's eyes flashed before I could finish the question. "Of course not," he snapped. "And—I was going to talk to Mercy about it, but then the whole thing with her dad and the Red Shark came up—I couldn't figure out how..." He grimaced. "And I didn't want to tell anyone else until I'd talked it through with her. I can't do it, but I'm not sure what I should do instead."

"Fuck," I muttered to myself. "Damn it." I'd had no idea that our attempt to protect Mercy would come to this. "What have you thought of doing? We're running out of time here."

"If I knew, do you think I'd be sitting here not doing it?" He exhaled harshly and then pinned me with a sharper look. "You weren't happy having her around at first, but you two seem to have worked out your issues. I take it you'll stand with me on this."

I didn't see any point in lying to him about it. "She's the only woman I've ever really cared about." The memories of our naked bodies twining, Mercy's gasp as I brought her to the peak of pleasure, flickered through my mind.

Wylder hummed to himself. "I guess she's made an impact on all of us." He paused. "You know, I didn't see this coming—how close all four of us have gotten with her. Heck, I never expected to have the same taste in women as Kaige. And it isn't easy sharing her when she's gotten under my skin like this..."

He trailed off, but I didn't know what to say. That was the first time Wylder had openly acknowledged our shared interest in Mercy—not just his and mine but Kaige's and Gideon's as well. I knew something had happened between her and the others, but his words were that much more confirmation.

I pictured her fierce eyes, the protective stance of her curvaceous body when she got ready to fight. I wasn't surprised the other guys liked her so much.

Jealousy gripped my chest, but only for a moment before it started to fade. Mercy had found a kind of home—a kind of *family*—with the four of us just as we had in each other. I wanted that for her even more than I wanted her all to myself. After everything her real family had put her through, she deserved it.

And Wylder obviously felt the same way. "Who the hell am I to say no to a woman like that?" he said with a shake of his head.

"She is one hell of a woman," I agreed.

"And you." Wylder clapped his hand to my back firmly. "My dad can go fuck himself if he thinks he's coming between us. If I haven't said it enough, let me make it totally clear now—I see you as a brother. I know how loyal you've been, how hard you've worked for me, and I value every bit of that. Maybe you joined the party late, but that doesn't make you any less than the others. You have my trust and I'll always have your back."

Pride more potent than anything Ezra's words had provoked swelled inside me. I smiled at Wylder despite all the anxiety still gnawing at me after his admission. "Right back at you. Since you value my input... can I make a suggestion?"

"Go right ahead," Wylder said, his tone going serious again.

I pushed my glass aside and fully faced him, my gaze intent. "You *have* to tell Mercy and the other guys what's going on with your dad. We'll have a much better chance of coming up with a good solution if we can put our heads together."

Wylder bristled for a second, his lips flattening. "I can't just—" Then he sighed, his shoulders coming down. "No, you're probably right. I just hate thinking about how Mercy will look at me when I tell her."

"As long as you're not trying to carry out your dad's orders when you do, I think it'll be just fine," I said dryly.

He rolled his eyes at me, and somehow everything seemed totally normal again. Like there was nothing unsurmountable in front of us—like we'd tackle this problem like we had every one before and come out on top.

"You're not alone, no matter what we're up against," I reminded him.

He raised an empty glass to me in a silent toast, a grin playing with the corners of his mouth. And just like that, I felt totally at home as well.

This life might not have been the one I'd have pictured myself living, but there was a lot of good in it too, in ways that mattered to me now. And not least of those was this brotherhood we'd forged.

Mercy

WHEN WYLDER FINISHED LAYING OUT WHAT HIS father had ordered him to do, for a moment my head just spun. My mind was foggy from interrupted sleep. I hadn't wanted to stick around any one place for even a whole night now that I was on the run, since I had no idea how easily Xavier might find me. I hadn't gotten enough rest in days.

Maybe I was hallucinating due to sleep deprivation, or this was all a bad dream.

"Your dad... wants you to kill me," I repeated. It didn't sound any better coming from my lips.

"He says that's the only way I can prove I'm loyal to him," Wylder said with a grimace. "Obviously I'm not going to do it."

He looked straight at me, his green eyes shining with the truth of that statement. Tendrils of warmth wrapped around my chest and squeezed me. I nodded at him, hoping he could tell how much I appreciated what he was doing for me no matter what it might cost him in the future.

I looked around at the other guys and Anthea, who I'd met in the back of Gideon's van just ten minutes ago. They all looked as shocked and upset as I felt. I wasn't at all worried about Wylder's intentions, because he'd never have admitted any of this if he was even considering going through with it. But still...

This was Ezra Noble's twisted revenge for crashing into his life and supposedly leading his son astray. As the initial surprise wore off, I found I was almost numb. It wasn't really that much of a surprise, was it? He'd gotten to be the head of the Nobles by knowing how to hit where it hurt.

Kaige swore and smacked the bench with his fist. "So what happens if—*when*—you don't do it?"

"I don't know," Wylder said, and grinned in a humorless way that made me wince. "Maybe he'll kill *me*."

Anthea's head snapped up. "Don't talk that way. He values you more than that. We've simply got to find a way around the problem." She rubbed her mouth and glanced at me. "What if you just took off? I could give you enough cash to get you a hundred miles away from here and set you up in a hotel for a while. You lay low, Wylder can say he couldn't find you, and hopefully it all blows over."

Gideon raised his eyebrows. "Since when does Ezra

let things just 'blow over'?" His tone was typically cool, but his hands had tensed around his tablet.

Anthea let out a huff of frustration.

Even with my life on the line, I couldn't suppress a yawn. Kaige's anger faded in the wake of concern. He passed me a packet of M&Ms from the bag of food they'd brought for me. "Here. Sugar plus caffeine is a great combination."

"Thanks," I said, but after I ripped open the package, I just stared at the brightly covered candies. My stomach had balled tight.

I looked at Anthea. "I'm not leaving my home anyway. Even if that home is pretty crappy right now." I held back yet another yawn and scowled at the thought of the early morning rain shower that'd soaked the hell out of me on the terrace where I'd spent the second half of last night.

"It wouldn't necessarily be for that long," Rowan started.

"No," I said firmly. "The Bend needs me—it needs all of us. The way Xavier came at us the other day just proves that. He knows we're the best chance the city has of stopping him and the Storm's people. I'm not cutting out on them."

When I rustled the candies in the bag without taking any out, Gideon held out a steel thermos to me. "Would coffee go down better? This is my own blend."

I blinked at him and accepted it. "Don't you need it?"

He shrugged, but there was a fondness to the gleam

in his eyes that warmed me more than the thermos in my hands. "I already drank some, and I think you need it more."

"Thank you." I unscrewed the cap and sipped some of the still-hot liquid. The bitterness seared down my throat—clearly an acquired taste—but it did jolt me into a higher state of alertness. Mission accomplished.

Kaige cocked his head. "In all the years that I've known you, why haven't you ever offered your special coffee to me?"

"You never asked for it," Gideon said simply.

Kaige grumbled something half-heartedly about inconsiderate friends, and I laughed. I'd missed their presence and their banter. Heck, I even missed watching Wylder lose against Gideon in their stupid continuing games of chess. I missed the whole stupid Noble mansion, not because of the huge rooms and fancy furnishings, but because it was where I'd been able to live with them.

Too bad Ezra lived there too.

"We can't do nothing," Anthea said, getting us back on topic. "There are other ways, if I pitch in. A little messy, but... we could find a corpse that's the right stature and age to pass for Mercy. I have contacts who could help with that. Then we disfigure it beyond recognizability and tell Ezra it's her."

Kaige made a gagging sound.

Wylder just shook his head. "No."

"I could come up with a similar approach that's not quite as gruesome," his aunt started.

He cut her off with a sharp motion. "*No*. Nothing that means faking that I really did kill Mercy. I don't want to pretend I'm the kind of guy who would. It's a coward's way out. Besides, Mercy would still have to stay in hiding then, or things would get even worse for both of us."

Anthea frowned. "Think about it very carefully. You're walking a thin line. I've known my brother even longer than you have, and he doesn't take kindly to having his orders outright ignored."

"We only have a couple more days before the time he gave Wylder runs out," Rowan said. "What are our other options? Is there any chance of convincing Ezra that Mercy's a useful asset after all?"

"Yeah, right," I muttered. "If he hasn't figured that out yet..."

Gideon recovered himself enough to poke at his tablet. The surveillance feeds on the screens flickered and shifted. "None of this talk does us any good if we get slaughtered by the Storm's people or the Red Shark's in the meantime," he said in explanation.

"If we knew how to get rid of them and could prove Mercy played a big role in making that happen, maybe Ezra would have to admit she's all right," Kaige suggested. "I know we kind of tried that with Colt, but this Xavier asshole did turn up right afterward... Ezra was happy for a little while before that."

"Then we just have to figure out how to crush all our enemies in two days," Wylder said. "Got any brilliant brainstorms?"

Kaige pointed at Gideon. "That's his area."

"And mine." Anthea tapped her lips. "Give me some time to make some calls, and maybe I'll have another idea by the end of the day."

"Nothing that means Mercy plays dead," Wylder told her. "I'll figure something out one way or another— something that doesn't mess up her life any more than it already is."

He spoke confidently, but the corners of his mouth had pulled tight with worry. My throat constricted. I didn't want his life getting messed up over me either.

Before I could say that, Gideon's head jerked up. He motioned to one of the screens. "Well, look at that."

We all glanced over at the feed he'd indicated. A few guys had gathered on a street corner in the grainy footage that must have been from a street cam. I immediately recognized one of them from the confrontation with Xavier the other day.

"Storm people," I said. "That one guy, at least, is pretty high up. What do you think they're doing?"

"I saw them stash a duffel bag right before they got into position," Gideon said. "Looks like they're planning on doing some major dealing. They're outside some apartment buildings, lots of foot traffic, people coming and going."

As if on cue, a couple of kids darted by, waving at each other. They didn't even glance at the Storm's people, but Kaige stiffened next to me. His jaw clenched. "We should shut them down. We can call the cops on them—they'll have no idea we spotted them, right?"

Gideon turned to Wylder. "We were looking to trace some of the key players to the Storm's local center of operations. One of these guys might lead us there if we keep an eye on them undisturbed. It's up to you."

Before Wylder could answer, Kaige spoke up again. "You've already been narrowing down the locations watching their activity with all this." He waved to the screens. "We don't need these pricks."

"We might," Wylder cut in with a bit of an edge in his voice.

Just then, another car pulled up at the edge of the screen we were watching. I leaned forward, studying the figure who got out. A chill trickled through my stomach. "Gideon, can you zoom in on the feed?"

"Sure." His fingers skimmed over the controls on the tablet.

As the view closed in on the men and the new guy who'd joined them, my eyes narrowed. "I thought so. It's that guy who works for Axel—he's hanging around the Storm's people again."

"What?" Wylder's head whipped around. "That's the same guy we saw with them at the arcade."

"Damn right," I said. "There's no mistaking that hair. But what the hell is he doing with the dealers now?"

"He's supposed to be investigating the Storm, isn't he?" Rowan said. "At least that's what Axel said."

"Yeah," Wylder said, but he knit his brow.

"He seems to be hanging out with them an awful lot," I said. "Look at how friendly they're being with him. I don't know."

"Axel didn't seem totally sure about what the guy was doing," Wylder admitted. "He's been so busy keeping an eye on us, I'm not sure how closely he's been watching his people. I wouldn't expect him to make a mistake *that* big, though."

Gideon tapped the screen. "Either way, I'm recording this. We'll have proof if he's up to no good."

"Fuck." Kaige swore so loud I startled on the bench. He leapt up and smacked his fist into the doors, making them shudder.

"Hey!" Gideon protested. "A lot of money and work went into this vehicle."

"And we don't want to be drawing attention to it," Rowan added, looking at the bigger guy with concern.

Kaige spun around. "Don't you see? Maybe Axel's guy is doing exactly what he's been ordered to. Ezra's heard about how popular Glory's getting. What if he wants to get in on the drug trade now?" The fury in his voice showed just how much that idea disturbed him.

Wylder stood up too. "Calm down. There's no point in jumping to conclusions like that. My dad's never been interested in dealing drugs before now."

"But now there's Glory. And we never thought he'd order you to kill Mercy either, did we?" Kaige stomped from one side of the van to the other, his face flushing. "Where's that intersection? I should head right over there and pummel that fucker and every other piece of shit involved in this into pieces." He slammed his fist into his open palm.

"Kaige," Wylder said with a warning note, "get yourself together and sit the fuck down."

Kaige swung toward him. "And do nothing? While they're poisoning the whole goddamned city?"

Wylder grabbed his arm and held his gaze steadily. "And how is charging in there going to help anyone, huh? How well did that work out for us last time? Your hotheadedness got us caught with Mercy, and the time before we were nearly nabbed by the cops. So chill the fuck out *now*."

Kaige stared at him. He'd gone still, but his whole body was rigid, his face still red.

Wylder dropped Kaige's arm but kept his gaze fixed on his friend. His tone hardened even more. "I know you've got shit from your past to deal with, but I can't tolerate you flying off the handle constantly. Going off the rails only hurts the rest of us. If you want to be part of this team, you need to get yourself under control."

"Maybe I should just leave, then, since all I do is screw things up," Kaige yelled abruptly. He shot a fierce but guilty look at me. Then, without another word, he shoved open the back doors and leapt out of the van.

"Kaige!" I said, but he'd already slammed the doors behind him. By the time I got them open again, he'd stormed out of sight. I turned back to the others, my heart heavy. What Wylder had said wasn't untrue, but I'd never seen Kaige so upset he'd leave us behind. "Is he going to be okay?"

Wylder sighed and dropped down on the van's floor, rubbing his forehead. "I'm sure he'll be fine. It's better if he clears his head instead of raining all that thunder down on us."

"But what if he runs into the Storm's people—what if he really does try to take them on all by himself?"

"I wouldn't worry about that." Wylder gave me a crooked smile. "Knowing him, he's headed for the train station. There's one place he always goes when he gets too close to the edge. I just hope this time he leaves a lot more there before he comes back."

Kaige

THE AMTRAK JERKED TO A HALT, ALMOST THROWING me out of my seat. I caught my balance, rubbing my eyes blearily. The conductor's voice carried robotically over the speakers. "Last stop, Festival Beach. All passengers must now leave the train."

I'd reached my destination. And in the two-hour ride, it felt like I'd slept a lifetime. In fact, it was the deepest sleep I've had in a while. The buzzing haze that usually filled my head, fueled by insomnia and too many energy drinks, had cleared, leaving me shockingly refreshed.

Wouldn't it be nice if I could feel this way without shelling out for a fucking train ticket?

I was in too good a mood from the rest to feel that sour about it. All the stress that had propelled me to the station had faded away. I yawned and grinned, and then noticed the kid from the family in the seats opposite me staring. He was coming out to the beach with Mom and Dad like I'd used to—about the same age too, four or five.

I aimed my smile at him, but he looked away to his mother, who was taking down the luggage from the overhead rack. "Mommy," he hissed, as if he thought I wouldn't hear him, "what's on that man's arms?"

He meant the vine tattoos that encircled my biceps, disappearing under the sleeves of my T-shirt. He didn't know they wrapped around my chest as well. They'd just felt right when I'd had them designed. I wasn't totally sure whether they reflected the trapped sensation that I was all too familiar with or an attempt at reining myself in for my own reasons.

The mother glanced at me and made a face. She dropped her voice lower than his. "Let's go, sweetie. And remember, you don't speak to men like him."

Men like him. As if I'd been so different from her son when I'd started out. As if it was strangers who'd mess you up and not the people who should have been taking care of you.

"Kid," I said. The boy startled but turned his wide eyes on me. "Monsters don't always look so monstrous. Don't go by appearances."

The mother's lips pressed flat, and the father urged the boy down the aisle away from me. Fine. I didn't want to hear any more of their shit anyway. I heaved myself out of the seat and headed down the aisle in the opposite direction toward the car's other doors.

As soon as I stepped out onto the platform, the humid air condensed against my skin. The train ride had only taken two hours, sure, but I might as well have come to another continent. The smells of sand and salty ocean water wafted over me with the heat, and the sun beamed down from a smog-free sky. I fucking loved Festival Beach.

I navigated the crowd heading out of the station. Most people around me were tourists, judging by their dorky sun-hats and Hawaiian shirts or sarongs. No one wanted to waste the last few weeks of summer.

The beach lay just across the street from the station. I walked straight across the road and the boardwalk, kicked off my shoes, and sank my feet into the sand. Hot on the top and cool down beneath, just like I remembered. The perfect combination.

The sun glinted off the deep blue water up ahead. Memories rose up as if tossed by the ocean's waves: running across the sand so fast it sprayed out around me in my wake, spreading my arms as if I were an airplane about to take off into the air. Mom and Dad laughing as they watched, their arms hooked together. Dad coming down to the edge of the surf with me and helping me sculpt a sandcastle.

I could still picture every detail of the last one we'd made, complete with four turrets and a ring of little pearly shells along the outer walls. Mom had applauded and snapped pictures. Then she'd swept me up into her arms and carried me right into the water, where we'd paddled around until my skin was sticky with salt and my fingers pruned. My eyes had started stinging, but I'd never cared about that.

I opened my eyes now to the squawk of seagulls

flying above me, and those flashes of the past disintegrated. Despite my train sleep, tension was starting to creep back into my chest.

As if I could outrun it, I walked down to the water and then half a mile along the ocean, rolling up my jeans and letting the foam tickle against my bare calves. The Atlantic water was chilly even this late in the season, but it kept my mind on the present. Plenty of people were splashing around in the ocean, enjoying the relief from the muggy weather.

Right near the train station, couples and families had crowded the beach with a patchwork of towels and umbrellas. Gradually, I left the babble of their happy voices behind me. That atmosphere didn't fit who I was now anyway.

I walked on until the beach got rockier, dark crags of stone jutting from the sand here and there after the boardwalk had ended. No one was venturing this far today—except me.

I wandered on even further just to be sure I wouldn't be disturbed, and then I hunkered down on the other side of one of the boulders. Folding my arms behind my head and stretching out my legs, I closed my eyes and just listened to that rhythmic hiss.

I didn't realize I'd fallen asleep again, but all of a sudden I was jolting awake to the sound of my name. A figure was standing over me, framed by the pink tones coloring the sky that was now shifting toward evening. Her ponytail tossed in the wind.

"Kaige?" Mercy said, crouching down next to me. "Are you okay?"

My pulse lurched, and I shoved myself upright. "Mercy?" It couldn't really be her, could it? I was still dreaming, or she was a hallucination. Frank would be so happy to know he'd been right and all those energy drinks had finally fried my brain.

But then her tanned, solid hands came down on my arm. Electricity buzzed through me as I registered her touch.

She was here. She was real.

The last of the sleep left my eyes, and I stared at her, horrified. Of all the places... "What are you doing here?" I asked.

She looked at me sheepishly. "Wylder told me about this place. You... seemed pretty upset when you left. I wanted to make sure you were okay."

I shook my head to make sure I was hearing her correctly. "Wylder told you?"

He had absolutely no right to. Irritation flared in my chest, followed by a jab of guilt. They'd both probably been worried about me doing something stupid—more stupid than the crap I'd already put them through.

Mercy looked at me with concern I couldn't quite believe I deserved. "Is that a problem? He isn't really angry with you, you know. He was just frustrated."

"*You* should be frustrated," I muttered, rubbing my forehead. "Because of me, you've got a bounty on your head. And you still came looking for me."

Mercy cocked her head at me as if I was being ridiculous. "I'm sure Ezra would have found a way to screw me over no matter what you did. And I was worried about you. In case you haven't noticed, I kind of like you a little bit."

Her wry tone brought a smile to my mouth even as my heart squeezed at her words. "Just a little bit?" I couldn't help teasing.

She socked me in the shoulder in answer and sat down on the sand next to me, close enough that I could tuck my arm around her waist. I watched her from the corner of my eyes, still having a little trouble believing she was real.

No one had ever cared this much about me before. No one had ever bothered to follow me here. It was partly that the guys figured I knew what I needed and could sort myself out on my own, but... it was kind of nice having someone track me down just so I wouldn't be alone.

Mercy drank in the sea air and gazed around us. With the nearby boulders sheltering us, the beach looked empty. I couldn't hear a single voice or laugh in the distance. Most of the families farther down had probably left for the day.

The cooling evening breeze played with a few stray strands of Mercy's hair. She tipped her face toward it. "So, why this place?"

I hesitated. Even Wylder didn't know the whole story.

Mercy glanced over at me. "You don't have to talk about it if you don't want to."

A stronger impulse rose up in me—to show her I could be just as real with her as she'd been with me. I wasn't sure I wanted her knowing all the fucked up stuff, but there were some things it wouldn't be too bad to share.

I motioned behind me. "When I was a little kid, my parents were friends with another family who had a beach house out here. They'd have us come out to stay for a week every summer. Best times I had in my whole childhood."

My throat had started to tighten. Mercy ran her fingers over my hand. "You don't sound so happy talking about it."

I shrugged, my other hand coming up to wrap around my dad's dog tags where they dangled from the chain around my neck. All kinds of uncomfortable emotions were swelling up inside me. I wanted to run away from them, away from Mercy's questions—but how would that be fair to her?

She deserved to know what kind of guy she was letting herself get tangled up with, didn't she?

I dragged in a breath and looked down at my knees. Something inside me hummed in tune to the waves, helping me gather my words.

"My dad never totally got over the stuff he went through when he was enlisted, before I was born," I said. "He'd have nightmares, wake up screaming. One time he punched Mom so hard in his sleep that he gave her a black eye. He didn't believe in shrinks, though, thought they just messed you up more. At first it was only now and then, but it started getting worse. He'd get edgy even when he was awake... I think that's why he ended up turning to the drugs."

Mercy squeezed my hand. "You told me both of your parents were addicts. I didn't realize that's why."

I nodded, my head feeling heavy with the weight of the story and all the awfulness that came with it. "At first it was only a hit here and there, and he encouraged Mom to give it a try—I think so he wouldn't feel alone, to convince himself it was okay. But they got hooked fast. We had one last good summer here when I was five. Then everything went to hell over the next winter. Dad lost his job. Mom's barely paid enough to cover the bills. They cared more about getting their next high than making sure we had anything in the house to eat."

"I'm so sorry," Mercy said, resting her head against my shoulder.

Would she still want to be this close to me when she heard the whole thing? I forced myself to keep talking. "The next summer, they brought me out here again. I was so happy, thinking maybe it was a sign that things would get better again. I was a naïve kid. I didn't realize my mom had just lost her job too. My parents showed up at the beach house and begged their friends for money. That was the only reason we'd come. And they tried to use me for pity points."

Mercy sucked air through her teeth. "Kaige—"

I shook my head. Now that I'd begun, I couldn't stop the truth from pouring out of me. Even the parts that hurt coming out.

"Things only went from bad to worse from there. Their friends obviously turned them down. Back in the city, I started grabbing whatever food I could out of park garbage cans when people would toss sandwich crusts or whatever. The electricity and then the water got shut off. My parents didn't seem to care about that or me. The only time they noticed I was even there was when they came down from a high and got angry. They would beat the shit out of me, saying they'd have it so much easier if they didn't have to take care of me. As if they even were."

"That's horrible," Mercy said in a choked voice.

And it wasn't even the worst of it. I inhaled shakily as darkness began to consume me, the same darkness that haunted the edges of my mind every time I started to relax back in the Bend. Drugs had ruined my parents and infected me with the ugly rages that I would have to carry for the rest of my life.

"Then they decided I was the solution to their problems," I went on. "They—They started hiring me out when I was eight. Letting men come and do what they wanted with me, as long as they paid. The first time, I didn't even understand what was happening till I felt the pain..."

The blaze of that pain had almost made me pass out. I'd begged the man to stop, but he didn't care, and neither did the one after him or the next one.

"They'd always come after I'd gone to sleep for the night," I said, staring at the ocean because I couldn't bear to see Mercy's expression. "When I got into bed, I never knew whether I'd make it through the night alone. I'd lie there, braced for another one to come... It fucked me up. Not just the sleep, but all kinds of ways. I can't stand letting anyone else be in control of me in any way now. I always have to be in charge when I'm hooking up with someone, and I don't even know how to take control of myself when my anger explodes."

"Kaige," Mercy said, her voice quieter now. Her hand squeezed tight around mine. I still didn't dare look at her.

Do you see me now? I wanted to ask her. Do you see how much ugly and monstrous stuff there is in me? Maybe that kid on the train and his parents had been right about me after all. They'd known what I was because I never could get rid of it.

"I wear Dad's tags hoping they'll be a good enough reminder," I said out loud. "Even someone who went through all that army training, all that discipline, can still totally fuck up his life and everyone's around him. I might have a temper and I might get into a rage sometimes, but I *never* want to let myself be so weak I'd hurt someone who didn't deserve it for my own gain. And maybe it's fitting too, because in the end Dad died a death worse than a dog's."

"What do you mean?" Mercy asked.

I grimaced, taking in the crash of the waves. "Eventually my parents' appetites got so big nothing was enough to keep them satisfied. They were getting their drugs from some small-time gang in the Bend. They ended up stealing some, and a guy came to collect. My dad lunged at him, trying to fight him over it—the guy shot him right in the head. Mom ran off. I never saw her again after that. But I didn't mind. I wasn't even upset at that point. I *admired* the guy who stood up for himself and blew Dad away."

My mouth twisted into a hard smile. "That was what

led me to the Nobles. I wanted to be like my own dad's murderer—to join a gang so I could learn how to be that strong and defend myself. I was only ten, so it wasn't like I could just sign up or something, but out on the streets, I heard pretty quick that the Nobles were the badass-est gang there was. I found ways to start doing little jobs for them when I could. Wylder noticed me and spoke up for me... and I finally had a life I didn't hate."

I swallowed hard and finally forced myself to turn toward Mercy. "There you go. That's my whole fucked-up life." I didn't think I wanted to hear what she'd say about all that, but it was too late to turn back now.

Mercy

I STARED AT KAIGE IN SHOCK, STILL REELING FROM everything he'd revealed. The abuse he'd suffered at his parents' hands... the way they'd let others do things even worse to him... I couldn't begin to fathom his pain.

He looked so miserable, so unlike his usual cheerfully flirty self, that it made my heart ache. He was tensed as if he thought at any second I was going to tell him to get the hell away from me.

I entwined his fingers in mine and gripped them tightly, sending all the assurance and strength I could to him. He had to know his past wasn't going to change how I saw him.

"It isn't your fault," I said. "You were betrayed by the people who were supposed to love you. That pain shaped you into the man you are today, but it doesn't mean something's wrong with you."

"But it is," Kaige whispered. "I feel the rage and—

and the fear inside of me almost like it's alive. I've tried putting it behind me so many times but it just takes over at the worst possible moments." He pressed his hand to his temple. "Maybe coming here was a bad idea."

I shook my head. "No. You faced up to your past and opened up to me. I think that means you're healing, Kaige. You just don't know it yet."

I rubbed his shoulder with my other hand. His unpredictable and erratic behavior made so much sense now. Kaige had been dealing with his trauma, not letting anybody in, not wanting to give anyone any power over him after how much his parents had taken away. "I'm glad you told me," I added.

He scoffed. "And how does it make you feel about me?"

"Nothing's changed," I said simply as I stroked my fingers across his back. It was ironic how I felt like I needed to be so gentle with this big man who was at least twice my size. But in this vulnerable state, I could almost see the younger Kaige, the six-year-old whose parents had led him out here one last time only to use him as a prop to try to fuel their addiction.

Kaige looked over at me. For the first time, I caught a hint of hope in his dark eyes. Affection swelled in my chest. Without thinking, I leaned forward and pressed a kiss to his lips.

He kissed me back only tentatively, as if he still wasn't sure he could believe that I was for real. I moved my lips to his cheek, then to the rough scuff of stubble on his jaw. A breath shuddered out of him, followed by an eager growl that sounded more like the man I knew.

I walked my fingers teasingly up his chest. "You know, I've had a lot of fun while you were in charge. But maybe it's time you learned how to let someone else share that role with you."

Desire still shone in Kaige's eyes, but I could see him debating my suggestion. It was probably incredibly hard for him to even consider it.

"You don't have to give up complete control," I said, and pressed another kiss to the side of his neck. "It'd just be a little back and forth. If it bothers you too much, you just have to say so."

Kaige let out a groan. "It's too hard to say no to you. You're a fucking enchantress, I swear. Come here."

He leaned forward, but only close enough that his mouth barely grazed mine. When he opened his mouth, the hot air of his breath played on my lips. I made an impatient sound, my panties dampening in anticipation of the passion I knew he could unleash.

"Why don't you demonstrate what you're thinking?" he murmured, his deep baritone so sexy I was instantly twice as wet.

I wasn't going to wait for a second invitation. My whole body was humming with hunger for him now. I glanced around, making sure we were well out of sight from the rest of the beach, and climbed onto his lap.

He adjusted me so my legs straddled his muscular thighs, then met my eyes as if to say, *Your turn*. I smiled and shifted forward, letting my legs ride up to his hips. My pussy settled against the bulge of his erection through our jeans. I wet my lips, holding back a moan at that first bit of giddy friction and the bolt of pleasure that shot up from my core.

I nudged his chest, and he tensed for a second before lying back on the sand. Splaying my fingers against the planes of muscle, I ran my hands down to his six pack and up again to tease along his jaw. "Is this okay?"

His hands came around to circle my waist. "More than okay."

I didn't want him just lying there, though. Maybe it was time he took a few orders from someone other than Wylder. "Kiss me," I said.

He cocked an eyebrow. "Where?"

I pressed a finger to my lips. Kaige eased back up on his elbows, meeting me when I lowered myself toward him. He gave the corner of my mouth a quick peck before sliding his lips right across mine with a flick of his tongue. I shivered eagerly and moved my head so that I could kiss him harder.

"Don't be impatient," Kaige chided. "I think it's my turn to call the shots."

I huffed my disappointment, and he chuckled. "I like this way too, wildcat," he said before gently pressing a kiss to my lips.

I sighed just as his tongue slipped into my mouth, gently playing against my own as he tilted his head to kiss me deeper. We made out like that, switching the tempo between shallow kisses and deeper ones, trading control back and forth.

My hips began to move against his, seeking out

more of that delicious pressure. Kaige growled and gripped my hips, but he didn't stop me. I sank down against him, putting my arms around his shoulders. The solid planes of his chest almost crushed my boobs. I liked the feel of them, the hardness against the soft curves of my body.

He squeezed my breasts as he kissed me harder and then let me go, resting his lips on mine so that when he spoke I felt the vibration of the words on my own. "What next, Kitty Cat?"

"I think you've neglected some places." I pointed at my jaw and trailed down to the valley of my breasts.

Kaige's gaze followed, hot and dark. He kissed down my neck, nipping and sucking at his whim, setting my skin on fire. My head fell back to give him better access.

He kissed across the path that I had shown him, lingering at the neckline of my shirt. I pulled it up without him asking and then tugged at the hem of his. He didn't hesitate. The second his shirt was off, he unhooked my bra.

Our clothes ended up in a bunch on the sand, but I was past caring. I ran my hands down his powerful corded muscles, tracing the vine tattoos that trailed across them.

"These are beautiful," I said.

"You think so?" Kaige glanced down at himself. "I keep changing my mind about whether I love them or hate them."

"Hmm. Let me worship them a little, and we'll see what you think then."

I slid down his body and dappled kisses along one

line and another, following the tattoos across his shoulders, pecs, and abs. When I traced the tip of one vine right beside his bellybutton with my tongue, he groaned and dug his fingers into my hair.

"See," I said. "It isn't so bad when you share control."

"No, it isn't," he said. "But I know where I want you right now." He hauled me up over him so that I could feel the hard press of his cock lined against my cunt again. I gasped at the sensation of it and then smiled. Yeah, he was definitely enjoying this.

Kaige tugged me even higher, cupping my breasts with his huge hands before bringing them to his mouth. When his hot lips wrapped around my nipple, the rush of pleasure made me moan. His tongue laved the hardened nub before swirling tenderly around it.

He tested the weight of my other breast in his hand, pinching the tip between his thumb and forefinger. I could feel his own impatience growing in the shifting of his body beneath me, the urgency of his movements. He sucked on my nipple hard, and before I could recover from the onslaught of his tongue, he rolled us so I was pinned under him.

"Okay?" he asked.

Oh, fucking, yes. I grinned up at him with a nod. "Fuck me. Fuck me with everything you've got. Everything you are. I want all of it."

With a strangled noise, he wrenched down my jeans and panties. As he nudged my legs apart, I reached for the buttons on his jeans and unzipped him. His cock sprang out, hard and wanting against my thighs. I rubbed the head, slicking the precum around, and then helped him into the condom he dug out of his pocket.

I had no idea if anybody on the beach was close enough to overhear us, and honestly at this point I didn't care. Kaige slowly eased into me. I gasped as my inner walls adjusted around his girth.

For a few seconds, he stopped above me, as deep as he could possibly get inside. Our past two encounters had been hard and fast, as if all that mattered was getting to the point of release. As if he was running away from things he'd rather not think about. But tonight he was taking it slower, like he was making the most of every second. Somehow that turned me on even more.

Kaige started to move inside me, stroking in and out. I rocked to meet him, humming encouragingly as his unhurried movements drove me toward my peak. He stretched my arms on either side, leaving me spread eagle beneath him. Sand clung to my skin, warm and grainy. It tickled against my skin as he increased his strokes.

His hips worked between mine as he picked up his pace, steady and sure, hitting a spot deep inside me. At the same time, his fingers went to work between us, rubbing my clit. A heady swell of pleasure was building inside me. When I moaned, he leaned down to capture the sound in his mouth.

Then all at once he pumped into me even faster, his motions becoming almost erratic. I clung to him, letting the first wave of ecstasy sweep through me. He continued to fondle my clit and didn't let his pace falter as my pussy began to quake, milking him. The second the aftershock of my orgasm subsided, he pounded into me again, kissing me at the same time. His hips rotated in a circle and drove him even deeper inside me, and I toppled over the edge again.

Kaige followed me with a loud moan of his own. Our mouths swallowed each other's cries as we came together this time.

Afterwards, we stayed wrapped around each other, listening to the sound of the waves. The cool, salty air from the sea teased across my naked back as Kaige played with my hair. The moon had risen above us. It was well and truly night now. I didn't know just how many hours we had spent together here.

I drew circles on his chest and heard his breath even out.

"Did you like that?" Kaige asked gruffly.

I raised my head to look at him. "It's never been better."

Something lit up in his dark eyes, so pleased and even joyful that my heart squeezed. An emotion I wasn't ready to name coursed through me from head to toe.

Was I falling for Kaige—was I falling for all four of these guys? I had a deep emotional connection with them, but I knew the bond that was growing between us was more than just friendship or loyalty.

How far would it go?

"Mercy," Kaige said. I heard the catch in his voice when he said my name. Did he know what I was thinking?

I leaned forward to brush my lips against his. "Yes?"

"I like this," he said. "Just—just lying here with you. Maybe as much as I liked making you come, if that doesn't sound totally insane."

A light laugh spilled out of me. "It doesn't. I like it too. Well, both things." I winked at him and then nestled my head against his chest again.

All I wanted to do was fall asleep and remain that way for the next few hours, but I knew we couldn't ignore the problems waiting for us back in Paradise Bend for much longer. I sighed. "We should probably head home soon."

Kaige nodded. "Yeah. But the trains run pretty late. Let's just give it a few more minutes."

I couldn't argue with that. We lay in our little cocoon of contentment, and I tried not to think about the hell that'd be waiting for us when we returned.

Mercy

"Look at that," I said, peering through the windshield of the plain Ford that Wylder had chosen for this drive.

Wylder's gaze jerked to follow mine. "Look at what?"

"Exactly." I motioned to the street ahead of us. "More nothing, just like we've seen all night. We haven't seen any sign of the Storm's people or the Red Shark's guys."

It was past eleven at night, and we hadn't even driven past any drug dealers selling Glory. I hadn't seen this little gang activity in the Bend in... maybe as long as I'd been old enough to notice.

"I guess we can hope that means our tactics have been working," Wylder said with a grin. "They got tired of fending off the police as well as each other and decided to cool it for a bit."

"Now we just have to get them to head right out of town," I muttered.

Wylder nudged me with his elbow. "Don't be so pessimistic. One step at a time. I, for one, would like to celebrate this victory."

He drove back toward Paradise City until we passed into the outskirts and pulled off onto a secluded side street. Then he dug a couple of wine coolers out from under the seat. He passed one to me, popped open his, and held it out to me. Shaking my head in amusement, I clinked the bottles together. "Cheers."

Wylder threw back a gulp of the stuff and grimaced. "Maybe I should have brought my brandy. Oh well." He sank into his seat, stretching out his legs, and glanced over at me. "Kaige has been much chiller since you went out to collect him at Festival Beach yesterday. What exactly happened out there?"

I shrugged. "We talked."

"Just talked?" Wylder said with an arch of his eyebrows, but I didn't think his interest was totally casual.

I wasn't going to feed his competitive side. "Yep. Talking helps, you know. Sometimes much more than you think."

"Well, all that *talking* seems to have helped Kaige a lot."

I rolled my eyes. "There's no euphemism to it, Wylder." Even if Kaige and I had gotten in some pretty spectacular not-just-talking afterward.

"Look, it doesn't have to be a thing." Wylder dragged in a breath and barreled onward with a rush of words I got the impression he'd rehearsed in his head. "You're into him, and you're into me—and Gideon and Rowan too. Well, I guess things never totally ended between you two, huh?"

Where was he going with this? I settled for answering the easiest question. "Rowan and I had a pretty complicated relationship."

"But you've figured it out, at least mostly." His fingers tightened around the neck of the bottle. "You have no idea how much I want to keep you all to myself. To know no one except me gets to touch you. The things I've imagined doing to you, *with* you..."

The vehemence in his voice sent a rush of heat through me. "Me being with the other guys doesn't stop us from doing all kinds of things too," I had to point out, holding myself back from squirming in my seat.

Wylder sighed. "It doesn't. And, even though part of me wants to make you only mine—I can also see that isn't fair to you. You're too much woman to be constrained to just one guy. As long as you're *only* with us, I can see the benefits to enjoying the extra help keeping you satisfied." He shot me a sly grin. "In all kinds of ways."

Okay, my panties were definitely soaked now. But I felt the need to clarify: "What exactly are you saying?"

"I'm not going to make you pick," he said with his usual air of assurance, as if the decision was totally up to him. "In case you were still wondering about that. I figure there's nothing wrong with you being 'our' woman. As long as you're willing to put up with all of us."

I cocked my head as if considering. "You *have* been a jackass for a pretty significant amount of the time I've known you."

Wylder snorted. "But it's been fun, hasn't it? Neither of us are easy people. I like when your claws come out, Kitty Cat." He rested his hand on my thigh and squeezed. "You spent a long time under your father's thumb in a shitty situation. Maybe between the four of us we can make up for all the time when no one in your life valued you anywhere near enough."

My stomach clenched, both at his words and his touch.

"That's definitely something to think about," I said as a strange but exhilarating emotion rose up through my chest.

Wylder glanced at me sideways with one of those cocky grins. "So, out of the four of us, who's your favorite?"

I gave him an incredulous look. "Do you really want to know that?"

"Of course. I love hearing my name from your mouth. Especially when it's accompanied by moans."

I smacked his arm. "That's a lot of confidence."

"It's called self-assurance," he said, wagging a finger at me.

"I still have your knife on me. Be careful what you say."

"A little blood never hurt anybody. Besides, you know I like it kinky." Wylder's grin only grew.

I laughed. It was good to know that no matter what happened, Wylder was never going soft on me. And I did like it that way. "Well, for the record, the position of favorite is still up for grabs. But I will make you work for it."

An eager glint came into Wylder's eyes as if he was going to start on that "work" right now, but before he could do more than stroke his hand up my thigh, his phone buzzed in his pocket. With a grumble, he drew back and pulled it out, hitting the speaker phone button when he saw the caller ID. "Hey, Gideon, what's up?"

Gideon's voice crackled through the line. "There's a problem."

Wylder frowned. "What are you talking about? We didn't have any operations planned tonight."

"*We* didn't," Gideon said. "But your dad had that deal going on tonight—the shipment coming in."

I glanced at Wylder. "I didn't know about this."

He waved his hand dismissively. "It didn't really have anything to do with you. Just typical business—some of our people bringing in stolen merch. There's a small cargo plane that's supposed to land at the private airstrip just outside of the Bend right around now."

"Yeah, that," Gideon said. "The cops seem to have found out about it."

"What?" Wylder said, sounding incredulous. "How the hell would they know anything?"

"I don't know, but they're closing in on the place. They'll be there and have it surrounded in five minutes or less."

Wylder swore and started tapping texts into his phone. "I'll warn the guys. What the fuck could have gone wrong? Axel was handling this one personally. He's a prick, but he knows how to keep his mouth shut about Dad's business."

"This is a particularly important shipment too, isn't it?" Gideon said.

"Yeah," Wylder muttered, still tapping away furiously. "It's one of the main reasons Dad was out of town so long last month. Fuck. If the first deal with his new associate goes sideways, the entire deal could fall apart." He stared at the messages he was getting back and banged his hand against the car door. "I'm not getting any responses. It's too far for us to get there in time to warn them in person. Who all would be out there with Axel?"

Gideon hummed thoughtfully. "All the usuals, I'd guess. Let me see…" His end of the conversation went abruptly quiet. Then he muttered, "Shit."

My pulse stuttered. "What?"

"I've been paying a little extra attention to that guy of Axel's we've seen hanging out with the Storm's people," Gideon said. "Put a tracker on his car a couple days ago. Right now it's out in that part of the warehouse district where we've heard the Storm's people probably have their headquarters."

"Why would he be out there when his boss has a major deal going on?" I turned to Wylder, a chill washing over me. "Unless he tipped the Storm's people off, and they sicced the cops on us this time."

"Fucking hell." Wylder sent off one last text message and glared at the screen. "I'm just going to call. Gideon, I'll have to get off the line."

"I'll keep monitoring the situation on my end."

Wylder hung up and clicked to dial Axel's number. He left the phone on speaker mode, the ringing carrying through the car. It took three before Axel picked up with an annoyed, "What the fuck are you harassing me about, kid? I'm dealing with enough problems already."

Yells and screeching tires carried through the phone line. Axel swore a few times as the sounds started to fade. The cops had already arrived, I realized, and he was heading away from the scene. He must have had lookouts who'd spotted them in time for at least some of them to flee.

"Cops are there, right?" Wylder said quickly. "Did you manage to get the goods?"

"No. Had to get the fuck out of there before— They managed to nab a few people even as it was... How the hell do you know what's going on here?"

"Gideon spotted it," Wylder said. "I tried to contact you and your men earlier. Of course, it looks like one of those men is the one who sold us out, so..."

Axel had started barking orders to whoever was driving, his voice muffled, probably with his palm over the speaker. At those last words, he came back on the line. "What's that supposed to mean?"

"That guy of yours you said was investigating the Storm," Wylder said, his jaw clenching. "Was he supposed to be there at the airstrip tonight? Did he know about the deal?"

"Who the fuck cares? I have a disaster to deal with."

"Was he meant to be there?" Wylder repeated with deadly firmness.

Axel paused, and in the momentary quiet, I sensed the understanding hitting him. "He didn't show. The cops must have grabbed him early."

"Then it's awfully funny that Gideon can trace his car to one of the Storm's people's main hideouts right now, isn't it?"

More silence. Then Axel switched over from shock to defensive anger like the flick of a switch. "How the fuck do you know about any of this? Seems like you've been awfully involved right when things went sideways."

Wylder let out a sputtered guffaw. "Are you accusing *me* of sabotaging things just so you don't have to admit you picked a rat for your team?"

"You're the one who said it," Axel snapped back. "Someone has to pay for this mess. I guess we'll just have to find out what Ezra says about it. I expect to see you back at the house when I get there. Have you even finished the last job he gave you?"

The job that was murdering me. We hadn't wanted to talk about it, but Wylder's time was up tomorrow. He looked at me, determined but with a question in his eyes.

He'd made a hell of a commitment to me just minutes ago. Certainty gripped me that I needed to show him I was just as all-in as he was. That I'd be here with him no matter what shit his dad rained down on us.

I reached to grab his hand and squeezed it. Then I took the knife he'd given me out of my pocket. Holding his gaze, I slid the blade across my palm like he'd done to his thumb when he'd sworn to help me take down

Colt if I cleared Kaige of the murder suspicions on him. A blood promise.

Wylder's eyes tracked the movement of the knife, the blood that welled up from the shallow cut. I held up my hand so he could see it clearly. "I'm in this with you," I whispered, holding his gaze when it lifted to my face. "All the way to the end."

Wylder gave me a tight little smile, but his eyes shone brightly. He turned back to the phone.

Axel was yammering again. "Did I hear someone there with you, kid? What kind of—"

"Axel," Wylder said brusquely, "shut up. You're not seeing me tonight. Possibly not for a few days. I have my own business to take care of, and maybe it's time both you and Dad realize just how much you need *me* after all."

He hung up before Axel could do more than start to sputter and tossed the phone on the dashboard. In one swift movement, he captured my wrist with his strong fingers. I kept my hand steady, ignoring the stinging in my palm.

"Blood for blood," I said, my voice still quiet. "We're in this together."

"Yes, we are," he murmured. Then he slowly leaned in and licked the blood clean from the small wound.

As his tongue made contact with my sensitive skin, I sucked in a breath, but I didn't flinch or pull back. He wiped a tiny smear of blood from his lips and smiled at me with the warmth of the sun. "I couldn't ask for anyone better to have by my side."

I smiled back and brandished the knife, the tip of

the blade still bloody. "Maybe it's time for the prince and princess of the Paradise Bend to become king and queen and reclaim what both of us really deserve."

Wylder's eyes heated. I saw lust in them, and resolve, and something else—just for me. "Damn right."

I didn't know how the hell we were going to deal with Ezra or the invading gangs or anything else we were up against, but in that moment, everything felt totally right.

Until Wylder's phone buzzed again.

Wylder let go of my arm with obvious reluctance and snatched the phone off the dashboard. He frowned at the screen before answering. "They've gotten out of there, Gideon. We were too late to salvage the deal."

"That's not what I'm calling about this time," Gideon said in an unexpectedly panicky tone. "Something's been set off in the Bend. The Storm's people came out of nowhere—they're all over the video feeds—they're attacking everyone they can get their hands on. It's a fucking massacre."

23

Mercy

THE EARLY MORNING SUN SHOULD HAVE LIT UP THE
streets of the Bend with a cheerful glow. Instead it
caught on splatters of blood staining the roads and
sidewalks—and here and there the wall of a building.
The legs of a corpse that hadn't yet been found
protruded from one alley we drove past in the van.
Several of the worst streets were cordoned off with
police tape, cops swarming the place and hauling away
bodies.

Other than a few other cars we passed, the police
were the only people we saw out and about. All the
businesses were closed; none of the regular civilians
dared to leave their homes.

As we cruised by a house that had its door bashed in
and pools of blood drying on the front walk, my
stomach flipped over. "How many people did they kill?"

"It's still not clear," Gideon said, peering at his

laptop. He had his full arsenal out today, the screens mounted in the back of the van all flicking from feed to feed, his tablet on the bench beside him. "I couldn't keep track of them last night. The Storm's people burst out of vehicles all over the place, broke into all kinds of buildings, shot the people inside or mowed them down as they tried to run. I'm not sure how many were even their actual targets vs. bystanders in the wrong place at the wrong time."

That possibility made me feel even more sick. That psychotic asshole Xavier had taken things even further, gone on some fucking rampage through my city, and now look at it. Who the fuck did the Storm's pricks think they were, anyway? My hands clenched into fists.

Then my gaze caught on a familiar store up ahead. I stood up abruptly. "Hey, stop for a second?"

Rowan pulled over. He glanced at the street ahead and then back at me. "Isn't that...?"

A man was carrying sagging boxes from a convenience shop on the corner to the back of a pick-up truck, where a few suitcases and pieces of furniture were already stacked. A woman and a little girl stood huddled off to the side of the door, watching him work, their gazes darting around nervously.

"Mercy?" Wylder prompted from the passenger seat.

I swallowed hard. "I used to come here with my Grandma. The owner was the son of one of her friends."

Mr. Phillips looked as if he'd aged a decade in only a few months. I remembered him a smiling man at the counter who always used to give me a lollipop even when I was too old for it. When he turned back toward the store now, I only saw exhaustion and fear in the lines on his face.

Another man poked his head out from an apartment window over the neighboring store. "Phillips, are you closing up permanently?"

"Yes, son," Mr. Phillips said, pausing by the door. "It's time to move on for good. Might be better for you to do the same if you can."

I stood transfixed as he grabbed one more box from the store and then locked the door. A FOR LEASE sign hung in the now-dingy window. As he put a hand on the small of his wife's back to lead her and his daughter to the truck, his gaze passed over the van as if he didn't see it at all. Maybe he couldn't see anything except the new horizons he was fleeing toward.

The urge gripped me to run after him and yell at him for abandoning his home to these monsters. But Mr. Phillips was doing the best thing he could, wasn't he? He was protecting his family the only way he knew how, taking them away from this hell before it was too late.

Anger flared through my queasiness. The Storm had changed my home for the worse, first by manipulating Colt into bringing chaos to the streets and then swooping in to claim territory. They had turned this place into a literal horror show, the streets red with blood. And what had *I* been able to do about it?

As much as I hated my father, I almost wished he was alive. He would see what his mistake had done to his home, and maybe he'd have done something to fix it. He'd been cruel, but he'd known these streets.

I couldn't bear to watch any longer. The guys were studying me, uncertain of my reaction. "Let's just keep going," I said, dropping back onto the bench and taking a few deep breaths. The combined scents of my four men wrapped around me, settling my nerves just a little.

As Rowan pulled away from the curb, Gideon looked at me, an expression I couldn't read on his normally impassive face. His mouth tensed as if he was about to say something but couldn't quite decide whether he should.

Before he could, Wylder motioned to him. "It was mostly Red Shark people the attackers were after, as far as you can tell?"

Gideon nodded. "They hit several locations where I'd already noticed Red Shark activity. My best guess would be that this was a concentrated effort to end the threat they posed completely." He frowned at the laptop's screen. "And it seems to have worked. There were at least a couple of Red Shark hideouts they mustn't have known about, and I have footage of several people packing up and driving off from those, right out of town."

Kaige turned from where he'd been standing with his hand on the back of Rowan's seat. "The Red Shark's guys took off?"

"What was left of them. The offensive worked."

The jolt of the van's wheels over a pothole made my gut lurch harder. "Then the Storm won that battle."

"And that means they're now in a perfect position to

focus all their attention on crushing the Nobles," Wylder said grimly.

"Not if we have anything to say about it!" Kaige declared, smacking his balled hand into his palm.

"Right," I agreed, wishing I had something—or better, someone—to punch right now. "We're not letting those bastards get away with this."

I didn't need my father. We'd beaten Colt, and we'd destroy these assholes too. The Storm and his men were going to pay for what they'd done to this place. If I had my way, by the end of this they'd wish they'd never even heard of Paradise Bend.

Wylder's green eyes were fixed on me. "You look like you're scheming something, Queen Katz."

My lips twitched into a ghost of a smile at his callback to our conversation last night. "I'm getting started on it. But I think we're going to need some help, and obviously we can't go to your father or anyone working for him for that." I paused. "Let's see what the rest of the Claws are up to."

———

Finding the former Claws members wasn't as simple as just showing up. We swung by the shop where I'd met with Kervos and his small crew earlier, but the basement was abandoned, pretty hastily from the looks of things. A half-full mug of coffee was sitting on the card table. Gideon glanced at it and wrinkled his nose as if he could already tell it didn't meet his stringent criteria.

Rowan turned to me. "Any idea where else they might have gone?"

I worried at my lower lip. "I can think of a few places we can try, but if they're trying to avoid being found after that massacre, they might not go anywhere that's ever been associated with the Claws. I did get Kervos's number. Let's see if he'll answer a text."

If he didn't, it might be because he was dead. I didn't want to say that out loud.

"Are there traffic cams in this neighborhood?" Wylder asked Gideon as we tramped back upstairs. "Maybe you can see which direction they took off in."

Gideon dipped his head in a jerky motion. He seemed more tense than usual. "I'll do whatever I can."

But we'd just piled back into the van when my phone pinged with a response to my text. *We're in the back of the pub your dad sold. Make sure no one sees you.*

My heart leapt. "Never mind about the cams. I know where to go."

My dad had owned the pub down on Morton St. until I was twelve years old. He'd used to hold meetings there, letting me play behind the counter as long as I didn't touch any of the bottles. Then the guy who was managing the place double-crossed him somehow or other, and even though he'd taken care of the traitor, the betrayal had soured the place for him. He'd sold it off and moved his activities elsewhere.

Business mustn't have gone much better for the later owners, because we arrived to find the windows boarded up. Rowan parked around the corner, and he and Kaige hung back to keep an eye on the street while

Wylder and Gideon joined me. We made our way over through the alley to the back rather than tramping along the sidewalk out front.

The lock on the back door was broken. As I eased it aside, a groan reached my ears. I pushed past it into the shadowy room.

Kervos was slumped on the floor amid the empty boxes that'd once held bottles of vodka and gin. Roy leaned over him, wrapping a bandage around his midsection. My pulse stuttered.

I hurried over. "Is he okay? What happened?"

"'He' can speak for himself, and he'll be just fine," Kervos muttered in a strained voice. "Although I'll admit I've been in better shape."

"It looks like it's healing okay so far," Roy told him, and turned to us. His face had gone wan. "You've seen what the Bend looks like. Those Storm jackasses went crazy."

"They attacked you too?" I glanced around and realized it was just the two of them. "Where are the others—Wheeler and...?" I'd never gotten the other two guys' names. Another jolt of panic hit me. "What about Jenner and the other Claws people you were still in touch with?"

Kervos sat up carefully, favoring his injured side. "We've heard from Jenner. He and a few people made it out. He's the one who warned us the pricks were coming."

"We just weren't fast enough," Roy added. "We only got a little way down the street when they were everywhere, shooting like mad—I'm surprised they didn't kill *each other* the way they were going at it." He let out a rough chuckle, but his voice was taut with fear. "That guy with the scarred cheeks was in the middle of it all, fucking *applauding* them in between firing his own shots. He's insane."

Wylder frowned. "Why would he come after you? I understand them wanting to take out the Red Sharks, but all you were doing was laying low."

Kervos shrugged. "Like Roy said, the guy's clearly absolutely fucking nuts." I thought I saw his muscular frame contain a shudder. It said something about Xavier that he'd unnerved even this experienced gangster. "I think he wanted to clear out anyone who'd ever had any loyalty that wasn't to him or Colt. He even—"

He grimaced and swiped his hand across his mouth before continuing. "He had a few of the Claws guys who'd stayed on with the Steel Knights contingent with him. They must have told the Storm's people where to look for us. But I saw, when Roy was dragging me out of there after I got shot—they died too. The Storm's men turned on them as soon as they thought they were done with us and blasted their skulls open."

"It was a fucking bloodbath," Roy said, looking away.

Gideon had been standing rigidly next to me during the conversation so far. Now, he started to pace the room, one arm tucked tight around his tablet, a wild light in his normally cool eyes.

"This isn't good," he said. "It's too close to spiraling out of our ability to control the situation. We need to hit back—hard and fast, before they can get any more of the upper hand."

Wylder shot him a puzzled look. "Don't forget smart. Hard and fast on its own is only going to get us killed too."

"Smart goes without saying," Gideon retorted. I'd never heard him speak to Wylder that sharply.

Wylder looked taken aback too, but Roy cut in before either of them could say anything more. "You've got to be crazy to want to take them on."

"What else can we do?" I demanded. "Look what they're doing to the Bend. Look what they've done to you! We can't let them take over everything."

Roy opened his mouth and closed it again before answering. "I'm not sure we have a lot of choice."

I set my hands on my hips, summoning all the determination I had in me. "We always have a choice. This is my home, and I'm not letting some psycho chase me out of it. Kervos, you said we could call on you if we needed you. Is that still true?"

Roy and Kervos exchanged a glance. Maybe they were thinking *I* was insane. Things had gotten a lot worse since Kervos had made that offer. But the thought of running away and abandoning the place where I'd grown up made my chest ache.

People like Mr. Phillips didn't have the skills or the resources to fight back, but we did. If we didn't stand up to Xavier and the Storm, who the hell would?

"I have a plan," Gideon said abruptly into the silence that followed. "We can do it on our own, but it'd be easier with a little help. It will be dangerous, though. I'm not going to let that stop me."

Kervos shook his head in disbelief. "You could be talking about a suicide mission."

"Hey," Wylder said. "If Gideon says something should work, it'll work."

I looked at both of the men who'd once served my father. "This is your home too. We could take it back. Put the fear into them instead of living with it ourselves. If I go down, I'm going to go down fighting. I obviously can't force you, but it'd mean a lot to have your help."

Roy sprang to his feet. "You know what? You're right. Those fuckers killed our friends, they're destroying the Bend. If you've got a way to take them down, I want in." Anxiety still glinted in the whites of his eyes, but I saw the same courage radiating from him that had brought him to warn us the night of Colt's ambush.

Kervos sighed. "Well, I can't let this kid show me up. Let's at least hear the plan."

A slightly manic smile curled Gideon's lips. "Xavier thinks he's terrified everyone in the Bend now, right? He'll never expect us to target him right in the heart of his operations the very next day. I've figured out exactly where the Storm's headquarters in the Bend are located." He raised his chin. "It's time to invade."

Mercy

As the van eased to a halt a couple of blocks away from the building he'd identified as the Storm's local headquarters, Gideon slicked his dark hair away from his forehead. With his normally blue locks turned jet-black with spray dye, his lip ring taken out, and bronzer rubbed on his face and arms to give his pale skin more of a tan, he looked like a different person altogether. It was kind of disturbing.

"Who are you, and what have you done with our tech nerd?" Kaige joked.

Gideon flicked his tongue over his lip where the ring should have been, the only sign he showed that he was nervous. "The tech nerd part of me is alive and well under the disguise. At least I *can* disguise myself. No one would fail to recognize you unless we invent a shrink ray."

As Kaige chuckled, Wylder squeezed past the seats

and put his hand on Gideon's shoulder. The discomfort in his gaze echoed the tightness in my chest. "Are you sure you want to do this?" he asked.

"Positive," Gideon said without hesitation. "I'm the only one who *can*. Believe it or not, my job is the easiest part of the plan. Let me pull my weight while you guys give them the hell they deserve."

Wylder turned to face Roy, who was sitting on a bench near the back door. "And you?"

Roy gave him a tense grin. "A little late to back out now, isn't it? It's all part of making these pricks pay. I'm glad to do my bit."

I peered down the street. It was a rundown commercial strip on the edge of the warehouse district, so nondescript and out of the way it'd have been easy for the Storm's activities here to go unnoticed. We'd parked around a corner so we weren't in view of the building, but I'd seen the exact area in photos Gideon had pulled up. They were using a small, three-story building that'd been a budget hotel until it'd gone out of business years back, wedged between a dive bar and a shoe outlet store. Classiness obviously hadn't been a consideration.

Rowan had come around to the back and picked up Gideon's laptop. Gideon moved to join him. "You've got it?"

"Everything's ready to receive the data you're going to send, right?" Rowan said, studying the screen. "All I've got to do is confirm that it's come in."

Gideon nodded. "It doesn't really need monitoring.

I'd just like to know someone's keeping an eye on things."

"Of course."

"All right." Gideon squared his shoulders and turned to Roy, grabbing a length of nylon rope we'd picked up on the way here. "Let's get on with this."

Roy stood up and let Gideon tie his hands behind his back. He tested the bindings and exhaled roughly. "Not too tight. They'll hold, but I should be able to shake them off fast if I need to."

"Perfect." Gideon tucked a USB drive and a few devices I couldn't have recognized into the pockets of the baggy cargo pants he'd put on and gave us one last glance. I couldn't help reaching for him and planting a kiss on his cheek. "For luck."

He met my gaze, his eyes momentarily flashing brighter. "Is that all the luck I get?"

I grinned despite my concerns and gave him another kiss, this one on the mouth and hard enough that Kaige let out a low whistle. "Are you sure we can't trade places?" he said with a laugh as I let Gideon go.

Gideon shot him a mock-glare, but a little smile played with his lips. He smoothed it out, took the gun Wylder handed him, and saluted his boss. "I'm just going to go in, get the goods, and head back out. I'll see you soon."

"I'm counting on it," Wylder said, looking like he was restraining a grimace.

Gideon clicked on the mic hidden behind the collar of his shirt and nudged Roy out of the car. As he ushered the former Claws member down the street, he held the gun to Roy's back. His voice carried through the van's speakers. "Have to make it look convincing."

They disappeared around the corner. Then all we could hear was the faint rasp of Gideon's breath and the rustle of his clothes.

Wylder stalked from one end of the van to the other. "Fuck. He had to insist." He shook his head as if shedding his worries and reached for the stash of weapons we'd gathered.

Kaige and I joined in, each strapping a couple of holsters over our shoulders and hefting another gun each. I settled on a pistol I could easily wield. With a fierce grin, Kaige grabbed a semi-automatic rifle. Wylder hefted the bag with the explosives.

We finished our prep just in time. A voice I didn't recognize carried through Gideon's mic. "What the hell is this?"

"Found another one of those Claws idiots poking around the neighborhood," Gideon said, putting on a tough, careless tone. The Storm's people had taken on so many new recruits from the Steel Knights and who knew where else lately that we figured they'd accept him as long as he acted like he belonged. "He didn't want to open up. I thought the boss might want to talk to him about any friends he's still got hanging around."

"Shit," muttered another one of the Storm's guys. "I thought we got all of them."

"Apparently not," the first guard replied. "Xavier isn't here. You really think this guy knows anything useful? We could just shoot him."

I tensed, but Gideon laughed with impressive confidence. My heart squeezed with affection at how well he was holding his own. "Yeah, I'm sure Xavier would just *love* us making that call without his say so. I'll stash him in one of the rooms and get back to work."

"Who are you again?" the second guy said all of a sudden.

"Terence," Gideon said, and snorted. "Come on, man. We did a drug run together on Ridge Street." Gideon must have recognized him from the feeds and known there'd been a lot of Storm people around that night.

"Yeah, yeah," the man said, sounding chagrined. "Take him inside and stick him in one of the rooms upstairs. He's dead meat anyway."

"I didn't do anything to you," Roy protested, playing up the prisoner act.

"You picked the wrong side," the first Storm guy retorted.

"Well, fuck you," Roy said. We heard a soft thud followed by a grunt from Roy.

One of the Storm's men must have punched him.

"Keep your mouth shut, dickhead," the guard warned. "The boss will deal with you once he gets back."

There was a sound of a slamming door and then muffled chatter. Stairs creaked. We stood braced, hanging on every sound. Gideon's breath was rasping harder now.

Another door thumped. He let out a sigh of what

sounded like relief. "Good to go," he said as if to himself.

That was our cue. "Be careful," I murmured to him, even though I knew he couldn't hear me. Wylder motioned to me and Kaige, and we hustled out of the van.

We ran along a side street at a sprint and burst out across from the old hotel. As the men in front of the door shouted an alarm and raised their guns, Wylder hurled two grenades one right after the other.

The guards dodged to the side just as one grenade blasted the door right off its hinges. The other landed on the hood of the car parked outside the hotel, where it exploded with a force that shattered all the vehicle's windows and blackened the frame.

The car's alarm began to wail. We dove down behind the vehicles along the opposite curb to wait for the Storm's people's response, guns at the ready.

It didn't take long. Yells were already carrying through the air. Kaige popped his head over the trunk of the car next to ours and took the first shot. Wylder took aim over the roof. I peered around the front bumper.

Storm men were charging out of the building, guns jerking in every direction, searching for their attackers. They didn't expect someone to make such a bold opening move and then retreat. Which meant they left themselves way too open in their hurry to defend their base.

Kaige and Wylder let loose a hail of bullets. I pulled the trigger on my own gun, aiming as well as I could at the men whose expression shifted from furious to startled in an instant.

They were responsible for destroying my home, every single one of them. I had absolutely no qualms about taking them down when they'd have happily killed me a hundred times over.

I managed to catch one in the thigh, another in the stomach, and a third in the chest. All of them collapsed. More fell with sprays of blood from Wylder and Kaige's shots. By the time they'd figured out that we weren't right on their doorstep but firing at them from fifteen feet away, more were slumped on the ground than still standing.

The few who remained ducked behind the smoking remains of the car. Another couple appeared by the front door. Wylder managed to pick one off before the other jerked out of view. We could hear the ones behind the car swearing.

Wylder shot me a devilish grin and grabbed another grenade from his bag. With a yank of the pin, he flung it toward the already burnt-out car.

At the clang of it hitting the car's roof, the men cursed again and bolted back toward the hotel. Kaige plowed them down with a frenetic series of bangs and a whoop of victory.

Then the street was silent, other than the ringing in my ears after all that gunfire. Wylder reloaded his revolver and pointed it at the blasted doorway, watching for movement.

My heart thudded wildly. The whole idea had been to distract—and destroy—as many of the Storm's people on site as we could while Gideon was at work, to make sure no one stumbled on his efforts. And to make it easier for him and Roy to get back out again when he was done. Had we bought him enough time?

That wasn't our only goal, though. "Do you think that's it for them?" I hissed at Wylder.

"Come on," he said. "Kaige, you stay ready to take down anyone who shows their face in the doorway."

Staying low, Wylder and I dashed forward to the bodies sprawled closest to us on the sidewalk and the edge of the road. I felt one guy's pockets and then another's, yanking out their phones. Wylder grabbed three more. I tossed the ones I'd gotten to him, and he stuffed them into his bag.

"Between these and whatever Gideon nabs for us, we should come out of this mission with info on every part of the Storm's operations here," he said under his breath with a triumphant grin. "Maybe we'll even find out where these assholes came from."

There was a stomping sound from inside, and Kaige took a shot over our heads. After he fired a few more times, I heard a body thump against the floor.

"I don't see any more coming," he said.

Wylder swung his arm. "We got what we came for. Let's go!"

We took off toward the side street we'd come up from. The plan was to meet Gideon and Roy back at the van. If he came out and joined us in full view, it was too likely the Storm's people would realize the full extent of our assault—not just on their men but on their computer systems. The longer they went without realizing what Gideon had stolen from them, the more use we'd get out of that information.

Hopefully our friends would be on their way out any second now.

The second we reached the van, we threw ourselves inside. Kaige leapt into the driver's seat and started the engine so we could tear away as soon as the others reached us.

Rowan was still sitting braced on the bench with the laptop on his knees. "I don't know half as much about this stuff as Gideon does," he reported, "but it looks to me like he's already sent a crapload of stuff. I think—"

A sharp voice crackled through the van's interior. "What the hell do you think you're doing?"

I flinched before I realized the sound had come from the speakers—from Gideon's mic. Then my heart hiccupped all over again.

"We were just—" Gideon's voice replied.

"Don't let him get away!" someone else hollered.

There were two ear-splitting bangs, followed by a thud. Bile shot up my throat. I clapped my hand to my mouth just as Gideon's voice carried through the speakers with a soft "Fuck."

Was he still okay? He hadn't been shot?

Another new voice reverberated from the speakers, but this one I recognized. "Who the fuck was that? And who's this prick?"

A chill swept through me. It was Xavier. The boss had returned.

"Some Claws guy," another man answered. "Better

off dead anyway. This one acted like he was with us—he said he was bringing him in for questioning."

"And you bought that lame-ass story?" Xavier demanded. There was a fleshy smack of knuckles meeting the side of a head and a pained groan.

I dropped my face into my hands. Roy must be dead —he was the one they'd shot. And they had Gideon cornered.

"I was only trying to—" Gideon started again, his voice rough. Something cut him off, the sound warbling. I realized Xavier must have grabbed him by the front of his shirt near the microphone.

"You're not acting alone, are you? The fucking Nobles or the Katz girl sent you? Ha!" Fabric tore, and Xavier chuckled darkly. "Can you hear me, Mercy? Or maybe it's Wylder Noble on the other end. Either way, listen up. I've got your man. What are you going to do about it?"

Then, with a sputtered crackling, the line went completely dead.

"Shit," Wylder said, spinning toward the doors. "Shit, shit, shit." He looked ready to rip right through the steel. I jumped up, wanting to race out there with him, all the way back to the hotel. What was that psychotic bastard going to do to Gideon?

Why had we ever let him go in there?

"Stop!" Rowan said, standing up, his voice harder than I'd ever heard it. When I looked at him, he was shaking, but his gaze stayed firm. "We can't get him out right now. You *know* you'd be running right to your deaths. If we want to get Gideon back, we have to pull back and regroup so we can figure out some way of beating them."

Wylder swore again and punched the wall of the van. Kaige had turned in the driver's seat, watching his friend with a taut and uncertain expression. I glanced toward the doors, but I knew Rowan was right. Running off to be slaughtered wouldn't save Gideon—it'd end any chance we had of rescuing him.

But the thought of leaving just about killed me too.

"We *are* coming back," I said, a tremor running through my voice. I had to say it out loud. "We figure out how to get the better of those assholes as fast as we can, and then we're getting him back."

"You'd better fucking believe it," Wylder snapped. He raked his fingers through his fiery hair, but he must have seen the truth as clearly as I had. With a haunted look in his eyes, he nodded to Kaige. "Let's get out of here before that psycho's goons come looking. We'll be back soon."

Kaige grimaced, but he hit the gas and swung the van around.

With every block we put between us and the old hotel, it felt as if another piece tore off my heart.

25

Gideon

THE PUNCH KNOCKED OUT MY BREATH AND LEFT ME panting on the floor. The two Storm men who'd dragged me across the hall kicked at me a few more times.

"Look at this weakling," one of them sneered. "Some bait. Who would bother coming for him?"

They stalked out of the room, slamming the door behind them. A deadbolt clicked over.

I tried to move my arms, but my lungs were burning. My breath was coming in strangled gasps now. When Xavier had ordered them to grab me, I'd tried to fight, tried to make a run for it—anything would have been better than ending up tied up and imprisoned like this. Better that they'd shot me than using me as a lure so they could kill everyone else too.

But I hadn't made it, and the effort had left me straining just to draw enough oxygen not to black out.

As I wheezed and coughed, my vision swam. Dark dots speckled it.

The image of Roy's slack face, his eyes staring glassy and unseeing, rose up. Blood staining his shirt and seeping over the floor. His dead body limp where the Storm's people had shot him. My stomach clenched almost as tight as my chest.

Fuck. Fuck. I'd been so close, but I hadn't made it, and one of our allies had died over my risky plan. It'd been my idea—I'd convinced Wylder. I'd convinced them all, and now look where I'd gotten myself.

I might die before Wylder even tried to get me out of here if I couldn't manage to drag more air into my lungs.

Each labored inhalation filled my nose and mouth with a stink like rotten cheese, which only made me feel sicker. *Just breathe*, I told myself. *Just fucking breathe, Gideon.*

If only it were so fucking easy. My lungs were shuddering as if threatening to collapse on themselves, and my pulse was going haywire. Sweat beaded on my forehead. The darkness crept in on my sight.

I had to snap out of this. I had to get my stupid, broken body under control.

I'd managed it before. A different memory wavered through my mind: Mercy, talking me down from an attack in my office just a few weeks ago. The unexpected softening of her tone, the assurance with which she'd spoken. The words came back to me, washing through my nerves.

Listen to me. Just focus on my voice. You're the smartest person I know. We'll work this out.

She wasn't here for me to really listen to her, but I took her advice as well as I could in my addled state. I thought of the kiss she'd given me before I'd left the van and the smile she'd offered afterward. Of her vehemence when she'd insisted she wasn't leaving her home to the Storm. Of the other kinds of passion she'd shown me.

I want to ride my dark god and do his bidding.

I'd felt so powerful in that moment with her in my bed, powerful and capable and wanting to do whatever I could to please her at the same time... She brought out something in me I didn't recognize, something no one else ever had. But it was good.

Abruptly I realized that the burning in my chest was subsiding. My breaths still snagged in my lungs, but it wasn't quite as hard to pull in enough air to stay alert. My vision had cleared. I wasn't outright wheezing anymore.

I lay still for several more minutes until my breathing evened out completely and my thoughts had unjumbled. A pang of affection shot through me.

Mercy had managed to be here for me even when she was nowhere nearby.

That was only my most immediate problem solved. A searing mix of guilt and panic trickled through my veins. I was still being held captive by our worst enemies. I'd still brought Roy to his death. I'd managed to send all the data I could scrape off the laptop I'd found back to my own computer, but I hadn't been quite fast or careful enough. They'd caught us before we could get out of there, and because of that I'd become an epic liability.

Because I knew my best friend. It might have been easier to leave me for dead—they had to realize that coming for me would be walking into a trap—but Wylder would never accept that. He'd come. And no doubt Mercy, Kaige, and Rowan would be right by his side ready to fight for me too.

Why the fuck had I ever thought I should step away from my devices and my screens to venture right into the lion's den? Total madness.

But I was here now. I was still alive. If there was any way I could turn this situation around, I had to find it, not lie here moping about my failure. Otherwise I really would be less than worthless.

With my hands tied behind my back, it took a little effort just to roll onto my side so I could take stock of the room. The space was small and dingy, with a matted carpet and thick curtains blotting out most of the light from the window at the other end. The only furniture was a bed with a stripped mattress and a boxy end table next to it. It didn't look like it'd been the nicest place even when the hotel had been open.

I couldn't hear a peep of sound from outside. Whatever Xavier and his goons were doing now, they didn't seem to be worried about me.

But maybe they should have been. As I squirmed and sat up, it occurred to me that I still had a couple of my devices on me. The goons hadn't patted me down all that carefully, only looking for anything large enough to be a weapon.

I'd shoved a couple of my tiniest trackers in my hip pocket in case I saw something good to stick them on, and those hadn't been found. Maybe I could do something useful with the trackers and get even more information to help the Nobles crush these pricks.

Of course, that meant I had to get the damned things out of my pocket. With my hands tied behind my back.

At least, since these were cargo pants, the hip pocket was on the side rather than in front where it'd have been even harder to reach. It took a hell of a lot of contorting to get my hands anywhere near it, though. I knelt on the ground, twisting at the waist and yanking at the fabric as hard as I could to pull the pocket closer, stopping now and then when my breath started to rasp again, hunching and leaning every which way until I found the right angle.

I ended up arching over on my back in some kind of demented yoga pose, tugging the flap on the pocket open, and shaking my legs until gravity pulled the little metal circles out to patter on the floor. With a sigh of relief, I sat back up and scooped them into my restrained hands.

Once I had them in my grasp, it wasn't hard to peel off the protective plastic on the adhesive side. I gripped them by the non-sticky edges and contemplated the room, debating the best spot to put them.

Nothing in the room right now was likely to go anywhere, so there was no point in tracking the furniture. I'd have stuck one on myself, but Wylder knew exactly where I was already. What might be useful is if I could get them stuck on one of the Storm's people's clothes without them noticing... Maybe they'd lead us to a secret supply building or even their home base outside of Paradise Bend.

The bottom of a shoe would be my best chance. I stepped closer to the door and carefully dropped one and then the other tracker on the floor a couple of feet from the entrance, where anyone coming in would be most likely to step. In the dim light, the thin metal circles, barely wider than the tip of my finger, just looked like a couple more stains on the carpet.

I'd only just had time to think that when footsteps thumped on the other side of the door. The lock clicked.

I scrambled backward, my heart lurching. I couldn't let them realize what I'd been doing. And once the light from the hall spilled into the room, I'd need to do my best to ensure they didn't look at the floor.

The door burst open to reveal Xavier's scarred face and broad-shouldered frame. He lumbered into the room with a maniacal glint in his eyes. "I thought it was time to check up on our guest. I hope my boys treated you well."

I couldn't hold back my urge for sarcasm. "Excellent. I got the VIP treatment." My gaze flicked across the floor as surreptitiously as I could manage.

Fuck, he'd stepped right past the trackers, missing them both. Maybe if I could get him to move around some more... but it was hard to concentrate on that with the psychotic monster looming over me.

He was carrying a knife which he flipped from one hand to the other. "So...Gideon, is it?"

"You know my name," I said.

Xavier's eyes narrowed, and for the first time I got a sense of the bubbling anger in him. The veins bulged in his thick arms. "I do," he growled. "I know a lot of things. You and your little friends have become very annoying."

"I'm going to take that as a compliment," I said, not knowing where this sudden burst of confidence was coming from, only that it was either let it loose or end up huddled on the floor in terror.

"You shouldn't," Xavier snarled. "I'm not impressed by this stunt your friends pulled out there today. I gave you all too much rope, clearly, but don't worry. Now I'm going to reel them all in, with you dangling on my line."

He poked me in the chest, forcing me to stagger backward, and stalked past me to pace the room. Which took him farther from the trackers. So much for that.

All at once, he spun on me again with another jab of his finger. "I don't like the mess you made of my men," he snapped. "And that little bitch and her dad stole the fucking world from me. I'm not even close to finished putting her through all the pain she deserves. And you're going to help me make them pay. The games are over. The Katz and the Noble heirs think they can pull one over me, but I'm going to crush them like the pathetic children they are."

Mercy and her dad had stolen *what* from him? Was he so deranged he thought the Bend should have been his to begin with—or he blamed her for fighting back and him for bringing in the Red Sharks?

Or maybe he really did mean the whole world. With the crazed look on his face, I wouldn't be surprised.

As if on cue, a cockroach scurried out from under the bed. Before it could go very far, Xavier smashed it under his boot. He didn't bother looking at the floor. "Crush them," he repeated. "Just like that."

I didn't want to fuel his fire by telling him he was wrong, but I had to point out, "This was our territory first. It's a little bizarre to blame us for defending against your attack."

Xavier snatched me by the collar and jerked his hand up to my throat. "Is that what *you* were doing here, little boy?" he said, hot rancid breath spilling over my face. "Defending yourself? What did you think you were going to accomplish poking around on my turf?"

Holy fuck. He didn't actually know what I'd come for—which meant he hadn't figured out what I'd done. I blinked, holding in my surprise as well as I could, and managed not to laugh, even though the whole situation suddenly seemed hysterical.

I must have shut down the laptop quickly enough when I'd heard the men coming that it'd looked like I'd never gotten it on in the first place. I'd been heading for the door with Roy when they'd caught us.

I sure as hell wasn't going to tell Xavier how much

of his operational data was now in Wylder's and Mercy's hands. I raised my chin as defiantly as I could with his knuckles nearly crushing my windpipe. If my voice shook, it was only because my heart was hammering so hard against my ribs. "I was supposed to assassinate you."

Xavier stared at me for a few beats. Then he threw back his head with a laugh so loud it rattled my ear drums. "And they thought *you* were the right one for the job? They're even bigger idiots than I thought. How've they managed to stay alive this long?"

He shoved me away from him, letting me go so my back banged into the wall. I gritted my teeth. "They picked me exactly because you wouldn't expect it. Here I am, and you still don't believe it. I'd say that's pretty smart."

"Hmm. Somehow I think there's more to it."

"Well, getting rid of a bunch of your men in the meantime wasn't exactly a loss."

"It was to me," Xavier snapped, and spun toward the door again. My pulse stuttered with the fear that he'd notice the trackers if he looked down.

"Maybe not," I said quickly. "We know you've got a traitor from the Nobles on your side. Anyone who'll double-cross for you will double-cross *you* as well."

Xavier swiveled back toward me with a fierce expression, his boot coming down just an inch shy of the nearest tracker. So fucking close. "What are you talking about? No one would dare bullshit me."

I was bullshitting him right now, wasn't I?

"How do you know?" I shot back, letting whatever

popped into my head spill out of my mouth. "I'm sure Ezra has heard all kinds of interesting things from his guy."

"Good thing I know not to trust a rat with anything important, unlike Ezra, isn't it?" Xavier waved me off and turned back toward the doorway. "It doesn't matter. I'm going to destroy the boy and the cat, and enjoy doing it."

His head started to dip, his gaze veering toward the carpet and the trackers, and panic blanked my mind. I spat the next thought that crossed my mind. "And that won't matter anyway. You won't even have gotten the real heir."

Xavier's head jerked up. "What the hell are you talking about?"

I opened my mouth and closed it again. But it couldn't hurt to say this, could it? It was mostly a lie anyway. It'd distract Xavier, confuse him, and maybe give us an opening. "Wylder's the younger brother. He's just a decoy. It's his older brother Roland who's the real heir."

"Really?" Xavier loomed on me again. "Then where is this real heir?"

"Oh, you know, he's got all his training to get through," I said, making things up as I went. "Ezra wants him totally prepared when it's time to take his rightful place. He moves around a lot, learning from all the best people."

"Liar," Xavier said.

I shrugged as if I couldn't care less. "There are these things called birth certificates. It wouldn't be hard to confirm that Wylder isn't Ezra's oldest kid." As for the rest, well... I'd either be dead or long gone before Xavier had any clue what was real there.

Xavier considered me for a few more seconds before he stepped even closer and raised his fist. I tried not to shrink away. He punched the wall right behind me, taking a good chunk of plaster off. "Whether it's true or not, your friends have been thorns in my side for too long," he sneered. "I'll enjoy slaughtering all of them."

He marched away from me toward the door. He was looking ahead, not down—but I could tell he was going to miss the trackers again with his feet as well as his eyes.

With a sudden burst of defiance and determination, I made as if to charge at him.

It was ridiculous—I didn't stand a chance even with all my faculties, let alone with my arms tied up. Xavier heard my footsteps and whipped to the side. He slammed his fist into my gut just before I reached him. I smacked into the wall and crumpled, agony exploding through my torso.

"Nice try," Xavier sneered, and stomped out of the room—with his boot landing right on the second tracker. It stuck on, vanishing underneath when he strode away. As the door closed in his wake, I let myself smile around the metallic taste of blood seeping from where I'd bitten the inside of my lip at his punch.

It was worth it. I'd accomplished one useful thing here. When I got out of this place, who knew where Xavier might lead us when he thought he was going unseen?

If I got out of this place. My stomach sank all over again. Xavier had talked about killing Wylder and Mercy with pure delight. What would that menace have waiting for my friends and my woman when they came for me?

26

Mercy

ANTHEA SIGHED AND LEANED BACK IN HER CHAIR, pinching the bridge of her nose. She'd spent hours sorting through the folders Gideon had managed to transfer from whatever computer he'd found in the Storm's local headquarters. Meanwhile, the rest of us had been pacing the abandoned pub my father had once owned. It'd seemed like a good a place as any to hold a meeting.

We were all too restless to stay cramped in the van. Of course, the stale boozy smell that permeated the air didn't exactly make for a comforting atmosphere either.

Nowhere in Paradise Bend would be comforting right now.

"What did you find?" Wylder demanded, coming over.

"Plenty of information about their past operations," Anthea said. "Businesses they've set up deals with in the

Bend, ideal locations for distributing the drugs, that kind of thing. Even some observations about the Red Shark's activities, which seems to be a moot point now. But I'm not seeing anything that exposes any weaknesses that'll help us get Gideon out of there."

"Keep digging," Kaige insisted.

Anthea shook her head. "I've gone through everything. They haven't kept any information that was all that vital in general on here—nothing about definite future plans, nothing about their activities outside of Paradise Bend."

The ache that'd been sitting in my stomach since the moment we'd driven away without Gideon intensified. "And we still have no idea who the Storm is or where his people came from?"

"Not a hint about that either."

"I guess it's not surprising they wouldn't have that stuff on a computer," Rowan said, though he looked just as worried as the rest of us. "Gideon's put us several steps above a typical gang in terms of tech, and even Ezra doesn't like to leave a digital paper trail whenever he can help it."

"Fucking damn it!" Wylder punched the bar counter and then shook his fist with a hiss.

"Hey, beating up on the furniture is my job," Kaige said, but he couldn't work any real humor into the joke.

"We're running out of time." I reached past Anthea to bring up the recording of the message Xavier had sent through Gideon's mic about an hour after his capture. The psycho's gruff voice carried through the speakers. "You have twenty-four hours to come retrieve

your boy, or you'll be picking his corpse off the street."
He followed the warning up with a chuckle that sent a
shiver down my spine.

That'd been twelve hours ago. We'd gone right through
the night without landing on a way to get Gideon back,
and now hazy dawn light was starting to creep through the
dirty front window. My hand clenched, but I knew
punching the laptop would be the opposite of helpful.

"You know this is a trap, right?" Anthea said gently.
"They're obviously going to be waiting for you to
show up."

"What's the alternative?" Wylder asked, his voice
strained. "We can't just leave him there for them to
kill!"

"I'm just saying that we have to come up with a solid
plan. Rushing right in there will only let them kill all of
you."

"Well, we can't just sit here and do nothing. He's in
there with that fucking monster." Wylder shuddered.
"God knows what state we'll find him in."

The comment echoed my own thoughts, but I
couldn't let hopelessness fill my head. "Gideon is
stronger than we think."

"We only need one thing that would give us an
advantage," Rowan said. He frowned at the computer.
We'd been counting on finding that advantage in the
files it held.

My gaze fell on the phones we'd grabbed off the
fallen Storm men. I motioned to them. "Maybe there's
something else on those. They'd need to be using their

phones for more immediate communication—they might not have been as careful about what they said in texts." That was the whole reason Gideon had wanted us to take the phones while we had the chance.

Unfortunately, he'd also been the one who could have hacked past their lock codes. Anthea grimaced and rubbed her forehead. "I know my way around a computer for the basics and a little more, but I can't break into a locked phone."

We glanced around at each other, but we all knew the rest of us wouldn't stand a chance. We'd already confirmed that all five of them were locked. Shit.

"The Nobles have other contacts," Anthea pointed out. "I'm sure there's someone on the payroll who could—"

"No," Wylder cut in firmly. "I told you what happened after the deal at the airstrip went sour. Dad knows I've sided with Mercy over him. I'll be lucky if he doesn't put a bullet in my head the next time he sees me. He's never going to offer up any of the Noble resources. So unless *you* know a specific person we can go to who'll support us over him..."

She sighed. "No. Most of my contacts are back in New York. I *might* be able to get ahold of one long distance, but they're not generally the type to want to discuss illegal methods in ways that can be recorded." Anthea paused, tapping her lips. "But we could still get what we need from your father. All you have to do is put on a show of having turned against Mercy after all—"

"*No*," Wylder said, even more vehemently than before.

"It wouldn't have to be as extreme as faking her death. We could always—"

He slammed his hand down on the table hard enough to make the laptop jump. "No. I'm done with Dad thinking I'm his marionette, dancing when he pulls my strings. It's time I stood up for what I believe in like the man who's one day going to be ruling the Nobles should."

He sounded like a leader then, so much that a glow of pride lit up inside me. Maybe I'd taken an unconventional route when it came to my current relationships, but I had found myself some awfully impressive men, hadn't I?

Now I just had to figure out how to retrieve one of those men before I lost him completely.

Anthea gazed steadily back at Wylder for a moment and then inclined her head. "I see your point. I don't entirely agree with it, but I accept it. So, what now?"

Wylder turned to Rowan. "You've handled a lot of the negotiations with the outlying gangs we associate with. Can you think of anyone who could handle the phones?"

Rowan rubbed his mouth. "With the current state of things in the Bend, I'm not sure how easy it'd be to get anyone to come out of the woodwork, especially when they can't be someone whose ties are mainly to Ezra. Let me think."

Watching Wylder step up as a leader sent my thoughts in a different direction, toward the men *I* was theoretically meant to inherit. One of whom had died for our cause yesterday afternoon.

I swallowed thickly. We hadn't told Kervos about Roy's fate yet. Before we'd set off for the Storm's headquarters, he'd managed to get in touch with Jenner, and we'd dropped him off with him and several other Claws members who'd survived the purge. In his injured state, he wouldn't have been able to pitch in with the attack anyway.

An idea tickled up through the twinge of guilt. "Maybe there's someone good with tech stuff still with the Claws," I said. "That's easier than tracking down someone who's got no stake in this war at all. We can go ask them now, before we lose any more time."

Wylder gave me a tense but grateful smile. "Lead the way, Queen Katz."

———

Jenner and the rest of the remaining Claws had holed up in an abandoned house in one of the more derelict neighborhoods in the Bend. Even with newspapers plastered over the windows, they were sticking to the large but unfinished basement to avoid any chance of being spotted from outside.

As we tramped down the steps to meet with them, the hushed conversations fell totally silent. A steady dripping echoed from a pipe at the other end of the dim space.

My shoes scraped against the cracked concrete floor as I came to a stop. Jenner and a couple of the others got up to greet us. The dozen or so other guys stayed on the blankets and sleeping bags they'd probably recently been sleeping on. Kervos stirred, just waking up where he'd been dozing in a corner. He sat up quickly and winced, clutching his side.

"Where's Roy?" he asked before we could say anything.

My pained expression must have given away the answer. Before I even spoke, he swore.

"The Storm's people shot him," I said, forcing my voice to stay steady. "They've captured our man who went in with him and are threatening to kill him too. That's one of the reasons we came to talk with you. But first—it's just about breakfast time. We figured you could use some food."

Rowan and Anthea held out the bags of groceries we'd stopped to buy on the way over. I wasn't going to show up and demand favors from my father's former people while offering nothing in return. Seeing the state they'd been reduced to living in, I couldn't help feeling I should have brought more. At the same time, my hope dwindled.

How much help were we going to get out of people who'd fallen so far?

As if to prove me right, one of the other guys muttered a curse and shook his head. "Why are we even staying here? These pricks are going to slaughter us all."

"No," I said. "We're not going to let that happen."

Someone else snorted. "What are you going to do about it?"

Wylder stepped forward, his eyes flashing, but I put

out my arm to hold him back, even though I'd bristled too. Maybe there *was* something more I could offer them. Maybe I needed to show them we didn't have to be this beaten.

"I can understand why you'd ask that," I said, drawing myself up straighter and pitching my voice so my words filled the whole room. "You haven't seen much of me before today. My father didn't let me get very involved in the Claws' business. But I can tell you that I was always watching and listening, paying attention to everything I could. I *wanted* to take control over my destiny. I'm here today as your leader and the true heir of the Claws. I'm here as Mercy Katz."

"Mercy," Jenner said, as if he was going to stop me. He moved to put a hand on my shoulder, but I shook him off.

"My father let you down. I can't put all the blame on him, but he reached out to the Red Shark, he didn't tell Colt what he was doing, and that set this whole catastrophe in motion. He let me down too by never trusting me enough to give me a chance to be a real part of the Claws. But I'm going to change all that now."

"What can you do that he couldn't?" one of the guys muttered.

"Well, for starters I didn't get myself killed," I retorted. "I'm here, standing with you, ready to listen to you. But right now, I want you to listen to me—really listen. The Bend is *our* home. I don't want to see some assholes barge in and ruin everything. I'm stepping up as the head of the Claws, and I intend to put everything back the way it should be, without bringing in outsiders who'll terrorize everyone.

"Xavier and his men thought they could break you, but yet here you stand, a testimony to the strength of the Claws. We can rebuild our home, take back the streets, and kick out the pricks who tried to destroy them. We can avenge all our friends and loved ones who already died in the fighting, every drop of blood that was shed. I'll do it on my own if I have to, but I'd rather have all of you on my side. I think you deserve the chance to show what you're made of too."

There was a momentary silence. My stomach twisted. Then Kervos spoke up in a hesitant but not hostile voice, glancing at Anthea and the guys around me. "Would that mean joining the Nobles?"

Wylder folded his arms over his chest. "Mercy is her own woman. I'm glad to have her as an ally, but I sure as hell don't expect her to bow down to me. We'll work together, but the Claws belong to her. You answer to her, not me."

A few murmurs passed between the assembled men. I held my breath. Would the things I'd said be enough? I didn't know how else to convince them, but I didn't know how much hope we had of winning this war without whatever help they could give us.

Jenner stepped in front of me and dipped his head. When he raised it, his eyes glinted with a wild sort of hope. "I'll recognize you as the new head of the Claws. I'll fight with you—for all our fallen brothers, but also for *you*."

When my lips parted in surprise, he gave me a small

smile. "Your father could be a great leader at times, but he was ruled by his ego. Every time you've reached out to us, you've given us a choice and treated us with respect and humility—even when we'd turned our backs on you. It would be my absolute honor to show the same loyalty in return."

"And mine," Kervos said. "I've seen what you're capable of. So did Roy. We can't let those fuckers get away with this, and you're the woman to take them down. I'll pledge myself to you."

A bittersweet smile stretched across my face. One by one, the other Claws members began to nod. "And me." "And me." The words echoed in the room.

I could feel their spirits lifting as hope lit their faces again. Goosebumps erupted down the back of my neck. Momentary tears pricked at the backs of my eyes. Here they were, battered and driven underground, but they were still willing to rise against their enemy one more time.

I pumped my fist in the air. "For the Claws."

"For the Claws," they echoed back. In that moment, I was one of them more than I'd ever been before.

"For the Claws," Jenner said, clapping me on the shoulder. "Let's take back the Bend."

"Thank you," I said quietly.

"You earned it. Now, what do you think we can do about your man they're holding hostage?"

I inhaled deeply and held up the bag with the stolen phones. "These belong to some of the Storm's men. We think there might be information on one or more of them that'd give us key information into how they work, something we could use to get the upper hand. Is there anyone here who knows how to crack the lock codes on them?"

A young guy near the back of the room held up his hand. "Toss them over here. I should be able to handle that."

I handed the bag to another guy who passed it on. As our volunteer got to work on the first phone, the other men dug into the food we'd brought. It was obvious they were starving.

I stepped back by the door with Anthea, Wylder, Kaige, and Rowan. Looking around the room at the Claws men—*my* men now—sent a weird quiver through my chest that was both anxious and excited.

"We're really doing this," I murmured. "*I'm* really doing this." I was going to lead the Claws. Dad would be rolling in his grave if he knew.

"You looked like a goddess telling them how it was going to be," Kaige said with a grin. "A goddess of blood and vengeance. The Storm's people aren't going to know what hit them."

"You were made for this life," Rowan put in. "I didn't always believe that was a good thing, but now I know you can turn it into something great."

I glanced at Wylder, who was frowning. "You don't look so happy."

He shook himself and tucked a finger through the beltloop of my jeans. "Not because of anything that happened here, Kitty Cat. I could watch you make declarations all day. You really are becoming a queen now."

A warm glow of affection sparked in my chest. I squeezed his hand. "And we'll rule together." I knew why that wasn't enough. The heaviness of our loss was weighing on my spirits too. "It won't feel right without Gideon here. We've got to get him back."

"We will," Wylder said fiercely, and Kaige and Rowan nodded.

Anthea let out a huff of breath. "I'll just be glad when this is all over and I can get back to killing people so discreetly no one can even tell it's murder, like everyone civilized should."

An unexpected laugh burst out of me. Kaige snorted, and Rowan took my other hand. I'd never been so glad to have all of them with me.

Just then, the man at the back stood up with one of the phones in his hand. "I might have found something. Come take a look."

My heart leapt. I tugged Wylder's hand, and he came with me. It was time to get Gideon back.

Mercy

ROWAN, WYLDER, AND I CROUCHED BY A BUILDING A block away from the Storm's headquarters. We watched as another Wylder, flanked by Kaige and several of the Claws members, walked up the street toward the old hotel. The Wylder on the street rolled his shoulders as if working tension out of them.

"That's the tenth time he's done that," the Wylder beside me—the real one—muttered.

"He's probably just nervous," I said.

"Maybe he should be. Does he really look that much like me?"

The three of us considered Sam, the Claws guy who was acting as Wylder, for a moment. A few of the Claws had volunteered to take on the role, but he'd been the one whose build was closest to Wylder's, and his blond hair had taken the auburn dye easily. We'd even gotten Anthea to trim it so it was the same style. He'd put on sunglasses so the differences in his features weren't so obvious.

I doubted many of the Storm's people had noticed much about the real Wylder other than his bright hair and his overall shape anyway. And having Kaige next to him helped sell the illusion. Sam had even spent a couple of hours observing Wylder back by the house, getting him to pace and move his arms so he could get a sense of his usual energy.

"I don't know," I said. "I think he's pretty good."

"That's not how I walk," Wylder insisted.

"Well actually—" Rowan began.

Wylder glared at him. "There's only one of me."

I rolled my eyes. "Of course there is, and thank God for that. It doesn't matter if he's not perfect. They've just got to believe it's you for long enough to stay distracted while we sneak inside."

Go in, take down as many of the Storm's people as we could—ideally including Xavier—and grab Gideon on the way out. Other than the show happening on the street, it was a pretty simple plan. I just hoped it stayed simple.

Fake Wylder, Kaige, and their entourage of Claws men came to a stop across the street from the headquarters. We'd warned them to keep a good distance from the old hotel so that none of the Storm's people would get a good look at Sam. He nodded to Kaige and shouted toward the building in a voice that was a decent imitation of Wylder's usual cocky tone. "Here we are, assholes. Now where's my man?"

"Is that how I sound?" Wylder asked.

"Yep," Rowan and I said at the same time. When Wylder narrowed his eyes at me, I had to smother a snicker.

I craned my neck to see if any of the Storm's men were coming out onto the street. It looked like they'd learned their lesson after our last attack. They stayed behind the walls of the hotel, where they'd hastily fixed the door, but we clearly had their attention. Faces appeared by the windows.

"So you're not a total chickenshit after all," one of the Storm's guys hollered back. "Good for you."

"Hand over our man now, and we'll leave peacefully," Sam demanded. "You're *all* chickenshits if you keep trying to win through pathetic tactics like this."

"Says the man at a disadvantage," called someone from inside the building. "Come inside and get him if you want him that badly."

"Okay, they're focused on them for now," Rowan said. "Let's get moving."

I nodded, and we ducked around the building to the alley that would take us close to the back of the hotel. It was empty except for the thick stink of garbage wafting to my nose.

We zigzagged around the dumpsters and reached the red brick building of the bar next to the old hotel. There, we stayed in the shadows and peered up at the back windows of Storm headquarters until we were sure no one was watching us. Then we made for the back door of the bar.

As I reached for the keypad by the door and tapped in the code we'd managed to find in the files Gideon had sent us, my heart thumped faster. It beeped, and the deadbolt flipped over. Relief rushing through me, I pushed the door open.

Cool but musty air washed over us. We slipped inside, closed the door, and spotted the stairs to the basement just a few steps away.

Wylder walked partway down first, his gun in one hand, his phone offering a little illumination in the other. "Looks clear. No one around this early in the day."

"The bar doesn't open until three," Rowan said.

I smiled. "Perfect for us."

As we descended into the stuffy basement storage room, Wylder wrinkled his nose. "I wonder how many deliveries Xavier's already taken through this route. Did the Steel Knights use this place before? We weren't aware of any activity around here."

"They might have kept it quiet," I said.

We'd only found out about the bar's secret thanks to the text chain the Claws techie had managed to dig up. One of the Storm's guys had told someone passing on goods to them to come through the bar and down here so it wouldn't be obvious where they were going.

"Ah ha." Wylder shoved aside a stack of crates to reveal a narrow door in the wall that faced the hotel. This door was older than the one in the alley, with a keyhole and nowhere to input codes. But that was fine. I'd done a little practicing of my own this morning— with Anthea, to warm up my lock picking skills.

Drawing out the picks, I took a deep breath to steady myself. Then I knelt down and fit them into the keyhole. Anthea's advice rolled through my mind as I adjusted them. *Take it slow and easy. Feel your way to the right spot...*

With a click, the lock disengaged. Grinning triumphantly, I straightened up and twisted the knob.

The passage on the other side was just as narrow, with crumbling brick walls that'd obviously seen better days. We slunk along it to the door at the other end, which should lead into the hotel's basement.

We stood still for a minute, listening, but no sound came from the other side. We'd figured it was unlikely they'd have guards down here when they didn't expect anyone to know about the secret entrance. I did my trick with the lock picks again, and in the space of several heartbeats, I had that door open too.

We closed it behind us as we came out into a larger storage room. A distinct chemical smell hung in the air. Wylder narrowed his eyes at the plastic boxes stacked along the far wall. "Glory?"

"No doubt." I had the urge to toss over one of the explosives from the bag slung across my back, but blowing up their stash here would only ruin our real plan. We didn't want the Storm's people to have any clue we were coming until we were destroying them.

They'd all be focused on the fake Wylder and the other men outside for now. Using the element of surprise should be easy.

It was getting out again that'd be the hard part.

Wylder tucked his gun into the holster under his arm and took out his knife. Rowan and I brandished our own blades. We crept down the hall that led into the storage room and found a set of stairs that would take us up to the first floor. A couple of voices carried down to us.

Rowan tapped his finger to his lips. We eased up the steps, feeling them out carefully to avoid any creaks. A couple of men came into view in what appeared to be a large kitchen, leaning against one of the counters with guns at their hips, just chatting.

Wylder pulled into the lead. He braced himself stock still on a step a few down from the top, where the shadows still hid him. Then he launched himself into the room so fast I lost my breath.

"What the—" one of the guys exclaimed. That was all he got out before Wylder had plunged the knife into his neck. As the first guy slumped with a deathly gurgle, the Noble heir was already lunging at the second guy.

The Storm's man had reached for his gun, but Wylder caught him with a knee to the gut and slashed his throat when he doubled over. That body thumped to the ground too. We froze, glancing around the room and through the doorway.

No one came running. More voices were carrying from the front of the building, along with mocking laughter and occasional gunfire. We'd told our guys to take a few shots here and there to keep the Storm's people occupied until we were in place. From the sounds of things, they were doing their job well.

A door at the other end of the kitchen showed the gleam of sunlight through its window. I added that exit to my mental map of the place.

We'd just started down the hall toward the front of

the hotel when a guy stepped out of a room closer by. Rowan acted immediately, springing at him and twisting his neck with a grunt and a snap of bones. The guy crumpled to the floor, his body slack. Rowan stared down at him, panting.

"I wasn't sure that would even work," he admitted in a whisper.

"Good thing it did." Wylder drew his gun again and nodded toward the rooms up front. "Sounds like most of them are gathered up there. We aren't going to get much farther without someone raising the alarm. Let's take out as many as we can before they realize we're here."

That was the strategy we'd discussed before. I readied my own gun, and we eased down the hall until it opened up into a larger foyer.

A broad staircase led up to the second floor. Straight ahead was the front door, where a few Storm men were staked out, peering through the panes of the small window. I could see several other men in each of the front rooms on either side of it, watching the street, a couple of them taking shots at the fake Wylder outside.

Wylder smiled thinly. Without a word, he caught my eyes and pointed to the door. Then he looked at Rowan and motioned to the room on the left. So he was going to take the right. I tensed, waiting for his signal to move.

He swung his hand and leapt toward the room he'd picked in the same instant. Rowan dashed to the left, and I stepped forward, raising my gun.

This was for Roy, and my family, and every other

person who'd died because of the Storm's arrival in the Bend.

We all opened fire at the same time. I squeezed the trigger again and again, braced against the recoil. The thunder of the shots made my ears ache, but I didn't give a shit.

One bullet and another hit the three men by the door. Before they'd managed to turn all the way around, I'd delivered at least one fatal shot to each of them. They toppled together in a heap in the front hall.

I grabbed another clip from my pocket and reloaded quickly. Wylder and Rowan were still shooting. I darted to Rowan's side in time to see him taking down the last of the guys in his room, planting a bullet in the man's skull just before the other guy could raise his own gun. The bodies lay in a row along the windows.

As Wylder fired his last shot, another sound reached my ringing ears. Footsteps thundered across the floor above us. Some of the Storm's people had been watching from upstairs, of course. We just hadn't known how many.

We ran back toward the staircase. Wylder and Rowan took shelter at the edges of the doorways, shooting at the figures charging down the stairs. Wylder aimed a worried but determined look at me and jerked his chin toward the kitchen.

We'd known Gideon would probably be farther up, and also that we couldn't take out more than one floor of Storm men before they caught on. Wylder and Rowan were going to hold off the pricks as well as they could on the bottleneck of the stairs while I made my way to Gideon around back.

I sprinted down the hall the way we'd come, fumbled with the lock on the back door, and shoved it open. My pulse pounded with the seconds ticking away. The faster I could get up there, the better.

I spotted a small dumpster heaped with garbage bags outside the shoe outlet store on the other side of the hotel, ran over, and shoved it toward the hotel with all my might. It scraped against the ground, but it moved. As soon as it was close enough, I flipped up onto it. It got me just high enough to jump up and hook my fingers around the ledge of a closed second-floor window.

The cracked stone bit into my fingertips. I scrambled upward and swung my body around, smashing the glass with my heels and diving through the frame in the same motion.

The shouts and the blaring of gunfire covered the sound of my entrance. I landed in a small room with a couple of twin beds, the covers rumpled. Empty beer bottles, cigarette butts, and fast food wrappers were strewn across the floor. The Storm's people didn't exactly live in style.

I stopped only long enough to smack my foot along the window frame, clearing the remaining shards of glass, since it might be my escape route too. Then I stalked to the doorway and peeked out into the hall.

I couldn't see the staircase from here. The shots echoed from around a bend in the hall. But as I stepped out, a couple of guys burst from a nearby room. They spotted me as my gun arm swung up.

My first shot hit one in the head, but the second went wide. The other man lunged at me, snatching at his own weapon. With a lurch of my heart, I whipped out my knife and heaved myself forward to meet him. The blade sank into his chest just before he could pull the trigger.

Wylder and Rowan weren't going to be able to hold off the men on the stairs forever. I hurried along the hall, trying each door I passed. The first three opened no problem to rooms a lot like the one I'd smashed my way into, all of them empty. The fourth doorknob jarred in my grasp—and then flew open to reveal a man with his lips pulled back in a snarl.

I wasn't sure what he'd been expecting, but he startled at the sight of me—just long enough for me to pump three bullets into his chest. He teetered and collapsed on the floor. I glanced past him to confirm Gideon wasn't in the room behind him and moved on.

Where the hell was our tech genius? They hadn't moved him to a whole different building, had they? Fear started to wrap a chill around my gut—and then I heard it.

Someone was singing an off-key version of "Hotel California" in a thin, raspy voice that sounded an awful lot like the guy I was looking for. Despite the odds we were up against and the blood already spilled, my lips twitched with a smile.

I raced down the hall, following the singing, which grew louder with every frantic step. There. I stopped at the door it was filtering through and fumbled for the lock picks. As soon as the pins clicked over inside, I heaved the door open.

Gideon lurched to his feet. His hands were tied behind his back, his cheek purpling with a bruise, but he was there in front of me and essentially all right. "Mercy?" he croaked.

I was so relieved I could have cried, but there really wasn't time. From the volume of the voices and thumping footsteps outside, some of the men from the stairwell were heading this way. I didn't even have time to untie him.

"Come on," I said, grabbing Gideon's elbow. "Nice singing, by the way."

As we hustled out into the hall, he sputtered a laugh. Even though I hadn't gotten him to safety yet, his face had lit up just like I was beaming inside with the joy of having found him. "I could tell something was going down," he said. "Figured it'd help you guys find me if you were looking, and at least annoy these jackasses if not."

A roar of pure rage split the air and shattered my good mood. I knew in an instant it was Xavier—and he was coming for us.

I kept looking over my shoulder as we dashed for the room I'd entered through. A couple of men charged around the corner of the hall, and I shot at them. I couldn't tell if I'd hit either, but they pulled back for shelter. The shots they fired thudded into the walls just inches from us.

I shoved Gideon into the bedroom ahead of me and

yanked the door shut just as several more shots rang out behind us. Bullets smacked into the wood, one of them piercing nearly all the way through. Shit.

When we made it to the window, Gideon froze up. "It's fine," I said urgently. "Just aim for the dumpster—it's full of shoe boxes. You'll survive. I'll be right behind you."

Gideon braced himself and jumped. He hit the garbage bags below with a *whoomph*. I was just about to climb after him when Xavier's voice broke through the shouts swelling in the hall outside.

"I'm going to skin that fucking cat!"

Oh, he thought so, did he? My pulse hammered through my veins, and I lifted my gun, sitting on the ledge and digging into my bag at the same time. If I could get in a good shot right before I jumped, if I could take out the menace who'd been terrorizing me before I'd even known he existed...

"Mercy," Gideon called from below, sounding worried. I swallowed hard. I'd give it one shot—

But I didn't get the chance. The door blew off its hinges, a swarm of men outside—but none of those at the front of the pack was Xavier. I caught a glimpse of his dark hair farther back, but I knew even as my finger itched on the trigger that I'd never hit him with so many people in the way.

I'd made it this far. I might have been willing to die to take that monster down with me, but Gideon wouldn't be safe until I got him farther away.

My teeth clenching with regret, I hurled the grenade I'd taken out of my bag instead.

When it exploded in the doorway, I was already jackknifing through the window frame. I landed on my feet next to Gideon, sinking into the bags with a groan of tearing cardboard. The bang of the explosion sent a puff of smoke into the air above us.

It wouldn't hold off whoever had survived for long. I helped Gideon clamber out of the dumpster, and we ran down the alley. I sent the quick text I'd had at the ready to Wylder—the special alert sound he'd programmed would tell him I'd gotten Gideon out.

We veered down a smaller driveway and hustled along a side-street, slowing when Gideon's breath turned ragged. Just as we turned the corner to double back toward the van, it roared around the corner to meet us, Rowan at the wheel.

As it screeched to a halt, the back doors flew open. Wylder and Kaige waved to us from inside. They grabbed us to help us in, and we sped away from the headquarters as fast as those tires could take us.

Mercy

I SLUMPED AGAINST THE BENCH, MY ENTIRE BODY
aching from the workout I'd just put it through. My
lungs were burning, so I could only imagine how
Gideon felt. He sagged next to me, his breaths labored
but starting to even out.

The van's tires screeched as Rowan took a sharp
turn, following the zigzag route we'd decided on to
make it harder for any Storm people to give chase. As
we swayed with its movements, Wylder crouched next
to Gideon and cut through the ropes binding his wrists.

"You're okay?" he asked, his voice gruff with obvious
concern.

"Fine," Gideon said, though he couldn't stop himself
from rasping a little more than usual. He took another
gulp of air and managed a shaky smile. "Those fuckers
had no idea who they were dealing with, did they?"

Kaige cracked his knuckles. "Hell, yeah. We painted that hotel red."

I pushed myself up straighter, my pulse still thrumming away with adrenaline. "What about the Claws guys? Did they all make it out?"

Kaige nodded. "As soon as Wylder and Rowan burst out, we knew to take off. Their cars were even closer than the van, so they must have made it to them no problem. The whole time we were there, the pricks shooting from the windows didn't manage to do more than clip one guy in the arm. He'll survive."

I should have felt relieved hearing that, but I was still keyed up. My body seemed to think the battle wasn't over yet.

I turned to Gideon, checking him over to make sure he hadn't taken any injuries worse than the bruise on his cheek. He had a little cut at the corner of his jaw too, and the ropes had rubbed the skin on his wrists raw. I frowned, inspecting them, and grabbed the first aid kit stashed under the bench.

"They're no big deal," Gideon insisted as I dabbed at the marks with an antiseptic wipe.

I elbowed him lightly. "It can't hurt to be careful, tough guy."

Gideon turned to Wylder. "I'm sorry. It was my fucking plan, and I—"

Wylder held up his hand before his best friend could go on, his gaze firm. "It was a great plan, and we got a ton of information out of it. Hopefully information we can use for more than just staging your rescue. You made it out, and you gave us an excuse to take down a whole lot more Storm men in the process. I'll call that a win."

The growl of the motor sputtered out. Rowan had parked outside the desolate strip mall where we'd decided we'd regroup, far from any of the Storm's holdings and anywhere they'd think Claws or Nobles might go. He squeezed between the seats to join us. "We accomplished a lot today. We took out a big chunk of the Storm's manpower in the Bend and showed we're a force to be reckoned with."

Gideon chuckled. "Whatever the hell you did to pull that off, it was pretty fucking spectacular." He aimed a shy grin at me. "Especially your part."

What felt most spectacular to me was having him here with us again, all in one piece, okay enough to even joke about what he'd been through. I squeezed his arm, a swell of urgent emotion rising up over me. "I'm just glad you're safe."

I didn't just want to tell him, though. The frenetic beat of my pulse urged me to *show* him just how happy I was to have him back. I cupped Gideon's face in my hands and kissed him.

I'd meant it to be a short peck, but as soon as our lips touched, something in me unraveled. Gideon tilted his head to deepen the kiss, his hand rising to grip my shirt with a similar urgency. Our tongues tangled, our breaths rushing together, and just like that we were outright devouring each other as if we'd starve if we couldn't absorb every possible bit of passion from the melding of our lips.

Gideon ran his fingers into my hair with enough

force to loosen my ponytail. He pulled me even closer, tugging me to straddle him. I kissed him harder, knowing the other guys were watching us and finding that not a single part of me cared.

Gideon eased back just enough to press a trail of kisses down my neck, tilting my head to the side for better access. He didn't seem to mind the audience either, at least not in this moment after the rush of our escape. He lowered his head to suck on the sensitive spot at the crook of my shoulder.

As I moaned, my eyes opened a fraction. Wylder, Kaige, and Rowan were standing over us, their eyes locked on us. A thrill shot up my spine. They were mine —all of them. And I was their woman.

I didn't just want them watching—I wanted every one of their hands touching my body.

I gazed up at them with a lick of my lips in invitation, my eyelids fluttering when Gideon bit my skin lightly. A whimper slipped out of me.

Kaige broke from the ring around us first. He sank down beside us, caressing my leg from my knee up to my thigh. Gideon froze for just an instant before shifting slightly to the side to give Kaige better access to my body. A giddy warmth flowed through my body, not just desire but the delight at seeing them accept each other.

As Gideon nibbled his way along my shoulder, Kaige teased his fingers into my hair at the back of my scalp. He leaned in to kiss me on the lips. One of my hands ran down Gideon's lean chest while the other slipped around the back of Kaige's neck.

Gideon nipped the lobe of my ear, and I moaned against Kaige's mouth. He pressed the advantage, dipping his hot tongue inside my mouth. Our tongues caught together in a frenzied dance, with each trying to gain control over the other. The stroking sensation made my pussy walls squeeze with a gush of arousal soaking my panties.

As Kaige's kisses became even more eager, another set of hands skimmed over the side of my hips. They were confident, knowing just where to touch me. I peeked from the corner of my eyes and saw Rowan kneeling at my other side. His eyes reflected the same awe as I felt. A breathless giggle escaped me, the sound vibrating against Kaige's mouth.

Rowan's hands climbed up to my breasts and fondled them, tracing my curves, teasing my nipples. Bliss rushed through me from every direction. When Kaige dropped his head to test my other earlobe between his teeth, Rowan claimed my mouth. Gideon gave my hair a little tug and kissed his way down to the neckline of my shirt. The three of them seemed to find a rhythm as they played with my body.

I tugged the hem of Kaige's shirt and pulled it off him, then ran my hands down the massive tattooed landscape of his torso. His muscles flexed as I circled a finger around his nipple. Gideon unbuttoned his own shirt, keeping his eyes on me. I kissed Rowan on the lips more urgently while my fingers skimmed to the crotch of his pants. He was hard, his cock straining against his fly. Kaige and Gideon sported similar bulges.

I stroked all three of them, moving from one to the

next while their hands ran all over my body. My skin felt as if it'd caught fire. Rowan pulled back so Gideon could yank my shirt off of me, and then Kaige ripped my bra open to lick down my spine.

I arched my back at the slick of his demanding tongue, gripping both Rowan's and Gideon's shoulder. Our combined groans reverberated through the van.

"Enough," Wylder said roughly, snapping me out of my trance. The guys glanced around to look at their leader where he was standing stiffly by the van's back door, but none of them moved away from me. I was surrounded entirely by their delicious heat and weight. Wylder had better not fucking ruin this moment.

The Noble heir stepped forward, forcing Rowan to move behind me to make room. When I saw the look in Wylder's bright green eyes, I bit my lip.

All at once, he caught me around my waist and lifted me right off Gideon. I squeaked as he whipped me around and slammed me against the wall over the bench, our heads just below the roof. Before I could recover, his lips were on mine.

The hard press of metal at my naked back made the experience even more raw. The heat of his kiss shot right to my core, which gushed as soon as his tongue came out to play against mine.

Wylder ground his cock into my stomach, and I growled against his lips. The wall of the van shook behind us at the force of our kiss. It was savage and take-no-prisoner, the force of it sweeping me away in the storm of Wylder's passion. I kissed him back hard, tilting my head so I could have deeper access to his sinful mouth.

Then he pulled me away from the wall and laid me down in the middle of the dense carpet. His gaze roved over my body, lingering on the swell of my naked breasts. I jutted my chest forward and looked at him with a challenge in my eyes.

A wicked smile curled his mouth. As he reached to flick open the button on my jeans, he glanced around at the other guys, who'd drawn back to give us space and see what would happen next.

"I think the new queen deserves a full celebration," he said in a low voice full of promise.

Answering smiles sprang onto the other men's faces —and my own. A quiver of anticipation ran straight to my cunt. Then my lovers closed in on me, discarding their shoes and kicking off their jeans as Wylder stripped me of mine. The avid lust in all their eyes made me dizzy. It was all for me.

They sat on their haunches around me. Four pairs of practiced hands roamed over my skin, touching me everywhere and sending tingles down my body. From that moment onward, we were all in this together. We were making something bigger than any passion we could have shared with only two or three of us.

We'd won against the Storm today, and we won a victory for our hearts right now.

Rowan kissed me again, his deft tongue tracing the seam of my lips. A mouth latched on to my left tit and sucked hard. A few moments later, another devoured my right nipple.

I closed my eyes against the onslaught of sensation. Fingers skimmed impatiently over my inner thighs before hooking around my panties and pulling them down to my knees, ripping the lace in the process.

My eyelids fluttered open at half-mast to see Gideon as he knelt between my thighs. He inhaled my cunt deeply before he lapped the center, his eyes staying fixed on me. As his tongue nudged inside my hot, wet slit, my eyes rolled back. Molten pleasure washed up from my core.

Rowan traced his fingers along my chin to tip my head so he could kiss me again. Kaige circled the mound of my breast with his tongue, while Wylder worked the hard nub of my nipple between his teeth. The pain and the pleasure made a heady mix.

Gideon continued to lap at my cunt greedily, as if he couldn't get enough of me. I writhed against the floor, the friction of the carpet tingling through my nerve endings.

Rowan pulled back just a few inches, his hand dropping to rub his erection through his boxers. "Condoms," he said, his voice coming out a little strangled. "I hate to break up the party, but before this goes any further—"

Gideon looked up from between my thighs, his lips shiny with my pussy juices. "The container next to the first aid kit."

Rowan gave him a quizzical look and reached under the bench. I tried not to whimper at the abrupt stillness around me. The other guys watched as Rowan retrieved a plastic container.

"I wondered what that was," Kaige said.

Gideon offered a satisfied smile. "Everything we might need is in there."

Wylder raised his eyebrows. "Even lube?" His gaze dropped back to me, nearly scorching.

"I said everything, didn't I?"

Kaige let out a guffaw. "Gideon had a sex kit in his van the whole time. Who would have thought?"

Gideon shot him a narrow look, but he was still smiling. "You know I like to be prepared for every possible contingency."

"And thank God for that," Wylder muttered, but his eyes hadn't left me.

The heat in the van seemed to have increased by about ten degrees. Rowan pulled out a condom, and the other guys moved as if agreeing that because he'd been the one to suggest this step, he should make use of them first. I couldn't say I had a problem with that.

As he rolled it over his jutting shaft, he nudged my legs apart and knelt between them. I slid my fingers into his ash-blond hair and pulled him to me. Our mouths collided, and in the same moment he pushed himself into my slick pussy.

He fucked me thoroughly, his strokes slow and deep at first before he switched to shallow but faster thrusts. Our bodies clung together, my legs circling his hips as he drove me towards my peak. Gideon's skillful tongue had already brought me to the verge. I clutched Rowan's shoulders as he bucked into me hard and fast. There was nothing sweet or gentle about this encounter.

The other three joined in every way they could, their

fingers trailing over the sensitive spots in my body. Rowan grunted, his strokes more and more erratic. I squeezed my legs around him, pushing him deep inside me just as he came with a loud groan. A wave of an orgasm tore through me. My pussy walls convulsed around his cock.

"Oh, fuck," Rowan murmured as he almost collapsed on top of me, his dick still throbbing inside of me, sending delicious aftershocks through my core. He panted as he rolled to the side.

Before I could catch my breath, Gideon was on top of me, kissing me. The nerves in my body came back to life in an instant. He pulled me up to a sitting position, my legs around his hips as I straddled his lap like I had before, but with no clothes separating us now. He rolled my nipples between his fingers as he kissed me and then rubbed the curved length of his dick along my slit where his tongue had traveled before. I wrapped my arms around his neck to hold him tighter.

Our eyes met, reflecting lust at each other, just before I lifted myself on my knees and impaled myself on his cock. My pussy was already sensitive from the first orgasm, and something about the angle of my current position hit a spot so deep and sweet inside of me I practically came again right then and there.

Gideon's breath stuttered out of him. Before I could worry that it was too much for his lungs, he gripped my waist and guided me up before slamming me down on his dick again.

Both of us let out a loud sigh, my mouth hovering over his.

I gripped his shoulder blades hard before we repeated the motion. My tits bounced as I began to ride his dick earnestly, my body catching onto a rhythm. Gideon's eyes were half-closed as he watched me. I circled my hips around his, and his hands slipped to my ass where he squeezed.

We kissed each other sloppily as I continued rocking over his dick, our moans mingling. Then impatient hands cupped my breasts from behind. I glanced back to see Wylder crouching behind me. The head of his cock slicked precum down my spine to the curve of my ass.

"How'd you like to have even more fun, Kitten?" he said in a voice so heated I nearly spontaneously combusted. One of his hands trailed down my side to my ass cheeks and dipped between them to circle the pucker of my other hole. He held my gaze with a question in his eyes.

His touch sent lustful shivers through me. I'd only tried anal once before and hadn't enjoyed it all that much, but this was Wylder, looking at me like I really was a queen. He wouldn't offer if he didn't know he could make it good for me.

I dipped my head in the slightest nod. A grin stretched across Wylder's face. He flicked open the lube and spread some over his fingers.

I continued to ride Gideon at a slightly more subdued pace as Wylder massaged my other opening. Gideon's eyes shone brightly as if he was nearly as excited to see us pull this off as I was. Finally, Wylder worked in a finger and then two, massaging me and stretching me to prepare me for his cock.

A low keening spilled from my lips. "Fuck, that feels good."

"Nothing but the best for Queen Katz," Wylder murmured.

I was momentarily distracted by Kaige lurching to his feet in front of me. He gazed down at us, stroking his cock at the sight. Taking in its huge, rigid girth, my mouth watered.

I reached out and curled one of my fingers around the head. Kaige hissed. I took that as encouragement to draw him toward my mouth. Why stop with two delicious cocks when I could have three at the same time?

I was Mercy Katz, and I took what I wanted.

Wylder eased out his fingers. He shifted me at an angle that let Gideon's dick hit a spot inside me that made me gasp. The tip of Wylder's cock nudged my asshole. I almost stopped breathing in anticipation as my lips wrapped around Kaige.

Wylder took it slowly. He pushed inside my ass bit by bit, letting the rocking of Gideon's thrusts draw him deeper. My eyes flew opened at the overwhelming sensation of fullness. He'd primed me well. There was a hint of pain and tightness, and then my body relaxed around him with a wave of sharper pleasure.

Wylder started to buck alongside me and Gideon, driving deeper every time I dropped to meet their cocks. For several seconds, I just floated on the incredible feelings rushing through me. But I couldn't forget Kaige.

I took him into my mouth again and sucked hard. Kaige's fingers dug into my hair. A moan reverberated through my whole body as I bobbed my head up and down on his cock while riding his two closest friends at the same time.

Gideon reached down and swiveled his thumb over my clit. Wylder put his hands on my hips and fucked my ass harder, while Kaige swayed his hips to fuck my mouth. I grazed his sensitive skin with my teeth until he swore helplessly. Then Rowan was there with us too, finding the space to fondle my breast, propelling me toward the most epic release of my life with the rest of my lovers.

Gideon flicked my clit at the same time that Wylder drove into me and Rowan squeezed my nipple. Another orgasm tore through me, shattering my vision and throbbing through my body. My pussy walls clenched to milk Gideon's dick.

"Mercy, ah," Gideon groaned as he lost himself in me, pushing me towards the peak again. Everything around me turned white with a blaze of ecstasy.

Wylder came with an animalistic groan while Kaige emptied himself half in my mouth and half on my breasts. They caught me as I sagged between them.

We settled onto the floor of the van together, tangled in the spent bodies of the four men who'd come to mean more to me than I'd ever expected. Their combined heat and weight lulled me. I stroked Gideon's hair softly and clasped my finger around Rowan's. My toe teased along Kaige's calf, and my heel nestled against Wylder's thigh. We all panted in unison as we caught our breaths.

"How was that for a victory party?" Wylder asked, pressing one last kiss to my hip bone.

A giddy laugh tumbled out of me. "That was the best fuck of my entire fucking life."

The others chuckled in agreement and nestled even closer to me. What I'd said was entirely true. Tucked there between them, I couldn't imagine ever letting them—or this—go.

If only there weren't still so many jackasses out there determined to rip us apart.

29

Wylder

As the van climbed up the hill to the Noble mansion, I glanced at Mercy. She had a speck of mud on her cheek that I instinctively reached out to flick off. Mercy looked at me, a wicked smile crossing her lips, and for a moment I almost forgot about where we were and the fact that we were about to confront my Dad.

Almost, but not quite.

Just hours ago, I'd had my cock balls-deep in her tight asshole as she writhed between me and the only guys I trusted in this world. It'd been some kind of heaven watching her come apart for us. But I didn't deserve any kind of heaven if I couldn't also make sure she was safe from my own family.

Rowan parked in front of the mansion. Immediately, the atmosphere in the van turned somber. Tight lipped, Mercy got up and shoved her gun in the back of her jeans. She touched her pocket where I knew she kept the little bracelet she always carried on her.

The rest of us kept our weapons in our hands. We weren't going to go in instigating a fight, but we'd be ready to defend her the second we needed to.

Anthea's favorite Mercedes was parked in the circular drive already. She got out when we did, moving to join us. I'd texted her letting her know we'd be coming, and she'd wanted to show her support.

We fell into a ring around Mercy, me in the front, Rowan and Gideon on either side, and Kaige behind her. Anthea stayed beside me. We marched through the crisp evening air up the stairs and into the stark light of the mansion's foyer.

Axel was already standing there, a cigarette dangling from his mouth. This time it was lit. A few other guys were hanging back closer to the wall.

"So the kid's come back," he said around the cig. "Your dad'll want to see you in his office." Then his gaze caught on Mercy, and his eyes narrowed. "What the fuck is *she* doing here?"

"She's with me," I said, firm but even. "And how many times have I talked to you about smoking in the house?"

Axel snorted. "What are you going to do about it?"

I walked up to him, snatched the cigarette from his lips, and crushed it under my heel. As I stepped back to rejoin the others, Axel scowled at me. "He's not going to want her getting any farther into the house."

"Then I guess we'll just have to talk here," I said.

"It's up to him. Are you going to tell him I'm back, or should we all go see what he has to say for himself?"

Before Axel could answer, Dad appeared at the top of the staircase. "I'm more interested in hearing what you have to say for *yourself*," he said in a cold voice that carried through the high-ceilinged room.

Apprehension prickled over me, but I held my ground. Dad strolled down the stairs as if there was nothing all that urgent about this confrontation, but I saw him take note of Mercy and watched his gaze harden even more.

It really was up to him whether we hashed this out here or in the greater privacy of his office, but I wasn't walking away from her, that was for sure.

"I had business to take care of," I said. "Protecting our interests. And that included making sure we have Mercy Katz on our side, no matter what you say about it."

Dad came to a stop at the bottom of the stairs. He made no move to usher us elsewhere. His hands were empty, but I knew he'd have at least one gun on him somewhere. I wasn't going to give him a single clear shot at Mercy.

"*I* decide what protects the Nobles' interests," he said in an icy tone. "You don't have that authority yet, as you've apparently forgotten. Or have you simply chosen this whore over your other loyalties? She opened her legs to you, and you forgot about family, just like that?"

Mercy shifted her weight behind me but stayed silent. I'd asked her to let me handle my dad, but I had to imagine that promise was burning her up inside now.

I raised my chin. "I haven't forgotten my place. I'm here, aren't I? We've been in the Bend fighting against the Storm's forces, and Mercy's been with us every step of the way."

Ezra snorted. "How honorable of her, considering the fact that she's the one who brought that psychotic man of his to our door in the first place."

"Her leaving hasn't stopped the Storm's people from targeting us," I pointed out. "We've been able to weaken their resources and steal valuable intel on their operations with her help. Help we're lucky she's willing to give, considering that you've been trying to get her killed one way or another for weeks now. She's shown more loyalty to the Nobles than practically anyone around here even with you treating her like crap."

"I don't owe anything to a stray who came begging for charity," Dad said even more coldly than before. "Besides, you haven't made all that much progress, have you? Xavier isn't dead, is he? And we're no closer to finding out the reason he and his people are here."

"Maybe not," I said. "But we've weakened them and we showed them we aren't going to go down easy. We're already putting together a plan to get them out of here for good."

"None of that matters. I gave you an order, Wylder. You went against my wishes and continued to align yourself with her. You have one last opportunity to rectify that now."

"No," I snapped. "*You* have the chance to get your head out of your ass and start treating her like the valuable ally she is."

"Or what?" Dad demanded. "You'll run off again like the spoiled brat you apparently are? I raised you better than this."

"Maybe Wylder should run," Axel sneered, and glared at me. "All your running around playing hero ended up with five of our men getting arrested and a major deal going sour. How're you going to make up for losing *that* ally?"

I blinked at him in honest disbelief. "Are you fucking kidding me? *You* were in charge of that deal at the airstrip, and it was one of your men who sold us out. Which we wouldn't even know to make sure the rat doesn't come back into the fold if Mercy hadn't noticed how suspicious he was acting."

"You have no proof it was—"

"Actually, we do," Gideon piped up. "And not just circumstantial anymore. There were records of him on the Storm's payroll in the data I was able to grab from their headquarters."

Axel spluttered for a second before recovering himself. "And he'll be taken care of, because I know how to do my job, unlike you." He cut his gaze toward Mercy.

"You don't get to tell me what my job is," I shot back, and turned to Dad again. "You might not want to see it, but we've accomplished a lot, and Mercy's been a part of it the entire way. We've gotten the cops off our back with their drug trafficking suspicions, we've gotten several of the Storm's men arrested and killed dozens, and now we've compromised their headquarters. Trust me, this once. It won't take much more to—"

Axel broke in with a rough guffaw. "Did you snort some Glory on the way here? You don't get to make those kinds of decisions. You've gone fucking rogue, and you come in here accusing *me* of shit?"

"Oh, shut the fuck up," I told him. "This is between me and Dad. You've never cared about the Nobles beyond pumping up your own ego."

The vein in Axel's temple bulged. "You're just a stupid kid," he spat out. "Waltzing in here like you can magically solve all the problems I've had to clean up after your crazy plans—"

"The only one who's made any mess around here is you with *your* stupidity."

"Maybe I haven't made enough of a mess, then," Axel growled with a flare of his nostrils. He whipped his gun from the waist of his jeans, clicking off the safety as he raised it.

My body reacted automatically. I couldn't tell whether he was aiming it at me or Mercy, but my response would have been the same either way. With a hitch of my pulse, I jerked up my own gun and pulled the trigger.

The bullet hit Axel right in the middle of the forehead. Blood sputtered from the wound, flecks of it landing on my shirt. My father's right-hand man collapsed to the floor in a heap, his glassy eyes wide open, his face caught in shock. Blood pooled beneath his head and seeped across the pristine marble floor. I lowered my hand with a weird rush of adrenaline and relief, but not a hint of regret.

"What the hell do you think you're doing?" Dad

said, raising his voice just a tad for the first time. His face was a mask of tension.

I met his gaze steadily. "What I had to do. Isn't this who you wanted me to be, Dad? A leader who's focused and ruthless? You wouldn't accept any member of the Nobles making accusations and trying to undermine you—and Axel's been doing that to me for *years*. This is my home too, and anyone working for the Nobles needs to be loyal to both of us. Or do you only have a problem with me getting fucked when it's not by one of your men?"

Dad stared at me as if he'd never seen me before. His jaw worked, but he couldn't seem to find his words. That was fine. Let it sink in.

I wasn't totally sure what I'd do if he told me to get the fuck out, but I was done cowering. I was done blaming myself for the shit *he'd* thrown at me. It was time to write my own story.

Before Dad could get around to speaking, someone pounded on the door. One of the lackeys poised around the room ran to answer it.

"Delivery for Ezra Noble," a man's voice said. "Do you need any help bringing it in?"

"We'll manage," the guy said brusquely, but he motioned over another lackey. We stepped back as they dragged a large crate, waist high and equally long and wide, into the foyer.

What the hell was that? The last time we'd gotten a surprise on our doorstep, it'd ended with a man's guts exploding all over our front lawn. A sense of foreboding washed over me.

Dad obviously hadn't been expecting this package either. Snapping out of his shock, he marched over. "What the hell is this?"

"I don't know," the first lackey said. "The delivery guy didn't say."

We kept a few steps back as they looked it over. There was no identifying information on the outside of the wooden slats, and when they tugged on the lid, it didn't budge.

"You'll need a crowbar," Kaige said.

One of the guys glanced at Dad, who nodded, his expression grim. The lackey dashed out of the house to the garage and returned quickly with a curved length of wrought-iron.

He looked at the crate with a nervous expression and then at me and Dad. "Maybe you should keep your distance."

Right. Who knew what opening the lid might trigger? We moved to the sides of the staircase for shelter, the other lackeys pulling back too. The guy with the crowbar winced when he must have realized he'd volunteered for the dangerous job, but then he wedged the flat end under the lid and started heaving at it.

After a couple good tries, a few nails popped out. He moved to the next corner. When he heaved up the third, the whole lid flipped off and crashed to the floor.

No explosions. No monsters springing out.

"What's inside?" Dad asked, reemerging.

"I don't know," the lackey said. "All I can see on top is packing peanuts."

As Dad walked right up to the crate, the rest of us

followed. He brushed aside the foam peanuts with a few brisk sweeps of his hand and then jerked it back as if he'd been bitten. All the color drained from his face.

"What?" I sprang the rest of the way forward.

My gaze caught on the bloody stump of an arm first. *He's sent us another dismembered corpse*, I thought distantly, remembering the rotting limbs Xavier had tossed through one of the mansion windows not that long ago. But this one was fresh, the only odor a sickening meaty one with no hint of rot yet, and—

My eyes slid over the arm and a protruding foot and landed on the face still half-buried in packing peanuts. My stomach lurched, and my legs wobbled under me.

It was Roland.

My older brother. How the hell— Why would Xavier— None of this made any sense.

I squeezed my eyes shut, but the image of my brother's decapitated head swam behind my eyelids. Nausea crawled up from my stomach, and a different burn caught in the back of my throat.

I'd always thought— I'd never gotten the chance— How could he be *dead*? I wanted to scream bloody murder, to punch someone, and part of me also wanted to cry.

But I couldn't. Not in front of Dad and all the men watching this spectacle. Not in front of *my* men. Even Dad was standing rigid, his hand over his mouth but no sound coming out, holding all his emotions in.

Cold and ruthless. It wasn't the kind of leader I wanted to be all of the time, but right now, it was who I had to be. The fucker who'd done this was going to pay in blood.

Anthea's face had paled, her mouth pressed tight, but she plucked a note out of the corner of the crate. *I hope you like my gift, Ezra*, it said in a hasty scrawl, followed by a signature that was simply *X*. As if we'd have any doubt about who this had come from.

"This is what we're up against," I said, pointing at the crate, relieved that my voice only shook a little bit. "This is what that psycho's capable of, and we need every asset we can get to take him down. I'm the only heir you've got now. From here forward, you'll respect that and me. We have to stand up against this asshole together and with everyone who's willing to stand with us, which includes Mercy and the Claws who'll follow her, or we're going to destroy ourselves before the Storm's people even have the chance."

Dad was silent for another long moment, though he lowered his hand from his face. My stomach kept churning. He looked as if he'd aged ten years in that instant. His face was blank, as if he was in a place far away, his grief locked inside of him.

All this time, he'd still been hoping Roland would walk back through that door properly and reclaim the throne that'd originally been meant for him. I'd always suspected it, but I could see it written all over Dad's face now.

He drew himself up to his full height and met my eyes. "Yes. This menace needs to be wiped right off our streets, right out of the county. Whatever it takes."

I nodded back at him, but my spirits didn't feel any

lighter. Dad didn't like being backed into a corner. I'd have to keep watching my back and Mercy's. The second the Storm's people were out of the picture, I had no idea how pissed off he'd be with me, but I didn't for one second believe he'd just forgive my defiance.

30

Mercy

I FLICKED ON THE BASEMENT LIGHT BUT THEN stopped there at the top of the stairs, my legs refusing to move.

"You okay?" Rowan asked from behind me.

"Yeah." I dragged in a breath. We'd been going through my old house, checking whether Dad or the Red Sharks who'd recently vacated it might have left behind anything useful. So far nothing. All that was left was the basement.

Nothing down there could hurt me anymore.

"This place just brings up a lot of bad memories," I added, and pushed myself to tramp down the stairs.

With nothing else left to do, all four of the guys followed me. Weirdly, I felt both comforted and unnerved by their presence. I wanted them with me, but I wasn't sure I liked them seeing the place that was the root of so much trauma—of the most fragile parts of me.

The small fixture in the ceiling lit the long, wide room with a yellow glow. Dust tickled my nose, the dank scents of old cement and long-dried bodily fluids traveling with it.

Kaige stepped past me and prodded a long metal pole mounted on one wall. "Was your dad a secret ballet dancer or something?"

My mouth twitched even as my gut twisted, looking at the thing. "He'd handcuff people to that to hold them up while he interrogated them," I explained. "It annoyed him if they collapsed on the ground where he couldn't hit quite as many sensitive places."

Avoiding looking at the floor at the other side of the room, I walked over to the locker in the corner. When I opened it, I found nothing but a few cobwebs. Either Dad hadn't stashed anything in there recently, or one of the gangs that'd come through since had cleared it out.

I turned around to find that Wylder had wandered over to the rectangular concrete slab fitted into the floor, the one I'd been trying to ignore. He nudged it with the toe of his shoe. "What's this?"

My heart was already thumping faster. I debated walking over to join him, but decided I was happier right here. "Open it up if you want."

"Mercy," Rowan started.

I shook my head before he could go on. "It's okay. They all might as well see it." I'd already told Kaige and Gideon about the pit, but somehow it'd never come up with Wylder in any detail before now.

Wylder heaved the concrete lid to the side and peered into the coffin-sized hollow underneath. "I don't get it."

I swallowed hard. "He'd dump people he was pissed off at in there so they'd be more... malleable when they came out. Or just to torture them until they bled out and died. When it's closed, there's no light at all, and the lid's way too heavy to shift from underneath." My thumb ran over my scarred fingertips of its own accord.

Wylder glanced at me, a flicker of understanding and then horror crossing his face. It must have been obvious I'd spoken from experience.

Gideon was studying the pit with an analytical expression, but a furious glint had sparked in his eyes. Kaige's muscles flexed as if he thought he could beat up my past for me if he took out his own fury on the source of my torment.

"It's where I learned to be afraid of closed spaces," I finished. "A long time ago."

Wylder sucked in a breath through his teeth, his own hands clenching. "Just when I thought I couldn't hate that prick more." He kicked at the lid, which didn't budge it, and then shoved it back into place with his hands. When he looked at me again, I could tell he was remembering the time he'd prompted my fear. "I'm sorry. I had no idea."

I shrugged. "How could you have? I didn't tell you."

"I didn't give you a chance to. I was such a shit about it." He let out a little growl and stalked over to me, clasping my hand in his, his thumb meeting my palm where they held identical scars. The cuts where we'd drawn blood might have healed, but our bond remained in place. "I am *never* letting anyone torture you like that again."

Gideon's jaw twitched as he caught my gaze. "What your father did was unforgivable."

"I wouldn't agree with throwing a grown man in there, let alone a little kid," Rowan said, his voice soft. "But you made it through. You didn't let him break you."

"You made yourself a total badass, in spite of that asshole," Kaige put in. He cracked his knuckles. "It's a good thing for him he's already dead, or I'd make him regret every fucked-up decision of his life, starting with that."

They closed in around me, but their nearness didn't make me feel at all claustrophobic. Instead, I was cocooned in the warmth of their bodies. They knew my weakness... and by now, I knew theirs too. Somehow we'd all become something more than we were before. It was thrilling even if it scared me how much I liked it.

Gideon's phone buzzed, breaking the moment. He dug it out of his pocket and grinned.

"What's up?" Wylder asked.

"Looks like the cops found the trail of evidence we left them," Gideon announced. "Very handy that the Red Shark's people fled town so they're not around to speak up for themselves—the perfect scapegoats. The Nobles have been cleared of all charges relating to the drug activity at the waterfront property."

Rowan breathed a sigh of relief. "Then we'll be able to resume construction."

"Too bad we couldn't pin it all on the Storm's pricks," Kaige grumbled.

Gideon frowned at his phone. "I'm still waiting to see if that tracking device I managed to get on Xavier's boot takes us anywhere interesting. It seems active, but he's only been going around the places we already know the Storm's people are active so far."

"One thing at a time," Wylder said, clapping Kaige on the back and then glancing at me. "Let's get the hell out of this place."

I smiled. "Yeah."

We climbed back to the first floor, and I stopped there to look around the kitchen and into the dining room beyond. "I'm thinking I might take this place back over for myself. Make it the new Claws headquarters. I'll need to set up security, obviously... I'll have to talk to Jenner and the others and see how they want to go forward from here."

"You're their queen," Wylder said, nudging me. "They've got to listen to you. And I'm sure it'll be more comfortable for you to have your own place without my dad lurking around."

He paused, a shadow crossing his face. A question had been itching at me ever since the night when that mysterious package had been delivered to the Noble mansion, and now it rose up again. It'd clearly shaken up both Wylder and his father. I hadn't totally understood the comments Wylder had made about heirs. But it'd seemed so painful that I hadn't wanted to bring it up, giving him room to do so.

But it'd been two days, and he hadn't said a peep to

me. I hadn't heard anything other than a few comments between the Nobles about a funeral being set up late this afternoon. Maybe Wylder was waiting for me to show I *wanted* to know.

"Wylder," I said carefully, "who was it Xavier sent to your father? I know you might not want to talk about it, but you don't have to shut me out."

Wylder's mouth twisted. He ran his hand over his face and seemed to gather himself. The other guys stood around us silently, and I got the sense from their awkwardness that they already knew what he was going to say.

"That was my older brother," he said finally, his voice gone a little raw. "Roland. *He* was meant to take over the Nobles from my father. Dad trained him for it since he was a little kid. But when I was thirteen— Roland was eighteen—he decided he didn't want this life. He took a bunch of money out of the Noble accounts and ran for it. I haven't even known where he's been."

My heart sank. That was even worse than I'd imagined. To lose his only brother, without even having had the chance to talk to him in so long. "I'm sorry," I murmured.

Wylder grimaced. "You don't need to feel sorry for me. I don't even know... He's basically a stranger now. And—all these years, I kept waiting for him to show up and say he wanted to rule the Nobles after all, and my father would have shoved me aside for him in an instant, even after everything..." He shook himself. "I gave in to more of Dad's demands than I should have trying to prove myself. I let him get away with what he did to Laurel. Never again."

I squeezed his hand. "You did the best you could."

"Maybe. Funny that when I finally got the guts to really stand up to him, Roland was already dead and gone, I just didn't know it yet." He raised his head, his tone darkening. "And no matter how I felt about Roland then or now, he didn't deserve to die like that. Xavier's added one more item to the list of things he needs to pay for."

"And we're going to make him regret every one," Kaige promised, baring his teeth.

"So let's get on with that." Wylder swung his arm to the door. "Pack up. We're grabbing an early lunch for a massive planning session."

We stepped out into the morning sunlight. I locked the door behind me, and I turned back around just in time to see something small and glinting whip through the air and sink into Kaige's neck.

"Kaige!" I yelped. It was some kind of dart. What the hell?

Kaige staggered, snatching at the thing. I was springing to help him when my ears caught several faint popping sounds in the distance. The next instant, pain jabbed into my own neck.

A rush of dizziness swept over me. I pawed at the dart, spinning around and nearly tripping over my feet. The other guys were stumbling too. My vision rippled and dimmed, and then the entire world faded to black.

ABOUT THE AUTHORS

Eva Chance is a pen name for contemporary romance written by Amazon top 100 bestselling author Eva Chase. If you love gritty romance, dominant men, and fierce women who never have to choose, look no further.

Eva lives in Canada with her family. She loves stories both swoony and supernatural, and strong women and the men who appreciate them.

Connect with Eva online:
www.evachase.com
eva@evachase.com

Harlow King is a long-time fan of all things dark, edgy, and steamy. She can't wait to share her contemporary reverse harem stories.

Printed in Great Britain
by Amazon